ARCHIPELAGOS:

Twenty Years in Labour

ARCHIPELAGOS:

Twenty Years in Labour

Christakis Georgiou

The Book Guild Ltd
Sussex, England

This book is a work of fiction. The characters and situations in this story are imaginary. No resemblance is intended between these characters and any real persons, either living or dead.

The Book Guild Ltd
25 High Street,
Lewes, Sussex

First published 1997

Set in Baskerville
Typesetting by Raven Typesetters, Chester

Printed in Great Britain by
Antony Rowe Ltd.
Chippenham, Wiltshire.

A catalogue record for this book is
available from the British Library

ISBN 1 85776 147 2

1

He climbed down the stairs that led to the basement cabaret as if hypnotised. He saw at the entrance the green and red lights that kept flickering and the message was recorded in his brain with extraordinary speed.

At the mine it was like living in exile, he thought. His old man, who had been digging in Latin manuscripts in the libraries of New York, always stumbled on deserted places. Copper and gold. From time to time a skinny American female came, forty years old, tall, slim. They made love, with tact.

To hell with that. He had wanted to roll on the ground, to feel the male sweat that accompanies love-making streaming along his skin, from his head right to the edge of his feet.

He was struck first by the red and then by the green. He understood. Until now he came down to Chora in company. This time he was alone.

'Mr Oriol is going to Chora?' one of the supervisors had asked.

He wanted to tell him going to go fuck but restrained himself. The Latin manuscripts which his father dug up were, in his mind, transformed into codes of good behaviour.

'Yeah, I'm going to Chora.'

His father and mother took care of everything. When they realized he was fed up with the forty-year-old skinny Americans they let him go to Nicosia. Always with company.

They turned three of his bodyguards into friends, they stocked him with money and let him go discreetly.

'I wanted to roam in the fields and they took me to the most classical dining rooms!'

This time, however, he dug in his heels. 'I'm going alone,' he said firmly to his father and mother. The tone of his voice allowed no room for objection. They looked at him imploringly but he turned away.

He pushed through a swing door that reminded him of cowboy films and found himself in a strongly lit hall. The harsh sounds of the band and the pitiless light gave the impression of a finale. He sat at a table.

'Yes, mister?'

He raised his eyes and looked at the crumpled waiter with his sweat-stained clothing. No slight bowing here. It's not dining rooms here but wild grazing fields, he thought.

'Champagne,' he said slowly.

With the edge of his eye he caught the waiter's eyebrows raised slightly in an expression of surprise.

'Champagne, mister?' His hand mechanically started cleaning the table. The shop has everything.

The waiter gave him the impression of wanting to start a conversation but Mathias Oriol, born in the depths of the South was not in the mood. He suddenly felt a deep boredom inside him.

'Yes. Champagne.'

The waiter left, almost running. He saw him skirting the floor skilfully, avoiding the dancing clients. What he saw was not dancing. The bodies loosened by booze moved as if unwound. The eyelids fell heavily. Only the hands behaved differently. They were charged with an electricity that the rest of the body had lost. They crept inside dresses, they groped thighs, they fondled breasts; in the grazing field it is the hand that counts.

'Have you a light?' As a man bent over him Mathias felt his breath heavy with whisky.

He looked at him. He was a fifty-year old Englishman, rather short who continuously tried to keep his head at a smooth angle with the rest of his body, but continuously he failed and continuously he tried. He raised his hand rather awkwardly to light the Englishman's cigarette. The latter's hair, straight and thinning, had been almost pulled out of his scalp and fell on his face. The lighter's click provoked an instinctive movement of his head that was accompanied by a broken bending of his waist. He belched deeply.

'I beg your pardon.'

He wondered why some people were called Belcher and they never belched openly. Others bear the name, others have the grace. The Englishman lit his cigarette at the third attempt.

'It's a bloody zoo,' he said and moved away.

He watched him infiltrating the dancing couples.

He bent his waist, tried to leap, grasped his genitals and let out some half-suppressed cries. The lights dimmed and suddenly became stronger. The band was finishing the piece it was playing.

'You fools,' shouted the Englishman. 'It's a bloody zoo!' He tried to grasp his genitals once more. But two hands grasped him by the neck and the arse, lifted him lightly amid the dancing couples who were beginning to leave the floor and, like a tray that a waiter balances at the end of his hands, brought him to the stairs that led up to the road.

Mathias Oriol looked at the gorilla who played the Englishman in his hands like a toy. It's a bloody zoo. Our friend is not a complete fool, he thought. He saw three or four waiters rush out from all sides and approach the clients who had danced and get two shillings from each. Next to the bar bench there was a tall, rather stooping man. He had a hooked nose, his dark hair shone with cheap hair tonic and his eyes danced strangely, embracing even the smallest corner of the shop. The boss, he thought. Everywhere someone should be at the helm.

Even in the grazing fields. How glad his father, Zacharia Oriol, would be at this last thought of his.

He brought the glass of champagne to his lips. Its familiar taste filled him with immense satisfaction. He had something to lean on. With the edge of his eye he caught the musicians caressing their instruments.

'Company?' Her accent was strange. She was wearing a green dress and her hair fell on her shoulders.

'Don't mind.' He waved to the waiter for another glass.

'Make that two,' another voice said. Without asking a second woman sat on his other side. He looked at her for a moment. Her flesh had something richly explosive about it. He remembered a film title – Rebellious Flesh. The place began to live.

The waiter had brought the two glasses and he filled them with champagne. With an abrupt gesture he ordered the astonished waiter to bring a second bottle.

'Anita,' said the first one.

'Not the Egberg one?' he said.

'Rather,' she answered.

'Bianca,' said the second, leaning against him and kissing his neck.

'Mathias. Mathias Oriol.' He raised his filled glass. They did the same: 'To our health.'

'To your health.'

The one with rebellious flesh bent her head on his shoulder while her tongue was searching for naked flesh to roam on. Her hands were caressing him everywhere.

The first one looked scared. The presence of the second girl had unnerved her. Mathias filled the glasses again, and emptied his straight away

'Darling, you me go together. After show.'

'Yes, yes. You come too,' he said to the one with the frightened eyes. 'Mathias Oriol wants to have fun tonight.'

The band began to play an oriental tune. In the smoky atmosphere the discordant oriental music awkwardly tried to find its balance, like an acrobat who felt lost. The lights almost went out and the smoke, thick wave after wave, rushed towards the partly opened small windows which were at the street level. The hands and the tongue of the first one worked on his flesh. A real massage. The other one drank silently. She looked scared and he wondered what was disturbing her.

'Ladies and gentlemen,' said the bandmaster, first in Greek and then in English 'We continue our attraction with Ziannette Manoleon in an oriental dance.' He had learned it by heart, word after word, phrase after phrase in both Greek and English and did not dare to deviate even the least. 'Ziannette Manoleon!'

The clapping rose slow, sleepy like the cigarette smoke – only there were no small windows to force it to leave suddenly.

The way she was dancing was rather awkward. She shook her rather non-existent buttocks, lifted her belly, waved her hair, travelled her eyes through the dancing floor and waited for her dance to come to an end.

'Manoleon, Kordelien,' shouted Mathias. 'Long live Cairo!' He turned to the frightened one. 'You never dance?'

'With the customers,' she answered.

A third bottle of champagne was ordered. On the stairs the Englishman made his appearance once more: 'I'm back again to the bloody zoo,' he slurred.

It was a question of minutes before the gorilla got to him, held him suspended in the air and then moved him like a broken banner towards the exit.

There was another break. The girls' dances were interrupted so that the patrons could dance, and the shop could make some half crowns. Mathias Oriol found himself on the floor in between the two of them, the one with the frightened eyes and the one with the rebellious flesh. The lights were lowered to the very minimum and the band played a slow oriental tune. Mathias was rocking on the floor awkwardly, without rhythm, and he felt the champagne roll from one side to the other of his skull. He leaned sometimes on the one and sometimes on the other.

To the hell with the Americans his father brought. They were tall, skinny, flat-chested.

'Four shillings mister,' said the waiter.

'Add six to the bill. Two for you.' He ordered another bottle of champagne. Only with difficulty could he keep his head upright. It fell sometimes on the breast of the one and sometime on the other's.

'You English?'

'I? No bloody shit. American, not English. Mine.' With his voice and hands he imitated the drilling machines. 'Copper, you know copper?'

'No, I don't'

'At two, we three go?'

'At two, at three and at six. One, two three, finish.' His tongue began to stumble on the words but he felt his head strangely light. And the cavern inside him assumed the dimensions of an underground pit, semi-dark, endless. Copper never finishes. Never.

His hands gripped Anita's and Bianca's breasts. (Sometimes he had a strange desire. In the summer afternoon as the sun descended towards the sea and the humid heat became thick like mist, he started running and climbed the wagons of the miniature railway; he filled his palms with ore and brought it near his face and a strange flash was trapped in his eyes and he felt a wave of pleasure unrolling inside him.)

The big underground hall began to empty and the smoke cleared. A corner of his brain recorded that the shop was closing. He clapped his hands. The waiter stood beside him.

'No more champagne!'

'Yes, yes. No capito, no speak, finito la mousica.'

'I pay you.' He stood, with difficulty.

'The bill.' He gave him a piece of paper.

'Just say how much.'

'Seven pounds.'

He threw to him two five pound notes. 'The change for you, Bianca and Anita. Finito la mousica.'

Suddenly he felt the killer wave unleashed inside him. A wild horse, a subterranean earthquake vibration was held imprisoned inside him. In his head, in his chest, in his knees. While Bianca and Anita were trying to hold him by the hands his eyes goggled, the pupils disappeared in an endless white. Foam was coming from his mouth and he was lying full length at the edge of the dancing floor. Bianca's and Anita's hands made the fall smoother. But suddenly panic seized them and they ran.

The waiter stood holding the two five pound notes. 'Fenk you ...' he had already formed the words on his lips but they stayed unfinished.

He found himself in the middle of the dancing floor. The boss, with his hawkish nose and the eagle's eye, was behind the bar.

'Why on earth did you drink the champagne?'

All looked in silence. Only Ziannette Manoleon – the oriental dancer – rushed towards him, lifted his head with one hand and tightly held his tongue with the other. He drifted, and when he opened his eyes he had the impression he was coming from afar. A place, he felt, marked by a huge moon. His first impression had been the white ceiling. He roamed for a few seconds inside it. Every time he came from afar, time assumed inside him an uninterrupted unity that gave it indefinite dimensions. He had the impression he had been travelling in the white a long time. He felt a bitter taste stick to his palate.

The champagne, he thought and then said: 'I'm thirsty.' The words sprang into the void, he was not addressing anybody, man or object. The void was both inside and outside him.

Ziannette came with a glass and a smile. He sipped a little and felt inside him a strange coolness:

'You slept well,' she said.

'What's the time.'

'Twelve, noon.'

He struggled on his feet: 'I'm late,' he said. His parents must have released his bodyguards. 'Where am I? Who are you?'

'You're in my room. I'm Ioanna, Ziannette. You remember the oriental dance?' Her body twisted in a snake's movement that remained suspended in the air for some seconds. Time continued its uninterrupted flow. The feeling, however, that he was coming from somewhere afar began to weaken. The white was broken by her face. Black, bright eyes, black hair that struggled to fall on her shoulders and a slim body on the point of losing its material existence.

'You're not Anita.'

'No, Ioanna, Ziannette.'

Of course. He had grazed in their bosoms. He remembered it now. On one side was Anita and on the other Bianca. They had swept aside all the tall, skinny, breastless Americans. And the vibration had started as sweet irritation in his legs and finally perched in his loins.

'What happened?' he asked.

'You didn't feel well. Taken ill suddenly.'

He understood. From half said things by his parents he had a vague idea of what was happening. Often he caught his eye stumbling in medical dictionaries over the term epilepsy but he never found the courage to read its analysis.

'I brought you to my room. It's not, of course, the Hilton but it has a bed and a bath.' She gave him a cup of coffee. 'Shall I pour some milk?'

'Yes, please.' When, at the mine, he was asked a question he nodded yes or no with a movement of his head or hand. Suddenly fear seized him. 'Did I pay the bill? I had promised something to the girls.'

'It's all right,' she said. 'You paid the bill, don't worry. The girls had left the place before you.'

Her voice was caressing his ears. It was the first time a voice had such an effect on him. He felt the words break into thin sands of particles and settle on him. Making him feel relaxed.

'I'm hungry,' he said.

'Okay. Do you want to have a shower?'

He went into the semi-dark shower room, two metres by two. He could only just stand. He remembered his own oval bath in the middle of a huge room. He laughed at himself. Everything to human measures. But where? His thought didn't specify. Here or there.

Ioanna was sitting outside waiting. In the small kitchen she had already boiled eggs and poured orange juice and plenty of coffee.

As she watched the American eat Ioanna remembered the men who had marked her life. She had come down to the town from her barren village. Perched on the slope of the mountain it suffered from a severe water shortage in summer and terrible cold in winter. The men were absent most of the time in the town or came up to the village every fifteen days or a month. The village was dominated by women. The coffee shops were closed most of the time and the children ran up and down the streets where there was neither car nor bicycle. But when those certain Saturdays and Sundays arrived and the coffee shops opened Ioanna would hear the women giggling and throwing half phrases to each other. And a strange atmosphere filled the houses which no woman could specify but which deep inside her appeared familiar.

They had sent her as domestic servant to a house. 'So that the village won't erode you and you shouldn't wither like me,' her mother told her.

Her master was the first to rape her. He passed most of the time at his grocery; he always left at six in the morning and returned at eight in the evening. He ate in silence, listened to the radio, glanced at the newspaper and he fell heavily on to his mattress. That night it was raining torrentially and was bitterly cold. Her mistress had gone to her sister, who was expecting a baby. Her master returned as always at eight. He lit the oil fire, put a deep plate in the middle of the table, threw pure spirit in, lit it and began to grill sausages over it. He uncorked a bottle of brandy and poured it into a glass.

'Ioanna, come and have something.'

He poured her some brandy. They ate and drank. The only thing that Ioanna remembered of what happened afterwards was his face with two eyes like the burning wicks of an oil heater and his lips cutting her breath short.

Having once tasted new flesh the grocer could not give it up easily. He found excuses to send his wife somewhere, to her sister or to her parents. He cornered Ioanna early in the morning before going to his shop. He never spoke about love. He simply threw her down, his hair fell loose down his face, he growled fiercely and did not stop before his joints loosened in a hedonistic trembling. From time to time he gave her a present or put some money in her name in a bank's saving account. Her mistress came to suspect what was going on and, since she could say nothing to the grocer she shouted at the girl. Then one day they threw her out.

She never went back to the village, not to wither. She found work in two other houses but the story was the same. Finally she got fed up and found herself in the house of Madam, a Turkish woman of around fifty with three daughters. The house was buried in a quiet street where the boys freely played football or in the evening sat on the pavements and told stories. But at night, after ten, when the road became deserted, there were discreet knocks on Madam's door.

Ioanna learned the profession's secrets quickly and Madam was pleased. 'You'll succeed,' she said. 'You're like my daughters.'

She stayed at the house for one and a half years and, strangely, she remembered nothing except that night when he came. Her movements until then were somewhat broken, were drowned in moments that had no continuity. But that night sealed the one and a half years. With the end of the Second World War the town was filled with demobilized soldiers. He came alone and knocked at the door. Madam sized him up and brought him to her. He was tall, brown, with a slight mark on his left cheek. The next night he came again. Madam looked sour, but Ioanna begged her to let him stay. In the tone of her voice there was something that took Madam by surprise. And she let him stay. For six months they were together all day, from ten when she woke up until eight at night when she returned to the house. Then Madam promoted her to a dance hall, although she could neither sing nor dance. She kept men company, she drank with them, she went with them to the back rooms. But at two in the morning he came. She went with him, she left darkness behind, her day started. It was strange that the hall, the drink, the back rooms did not even touch her. She felt him upright like a bronze statue. She would find employment; there would be an end to the houses, the halls and the back rooms. On one morning he did not come. She ran anxiously and found him burning in fever. She never left him for a moment in fifteen days. When he died they told her it was 'galloping consumption'. He died in her arms in an isolated room of the hospital. Behind her Madam looked on with big, rather melancholy eyes.

The noise of the shower brought her back to reality. For a while.

There was a third one too. He was a fisherman. He always came to the hall at eleven, shortly before he went out in his boat for his daily fishing. He had one or two drinks, teased everybody and laughed noisily. The crazy Pipis, they called him. He threw his arms around her and kissed her, and then left for his boat. Sometimes he took her with him, especially in summer when the humidity and the heat became unbearable.

He threw his nets in a hurry; his half-naked body shone strangely in the semi-darkness. She was sitting at a corner of the boat listening to the silence and the monotonous noise the nets made when sliding into the water. Then they made love on the wooden floor of the boat huddled in their own heavy breathing which in the general silence assumed new dimensions. She then slept by the engine and when it turned colder Pipis threw his coat over her. The morning sun did not wake her. It was only when the engine started working for the return journey that she lazily opened her eyes and looked at Pipis, who stood at the steering wheel with the air of an emperor.

The shower door creaked and the American filled the empty space with a wide smile. 'I'm starving, like a wolf.'

'Boiled eggs, orange juice and coffee,' she said smiling. 'Or we go to the restaurant next door.'

'Boiled eggs and the rest,' he said smiling. 'I don't want anything better for breakfast.'

They sat at the small table facing each other.

'Mathias and Ioanna Ziannette Manoleon. He could have turned you into Napoleon. You've got something in common, you and Napoleon,' (he meant the brandy). She stared at him with a half idiotic smile which Mathias felt filtering inside him releasing all the devils that were trapped in his loins: – You want to swallow both of them. They cracked their eggs and laughed as if children.

'I rarely have breakfast at the mine,' he said.

'I never do. Professional habit.' And then she added at a low tone: 'And necessity too.'

'I don't know if in my case you can call it professional habit. My profession is not to have a profession.' And he laughed at his own joke, a big laugh with no trace of pretence. He was eating with appetite. He ate the first egg and then cracked the second. 'I never sleep before one or two,' he said.

'I never do before three or four.'

'I like just after midnight when my parents go to bed and the flatterers leave and discreetly the servants retire one after the other. I like it when the last one brings me a bottle of champagne in ice: "Goodnight Mr Mathias. Anything else?" I look at the champagne. The words usually come – through my teeth: "Goodnight." I look at the night through the lit window. Sometimes I feel scared. This contrast between darkness and light shatters me. It kills me. I open the champagne in a hurry. I drink the first glass at a stretch. The darkness outside my window disappears. I play for an hour or two watching the radiation of the liquid in my glass. I empty it slowly. When I finish the bottle I'm ready to go to bed. The lamp that is on in my brain goes off.' He suddenly stopped talking and silence felt awkward in the small room. He drank some coffee. She did not know what to say.

'Do you drink champagne?'

'Whenever I am offered.'

He drank a little more coffee. 'Won't you offer me a cigarette? I'm in your hands today.'

'I'm sorry.'

He was surprised at her politeness. So there was room for manners at the grazing fields. He thought about it.

She stood up and went to the other corner of the room to bring cigarettes. 'I never smoke during day time. Night time is enough.'

She stretched her hand to offer him a cigarette. He kissed her and she kissed him. He pressed her to him and they found themselves rolling on the small carpet. And each one's heavy breath cut short the other's. They remained silent and motionless on the carpet for some time.

When they got up he looked at his watch. It was past two. The bodyguards must have been unleashed.

'I'll see you tonight. Definitely.'

'At the music hall,' she said.

He kissed her, opened the door and vanished in a hurry.

'Another one,' she whispered to herself. 'What difference does it make? It's always like that.' She shut the door, crept into bed and in a short while she was fast asleep. She always liked lying in bed lazily after making love and she slept for hours.

At eight o'clock in the evening she stood in front of the mirror . She first took special care of her face, then her hair and then stood absent-mindedly for some minutes staring in the mirror. She looked at her full breasts, and was impressed, as if seeing them for the first time. She looked at her watch. It was a quarter to nine. At nine the hall opened its doors. She switched off the light and went out, pulling the door behind her.

At the cabaret was the same air of expectation. The girls were wearing evening dresses. Until eleven they would be dancing with the customers and each dance would mean two shillings. Then they would get dressed for the special attraction, their specific dances. The waiters were talking in low tones. They had long since arranged the tables and now they were attired in their white shirts and black trousers. Their neckties pressed awkwardly on their throats. Their hair shone with cheap dressing. The two barmen played with their bottles, they arranged them in one way, they changed their position, just to do something. The musicians tuned their instruments. And above all the presence of the owner, the Boss as they called him, with his hooked nose and black hair. His glance embraced everything and he did not want the usual order to be disturbed in any way.

At nine the doors opened and at five past nine Mathias Oriol appeared with an older couple. The man and woman appeared awkward as they descended the stairs, but Mathias was euphoric. They moved to a table and sat down. Someone slid down the stairs like a shadow and whispered something in the Boss's ear. His eyes opened wide but then settled into their usual expression. The Americans had arrived at the cabaret in two limousines. The bodyguards did not come down with them, they remained up on the road.

Mathias greeted the Boss and the latter bowed slightly. A waiter approached timidly.

'Champagne,' said Mathias. 'And glasses for four.' When the champagne arrived Mathias whispered to the waiter: 'Tell your boss that I invite him to my table.'

When the man came Mathias invited him to sit, and he filled four glasses.

'To our health.' said the Boss.

The older Oriols kept silent. They just sipped their champagne.

'What profit do you figure you'll have tonight?' Mathias suddenly asked the Boss.

A good night brought him something like fifteen pounds, but there were nights on which not even the expenses were covered. ' Twenty-five pounds,' he said.

'Fifty,' Mathias said, and ordered the doors to be closed. 'The girls will dance tonight for me, my mother and father.' He threw ten five pound notes down and the Boss cast for a moment a glance of wonder but then gave the order. A notice was hung at the door: 'Closed due to circumstances.'

One after the other the girls began their speciality. Mathias Oriol drank his champagne and laughed. His father sipped his champagne more slowly. Among the girls who danced was Ioanna Manoleon or Ziannette Manoleon with her oriental dance. At about eleven the show came to an end.

'Call Ioanna,' Mathias ordered.

And she came. For the first time she felt so shy.

'Sit down Ioanna.' He took a long draught of champagne,

turned to his parents and said: 'Your daughter-in-law.' They exchanged a quick look and his mother made an imperceptible movement, as if she wanted to say something. But in her son's eyes flames were dancing.

Ioanna felt her knees trembling.

'Champagne for everybody. I'm marrying Ioanna tonight.'

The waiters started opening bottles, the musicians all of a sudden caught fire and started playing a gipsy tune. Holding glasses of champagne the waiters, the girls, the musicians all talked at the same time.

At midnight, holding Ioanna by the hand, Mathias Oriol followed his parents to the stairs that led to the exit. In the middle of the stairs Mathias lingered. 'Send the bill for tonight to the Oriols. Whatever bank you go to they'll tell you where.'

The party entered the two limousines and disappeared into the night.

The next day Mathias Oriol led Ioanna to the biggest law office of the capital. They opened a door at the end of a narrow passage and the lawyer in charge, a middle-aged man with thick lenses and straight hair, stood up to welcome them.

'Madam,' said the lawyer, giving her a typed sheet of paper. 'Your property data, according to a statement under oath of your husband. I'm always at your disposal for whatever problem and it will be a special honour for me to be of service.'

Thus Ioanna Manoleon became Ziannette Mathias Oriol and from the semi-basement of Amaryllis Street she found herself in the Oriol's mansion, at the edge of the Morphou plain, getting ready for her honeymoon in Europe and America. She sat with Mathias until late into the night sipping champagne. Then he made love to her in the unbroken silence of the night and when he left, she fell asleep in her separate bedroom.

They never talked about Mathias' illness. In the presence of her parents-in-law she felt somewhat uncomfortable and sometimes she felt a wave of fear that was on the point of unrolling itself inside her when the Madam Oriol's cold glance was focused on her. Mathias never woke up before one or two in the afternoon. After the post-midnight champagne he had a sleeping pill and this created chaos in his head. He found in sleep a way out. Ioanna woke at ten and they served her breakfast at ten-thirty. Her memory worked incessantly during those three or four hours until Mathias woke and came to take her for lunch and the afternoon wandering.

2

(From Ioanna Manoleon's diary)
Mother always got up at three in the summer. In winter she enjoyed the luxury of getting up at four. Our house consisted of only one room, huge as it appeared to me then. In one corner there slept mother and father, at the other end, we children were piled up, Dina and me on a huge bench, my two brothers and elder sister on the floor, on sacks full of wool. At nights when father returned drunk and we heard him opening the door noisily we tightly embraced each other lest shouting and beating would start. Sometimes he went straight to bed, and we heard his heavy panting, and we felt him moving in a way as if he was riding his mule, and the atmosphere was charged. And my mother's broken voice: 'Quiet, the children will know.' And him saying: 'Who cares?' And the silence being broken by his movements. We held our breath lest he should know we weren't sleeping. And then we heard his breath losing gradually its tension and in the end we slept and he slept.

Mother got up at three in the summer and four in winter. It was like a ritual. She slid through the room like a shadow, her hands touching various objects without making the slightest noise. Equally noiselessly she opened the door. In the yard we had a small barrack made of tin that we used as a kitchen. Its only furniture was an old table with a brasin at one end, and a small wire cabinet at the other, which was permanently empty because there was never money for us to store food. At the corner there was a crude fireplace with a hole on the tin roof for the smoke to squeeze out. Every morning mother drank camomile tea, she drank it with or without sugar, according to circumstances, she ate a piece of bread and two or three olives. When there was some money she might eat a very thin slice of halloumi or cheese. This was so rare that it was with difficulty we could remember its taste. And then mother attended our own animals, a few chickens, a goat, a small pig. The pig was part of the 'domestic economy' as the man from the Agriculture Department used to say. The English sent him round the villages to explain how we could improve our domestic economy. Around five, mother left. I don't remember having seen her home in the morning except at Christmas or Easter, or when she was ill. On those days she lay covered at the edge of the bed, not to make in any way things difficult for father.

He used to get up heavy, fastened his trousers and without even casting a glance at our side, he lifted to his lips the pot we had at a corner and drank water. Then he belched deeply, repeatedly.

'You've started pretending again,' he would say. He had spent some time in Egypt and picked up some words and expressions we didn't understand.

'Don't get angry Manoli. I'm ill.'

'Theatre-theatre. I'm fed up with all of you. Hear me?' Sometimes he took a swing at her and his hand fell so heavily that I thought he would split her in two.

Sometimes he jerked open the door and left with anger in his eyes. We then heard him swearing for long in the yard. And then he rode his mule and disappeared among the morning noises of the village. However, this scene was the exception and if I remember it in particular it's because it is so vivid. Mother left at five. Winter or summer. According to the season she worked at either houses or fields or gardens. She cleaned stables, swept yards, dug, weeded, harvested vegetables or picked fruit. She came back in the evening, exhausted. She always brought some foodstuffs and plenty of vegetables. Father never returned before ten or eleven. All the money he earned as a mule driver was spent in taverns. Sometimes he spent it on his mistresses.

Dina and I were too young to go to school. She was six and I five. My eldest sister left often for the town and it was days before she came back. She sometimes worked as a domestic servant and sometimes she worked in factories. Whenever she came she brought food, mainly beans, and for a few days the cabinet with its wire net justified its existence. She was then only sixteen. My two brothers, thirteen and twelve, had gone. They went as apprentices, one to a carpenter, the other to a builder, to learn a trade and escape from the misery of the village. I saw them only on Christmas and Easter for the next few years. Then they remained only names on my mother's lips – Nicolas and Jacob. I tried to remember their faces but at that age memories were rather faint. What counted most was the day's impressions.

All day we roamed outside the village. Its houses, about fifty, climbed a slope and all around were hills. We tried to comprehend with our childish imagination the world beyond the hills.

'The town is big. It's all houses. Cars too,' said Dina.

'Ever been there?' I asked.

'No, Ireni told me.'

'Cars?'

'It's one thing to tell you, another to see.'

For me car meant the only bus of the village which three times a week covered the distance to the town and vice versa. On the remaining four days it stood silent by the coffee-house watching the villagers. Dina and I went round the fields and the hill slopes and we picked wild vegetables. We had become great experts on wild vegetables. Our eyes had been trained to such a degree that no edible plant could escape us. With our small knife we cut it or we uprooted it and put it in our paper bags. At around eleven we came back and Dina lit a fire at the fireplace. Dina was afraid of the brasin and if father returned and found it burning he beat us.

'Wasting our resources,' he said. And his hand came down heavily, sometimes on one, sometimes on the other. Thus for us the brasin had unpleasant associations. Sometimes when Dina tried to light it the paraffin overspilt and flames danced round its top, and we were so much afraid that we clung to each other and shrank in a corner. And the flames danced in our eyes. The minutes seemed hours. Eventually the flames weakened and finally died away, but the paraffin smell lingered and Dina opened the little door for the atmosphere to clear.

She lit a fire in the fireplace, and threw on it two or three pieces of wood. She put a pot with the wild vegetables on the fire and we ate them without oil and lemon, only with a little salt and bread. With closed eyes I could identify each of those vegetables.

Towards the end of November or the beginning of December, after the first heavy rain, we entered the forest, at the very edge, and searched for mushrooms. Sometimes there was olive oil at home for us to try them. When there wasn't Dina lit some pieces of wood and waited until they turned into burning embers, then she put the mushrooms on them and sprinkled them with salt, and we ate them with a slice of bread. When Dina became seven mother enrolled her at school. She begged the teacher to accept me as an 'observer'.

'What do females need education for?' was father's reaction. But he said no more since school cost nothing. But when there was nothing at home for us to eat we pretended we were ill and vanished into the fields to pick wild vegetables. We took some paper bags and two rusty knives and every time our eye caught something we thrust the knife into the soil, uprooted the vegetable and put it quickly into a bag.

One day, as we looked at the distant indigo sea, I said: 'Shall we go to the sea sometime?'

Dina stopped abruptly. 'No.'

'Why?'

'There are eyes,' Dina said, and seeing the wondering expression of my face she said, 'the teacher called them swallowing pools. The water,' she stopped as if searching for the word, 'whirls and – swallows you.'

I stared at the sea, an indigo line, and I wondered how the water swallows you. And after swallowing you?

'Oou,' said Dina, and drew a circle with her hand in the air. She turned abruptly and made for the village.

'The daughters of Iste,' I once heard someone call us. Iste was father's nickname. We did not even look at him. We disappeared behind the bushes, turned a little and made for the edge of the forest where there were many wild vegetables.

That morning we set out as always, Dina in front, I a metre behind. We carried only paper bags. The whole night, in spite of the fact that summer was already here, had been torn by lightning, thunder and a torrential downpour. Now, in the morning, the sky was clear and the sun was already burning hot. We went for snails at the fringes of the forest. With last night's rain they must have been on their morning stroll. Beyond, towards Turkey, the sky was becoming thick with clouds and was torn by lightning. We followed a path, crossed a second, took a third but Dina carried on. I began to feel hungry. I don't know if Dina experienced the same but she never showed it. She went on in silence dragging me behind like her shadow. Time passed and I wanted to ask where we were going, but kept silent. We buried ourselves amid bushes and I began to feel afraid because all I could see were bushes and sky. But suddenly, the bushes became thinner and when we emerged from them we found ourselves at the other side of the mountain and the sea before us.

'There's the sea,' Dina said and stopped.

'You have been here before?'

'Yes, with Mother.'

We went on a bit more through a rocky pass, thick with reeds, raspberry bushes and vines. And then we came to a sandy beach where half-naked men sat on the sand or walked up and down.

'Shall we go to the sand?'

'No,' Dina left no room for objection.

Suddenly my eye caught the white house. It covered the entire top of a hill.

Dina looked at me. She understood just like that. Without saying anything she set out for the white house. When we came near she said: 'The Englishman built it.'

'Which Englishman?'

'Him,' and with this word it was as if she explained everything.

The wall was taller than me and surrounded the entire top of the hill. Dina took me near a corner. Some crude holes could be used as footholds. We climbed and mounted the wall, and in the distance I saw the house. Two huge dogs, were lying in the shade. Sometimes they rose lazily and leapt on each other in mock battle, they licked each other and then lay down again.

'He built it for his wife,' said Dina. Just then Ikkis a Turk ex-policeman walked out of a door holding something in his hands, and went towards the dogs. We jumped down.

'If he sees us he will turn the dogs on us.'

'Let's go.'

'Don't be in such a hurry.'

Five minutes later Dina climbed the wall again. With fear I climbed it again too. Ikkis was now going away towards the house.

'Ikkis works for the Englishman.'

'Isn't he a policeman?'

'No, not now. He was two years ago.' Insinuation, heavy as ripe fruit, hung in her tone.

'Do you see her?' Dina said.

I saw the Englishwoman walking to the verandah. She appeared to me tall and thin – thin like fern.

'They say she is ill,' Dina said. 'The Englishman built the house for her.'

'Only for her?' The woman was now standing in the middle of the verandah, staring at the sea.

'And the dogs,' Dina added.

The Englishwoman had blonde hair falling over her shoulders. Since that day every time I went to the sea, for a second I saw her standing in the middle of the verandah. I was reminded of the blonde woman on the verandah.

We jumped down the wall and I had another look down at the sandy beach and beyond that the sea. I would carry the image with me for years.

We set out for the path to the forest and the village. I had, however, the sense that I felt less hungry. We had found something to put in our paper bags. The sun beat on us mercilessly. In a short while, the naked rocks that hung over the village would radiate the heat. Without saying anything we sat under a tree. We felt very hot.

'The Englishwoman, they say, suffers from asthma,' said Dina.

'And what is asthma?'

'Something here,' Dina said, putting her hand on her breast. 'That's why she doesn't stay long. Three, four, five months. Then she leaves with her husband. Ikkis stays alone with the dogs. He trains them morning and afternoon. To climb on the wall and let no one come near.' She stopped.

We were both staring at the sea. It was now just a line on the horizon. In the strong light of the sun the colours became paler. Only the blonde line of the English woman still danced in my eyes.

'Does Ikkis stay always there?'

'Yes, winter and summer. He has nowhere to go. He serves the Englishwoman and the Englishman; and the dogs.'

'Hasn't he anywhere to go?'

'His family scattered. He killed the lover of his eldest daughter. They sent him to prison for two or three years. After one and a half months the English commissioner got him out. Good behaviour.'

'And what's good behaviour?'

'He neither cursed nor spat. And he did what he was told. Sine he came out he has been in this big house with the Englishman, the Englishwoman and the big dogs.' Dina stood up.

'His daughter's lover, why did he kill him?'

'I don't know. He was one of us.'

When, some years later, my mother brought me to the town for work, she found me what she said was a good home where I worked as a domestic servant for food, accommodation and a pound a month. They should deposit it for me in a bank – so that my father wouldn't take it, she told them. In that house there was an old attic where my master threw all the discarded furniture, old tables, broken chairs and old newspapers. I still don't understand why he kept them. When my master and mistress were absent I liked to hide myself in that room. I climbed a table and opened the small windows. Two or three, at different points. On the window glass, so much dust had been piled that the light stumbled on it. But when I opened them, light and air rushed into the small room. And I liked to scan the old newspapers. I read the titles. I looked at the photographs and I had the impression that I travelled into time. In an evening paper, *The Progress*, I found Ikkis' story.

3

Ikkis' wife came from Egypt. A gipsy. The English had taken Ikkis to Suez for work. It was there that Ikkis had come across her. He brought her and settled her in his house. There, at the fringe of the town, the houses were widely scattered and buried in trees. On every house there was a windmill. In the summer they planted cannabis and maize. They grew so quickly, they reached man's height. There were also some huge trees called tsoumezies which threw their thick shade on everything, and hid the sky. In winter they shone strangely, washed in the rain and dried in the sun. In summer they lost their bright colour and the dust settled on their leaves and their fruit. When summer came Ikkis climbed the heavily laden trees; and with a small knife he operated, one by one, on the fruit. There was no other way for them to ripen.

'Why Ikkis?'

'Sounnet - circumcision – like our male ones,' Ikkis answered.

In summer the gipsy woman luxuriated sensually in the heat. In winter she buried herself inside the house.

'I feel cold,' she told Ikkis.

'Summer won't be long.' He laid her softly in bed to warm her up. In her half-open eyes the Nile danced playfully and the Egyptian sun was trapped. But there were nights when Ikkis was on duty.

The gipsy woman could not understand why men should be

obliged to work at night. He put on his police uniform, made of thick, blue flannel, girdled himself with wide belts, put on his boots, buried the edges of his trousers into his chaki puttees, and tilted his wide-rim hat. And the gipsy woman stayed alone to feel cold in the night. He returned in the morning sleepy after a sleepless night. But his wife was asleep. No matter how much Ikkis caressed her she didn't react.

One morning Ikkis didn't find her. He had returned from his shift. He opened the little gate and entered the yard. His two daughters, seven and four, indifferent to what happened round them, played in the yard. But his wife was nowhere to be found. He thought, she must have gone to his mother.

Early in the afternoon when he woke to have lunch he saw the girls playing but his wife was not there. He went to his mother's. He asked the neighbours. But no one had seen her. The police looked everywhere. In the end they said: 'She left with some gypsies. We can do nothing.'

Thus Ikkis brought up his daughters with the help of his mother. Altinai, the elder, took after her mother. She had big eyes which now, at the age of fourteen, were half-closed, full of premature sensuality. Her body ripened, her hips swelled, under her cheap dresses her breasts could clearly be seen. Her sister, Sarize, was thin and weak. She struggled to remain in her clothes just as her sister struggled to come out.

'And our mother?' asked the younger.

'She left,' Ikkis answered and gestured towards the horizon.

'Why?'

'She had something in between her legs.' He always said it through clenched teeth, and the girl never heard it. 'People leave, you can't hold them by force.'

The elder one never asked. She heard the younger one asking but she stared persistently with her half-closed eyes. She gave the impression that she was trying to keep her flesh within her dresses. She only stared and kept silent. Ikkis felt strange with this silence of hers.

Does she carry the Nile inside her? His mind recorded the big question but he didn't find the strength to put it straight, even to himself. He apprenticed her to a Greek seamstress. It was the first house after the orchards towards the town. Altinai got up at six-thirty every morning, she threw water on her face, she combed her hair, cast some furtive glances in the mirror, drank a coffee and hurriedly ate breakfast.

'I'm going father,' she said, if he happened not to be on duty. 'I'll be back at one.'

In a short while the younger girl left for school. And soon after, his mother came to cook for them, to have a look around the house. She carried her years like her flesh, loosely, horizontally.

'Mother's getting old,' Ikkis said.

The Greek dressmaker's house had two big rooms and a hallway along the street. Beyond were other rooms and an enclosed yard. The two rooms and the hallway were filled every morning with apprentices. They bent over their sewing for hours, or ironed on a big table. The Greek woman never sat down; she was always shouting, checking what they did, giving instructions. Sometimes Ikkis came riding his bicycle at one and took her home for lunch. Sometimes he turned abruptly to catch the eyes that followed their backs. But he never did it.

And Altinai who carried the Nile inside her, and held the desire trapped in her half-closed eyes, and who at sixteen had ripened to such an extent that she overflowed her girlish dresses, found herself trapped in the juices that circulated inside her. She saw him every morning riding his bicycle, a new green one, with an extra seat at the back and a small yellow flag with the word RUDGE stamped on it in black paint, fastened somewhere on the back wheel. As the wheel revolved the small flag marked its horizontal movement second after second, minute after minute. It was a game that Altinai enjoyed at the beginning. But then she passed on to the rider. He was tall, blond and couldn't be older than eighteen. Wearing a chaki engineer's uniform, he always passed outside the dressmaker's house at a quarter past seven. He finished work at six and emerged just before the apprentices closed the windows. One day he was waiting for her a short distance from the windmills.

'Finished work?'
'Yes, you?'
'I leave at six.'
'Me at seven.'

She walked on and he remained behind. She felt his eyes on her, and she shuddered.

Every night he waited for her a short distance from the windmills. She expected him, too. She always found him near the waterworks, a long building full of engines that collected water from different areas and sent it to the huge water tank – a metal tower in Gladstone Street – that rose above the town like the water dragon. She expected to see him, yet every time she had the same feeling of shuddering starting from her breast and descending to her legs. In that area the houses became more widely spaced. They were small square cottages buried under huge tsoumezies and fig trees. A sycamore, here and there, dropped its fruit on the ground. In summer the clay-brick cottages were surrounded by maize and cannabis plants and yellow sunflowers.

'Has anybody told you you're beautiful?'

He touched her hand and they both laughed and her half-closed eyes opened wide. At a corner of the orchard he kissed her.

In November when darkness began to fall at six and the clouds closed on the small houses and the streets, he became more daring and walked at her side. At the beginning without talking. Then he started to talk about his job, the garage where four men worked, and she talking about her Greek boss and the girls who made dresses and embroidered their dreams on clothes that belonged to others.

On a night when Ikkis was on shift duty and fever was trapped between their legs Altinai said: 'Tonight.'

'Time?'

'Nine. My sister goes to bed at eight.' Sarize slept at eight. She was so active at school and the orchards during daytime that at night after dinner she sat for a little while at the table staring at the oil-lamp. From absolute mobility to absolute immobility. She began to doze continuously and then rose as if hypnotised and went to bed. Altinai blew off the lamp and moved to the kitchen. She read cheap romances until the clock hands rode eleven, and then she went to bed.

At nine there were three knocks on the window. Altinai opened the window and all the fever that swept their bodies dissolved on the kitchen floor, in the faint light of the half-lit oil lamp. Until eleven they were lying on the floor.

'We'll leave Limassol.'

'For where?'

'Does it matter where? Larnaca, Varosi, Nicosia. We'll think of something.'

Altinai blew off the lamp. He kissed her in the darkness, opened the door, took the bicycle he had hidden behind a tree and disappeared into the night.

Altinai's time was split in two. The long days at work, trapped between reality and dream, she looked on as a preparation for her two hours each night. However Ikkis' shift was coming to an end and Altinai and the bicycle Samurai began searching for corners in the orchard. Their inventiveness knew no limits.

Ruffian (Pesevengi).

It was a cry-stone that hit Ikkis as he was riding his bicycle from home to work or vice versa.

Ruffian and policeman. At the beginning they passed left and right without hitting their target.

Policeman and ruffian. The game lasted too long to miss its target. And as the cry hit him on the back he felt explode inside him like a bomb.

But they were seen and soon the whispers started. Eventually they reached Ikkis' ears, and he felt a bomb explode inside him, break into a thousand pieces and hit the walls of ego. After such a long time he felt the gipsy woman was born again in the movements of Altinai's body, her dreaming eyes, in her voice that was acquiring such depth that it frightened him. One night, having said he was on shift work, he left at seven-thirty. That afternoon he had taken out his hunting gun and cleaned it. He saw the steel shining in his eyes. But he wiped clear the grease. The hunting period, anyway, would soon start – Sunday if he weren't wrong. What's two days earlier? He buried it into some bushes.

Sarize was already asleep by eight-thirty. Ikkis was waiting behind the bushes. A small barrack made of tin attached to the rest of the house was used as a small store-kitchen. When it rained the thick drops raised such a noise that they multiplied inside you, and Ikkis ran to shelter in another part of the house. The three knocks on the window broke the silence. The shadow jumped in and the dim light that attempted to invade the yard was drowned in the darkness that was released by the house itself.

Ikkis passed into the little barrack.

'I'd have killed you.' (For whom did he say that: the gipsy woman or Altinai?)

For two hours he sat in a corner in the darkness. His eyes danced like two trapped mice and there was no way they could rest on the iron walls. His mind, however, roamed. It got caught on the *Police Chronicle*, the police magazine or the relevant column of his newspaper . . . He came to the kebab house and they talked, amid the smell of the roasting meat and the orders of a souvlaki or a mixed one–three shillings it cost. She also offered him a coffee.

'What do they talk about for so long?' And he felt the first wound inside him. They never talked and she never made coffee for him. He wondered what they were saying at the other end of the shop. Both of them had been bending over the burning coal, sweating and drying their sweat, for a piece of bread. They felt dry inside. They worked side by side but they were never near each other. And this salesman with the cologne and the well-combed hair – the brilliantine made it even more black. And the shiny shoes.

'Sihtir.' (To hell)

The gipsy stood erect inside him like a pillar. The gipsy woman stood inside him – a sword-cut in his intestines.

She neither talked to him nor made coffee for him. Their talk was always about meat, tomatoes, parsley and cucumbers. Who should be put on the list of debtors. And their trivial talk became an interrupted line, something concrete and abstract at the same time . . . And then boiling water every now and then in the small copper boiler, she waited for him to leave so that she could have a bath. He had not for long felt a flea in his ear.

'Shit. Trampled over. Even if they are not trampled it makes no difference,' Ikkis thought. With his butcher-knife he hit her in the middle of the shop and when she tried to run he stopped her in the middle of the asphalt.

'Ruffian.' (Pesevengi)

The hours in the barrack appeared to him endless. By his side was his hunting-rifle. He stroked it from time to time. And the other one? His mind pumps out ceaselessly memories he carried inside him. *Police Chronicles* and newspaper columns become one inside him. It's strange to find out how big the storage room is inside us.

He came in his car. An old Ford he had inherited from his father. She worked in a factory a short distance outside the town. It was noon and he knew the girls would be going to the opposite shop for an ice-cream, a lemonade or a coke. The sun at the beginning of June scorched everything. He parked the car under a tree and watched the flames dancing in the middle of the asphalt. (Ikkis' mind for a moment jumped to Egypt, to Port-Said where the English had taken him for work . . . The belly dance had something of the flames in the middle of the asphalt.)

'It was you, first,' he thought. 'It's her now.'

When the women emerged from the factory the other one left his car under a tree and advanced towards them. She stopped abruptly. The others went on. They had hardly time for an ice-cream or lemonade.

He stared at her entreatingly. At the centre of the entreaty, there was another tone, a harsh one. (It was the same feeling Ikkis felt spreading inside him, intangible and tangible at the same time.)

'You coming? I'll be waiting at four.'

'Are you leaving your home?'

'Let it alone. It has nothing to do with us.'

She left him. She walked to the others.

'Rebecca, are you coming?' Her steps trampled on his words. He opened the boot of his car. 'Are you coming Rebecca?' He took his hunting rifle. 'The others have nothing to do with us.' She did not even bother to look back and she fell prone in the middle of the asphalt.

'You coming?' The cry leapt wave-wise, like an echo which deviates from its course and hits one wall after another, one hillslope after another. She then remained stiff, breathless in the middle of the asphalt. He opened the car boot again and threw the rifle in. He did not bother even to close it. He strode over the walls of ego and found himself in some neutral, grey spaces.

The door creaked slightly. Night and silence act as an amplifier. A scar in the darkness. He felt it for a second marked on the night's body. And the shadow danced for a few seconds in front of his eyes. It was immobilised in time, a strong state of non-existence. Further away the reflection of the distant lights of the town landed smoothly on the asphalt, the tree tops, the flagstones of the yard.

Altinai rushed from the dark mass of the house, she jumped into the vacuum and landed on the yard flagstones. A heart-rending cry tore the night and then a lamentation full of tension.

Ikkis crossed the walls of ego. He disappeared amid the trees of the yard. He wandered in the streets of the town until four-thirty in the morning. When dawn started breaking he surrendered at the first police station.

'It had to be done,' he said, as if waking from lethargy.

He was sentenced to three years' imprisonment. Altinai vanished in the streets of the small town and then roamed in the streets of the other small town and then roamed in the streets of the other towns. She never came back home. Sarize went to live with her grandmother. After eighteen months Ikkis found himself out of prison. With a grey internal world. The gipsy woman and Altinai vanished in a corner. The Englishman who had built the big house at the edge of the forest on the small hill employed him as a guard. Thus Ikkis became one with the dogs. He roamed in the yard and the huge house. He had become the shadow of the Englishwoman – a discreet crutch, on which she leaned any time she needed it. When the Englishman took the Englishwoman and left, Ikkis was alone in the huge house with the yards, the thick wall and the dogs. Rarely did he go down to town – there was a time when the gipsy woman woke in him. He was in a hurry to finish off with the town. When he closed the gate of the thick wall behind him he felt a strange relief. He felt his inside a horizontal plane again. He had the impression that the huge house was digested inside him; in reality, he felt more tense with the passing of time.

4

From Ionna Manoleon's diary

Father had not come home for some days. He would ride his mule from village to village doing various light jobs, spending the money he earned on drink at one or the other tavern. Mother worked here and there for a little flour, a few beans, some olive oil, a few olives. Dina and I went to school – except when we decided to play truant in the fields. Sometimes the teacher gave Dina a book, full of black and white pictures and big letters. Dina spoke, about the pictures and the stories of the book, and her eyes shone. Sometimes I interrupted her with a foolish question.

Father's dark shadow filled the half open door. Neither of us realized that he had entered the yard on his mule nor that he had already dismounted and tied it in the roughly built stable.

'A reading club we've turned the house into? Where's your mother?' Dina had an expression of wonder on her face. 'Work,' she said. 'Left early in the morning.'

He threw himself on to a chair and stared at the wall. From his bag he took out a bottle of cognac.

'A glass,' he said, without taking his eyes from the wall. I noticed that the book was trembling in Dina's hands. I felt a mouse going round in my stomach, descending in a little while down my feet. Dina took him a glass. He filled it and drank it at a stretch.

'Get some food for the mule,' he told me.

I stood up and noiselessly went out. At a corner of the yard there was hay. I took an armful and took it to the mule.

'And water,' his voice came again.

I poured a bucket of water into a tub that was at the edge of the stable. I came in noiselessly. Dina was sitting holding the book in her hands. I sat beside her and unconsciously drew close to her. Father had lit a cigarette and was drinking his second cognac.

'Bring me something to eat,' he said.

We huddled together. Four or five minutes passed. Then his dark glance fell on us.

'You haven't moved yet.'

'We've nothing at home,' Dina whispered, and her lower lip trembled, like her hands that were holding the book.

'When you talk, stand by me!'

Dina stood up and it was a struggle to hide her nervousness, to control the trembling. I shrank even more. Five more minutes passed.

'When are you going to bring me something?' Father almost shouted.

'No . . no . . thing, there's . . . no . . . . no . . thing.'

I dared not even breathe. The air came in and out of my mouth without me making the least effort. Dina returned by my side. She sat, I didn't dare even to huddle against her. Father was lost again in his thoughts and the opposite wall. Dina felt the silence heavy on her and she could not bear the pressure for long. She wept silently and from time to time a sob was heard. Father descended suddenly from his silence and the wall. 'Stop crying. I just asked for something to eat.'

At the door mother's silhouette appeared. Slim, tired she gave you the impression of not belonging to this world. She cast a look at father: 'You came back.'

'Noou, don't you see?'

Mother's glance towards us enveloped us like a protective umbrella. She saw Dina's tears, felt our fear but said nothing. She went out. She pulled from the pile of branches some thick ones, and put them erect in the fireplace leaving a small empty space under them. She put kindling wood in it and struck a match. She blew at it several times and through the door we saw smoke filling the yard. Some of it came into the room.

Father pulled at his thick boots. 'Bring me a chair.'

Dina stood up, took a chair from the corner and took it to him. She was sobbing.

'Stop it. Three days and three nights I go round the villages. I came to rest and instead I find you.'

The thick burning branches were reduced to embers. Mother came in, took a big pan and put it on the glowing fire. She came in again took some flour, put it in the bowl, added some water and a little salt, to make it more tasty. She went out. She threw some of the mixture on the hot pan and made a kind of bread. She piled it on a big plate. Father had already drunk half the bottle. Mother came in. She placed the plate on the chair in front of father. She took four pieces and gave two to each of us. She also took a piece for herself and sat in a corner on the only chair that was free.

'Specialist on baking bread. Water and flour. What a cook!'

However, we began to eat with great appetite. Dina stopped crying. We ate our bread and in our fear we enjoyed the flour and the water. Darkness began to fall.

'Light the lamp,' father said.

'There's no paraffin.'

'No food, no paraffin. What the hell do you have?'

Mother opened wide the door. The moon's rays fell on the centre of the room. And father, there at the edge, between light and darkness, sat and drank. His face became even darker. We buried ourselves in the bed in the corner, pulled a sheet over us, huddled together in spite of the heat and remained silent. Father drank and ate. Mother sat without saying anything.

'I'll go for sleep too. Tomorrow I'll be up at four,' she said eventually. Without undressing, she simply took off her old shoes and lay on the bed opposite ours.

'Shut the door when you come to bed.'

Father did not even bother to answer. We were almost asleep when father's shouting woke us up.

'No food, no paraffin? And you lie in bed, dresses and breeches on. What do you have? Nothing. What the hell do I come here for?' He tried to ride mother.

'I want response, you understand?' His hand felt his trousers but could not find the buttons. 'You never touch it any more. Whose toy you play with?'

'Manoli, you'll wake the children.'

'The children! They're turning out sluts, like you.' He tried to rise but the abrupt movement shook his head and he fell on to the floor.

'You push me?' He half rose, took a chair and threw it at my mother. She seemed to have been hit because she leapt with a cry of pain. 'I'll kill you. All of you. Why do I come here?' He got hold of the chair once more. We didn't dare even to breathe.

Mother slipped from the bed and instinctively made for ours. Father brought the chair down on the bed with force.

'Sluts. I'll kill you all. With whores we filled the room.'

Mother pushed us quickly under the bed.

'I'll shoot you all.' He stumbled. He fell and stood up again. Every time his fall caused him pain he screamed. He gave up the chair and began to search for his hunting gun.

Mother was by now pushing us through the open door and came out herself after us.

A shot rang through the night. But we had already started running and since our house was at the edge of the village we found ourselves running through the fields stepping with our naked feet on dry thorns and straw. Mother was running as if hunted. And without a word she pulled us behind her. She was holding me by the hand and a little behind followed Dina. I could not wipe out of my mind father's face, which I saw fixed on the wall, becoming one with it. Without realizing it we found ourselves well outside the village. It must have been close to midnight. A cold wind was blowing in the burning heart of June. All day the earth was inhaling fire and around five or six began to exhale it, but around eight or nine a cold breeze began to blow from the sea, that cooled the burning face of the earth. Sometimes there was no breeze at all, the fire refused to take off, it remained suspended three metres above the earth and the dull heat combined with humidity left no room for relaxation. The clothes stuck on you and you felt as if swimming in your own sweat. Tonight fear reigned inside us and the cold breeze blew without touching us. We found ourselves outside the cemetery. A bare enclosure with few dry thorns with the single cypress tree bending on the opposite direction from the one the breeze was blowing. A few bent, semi-rotten wooden crosses. At the corner a small room with all the signs of abandonment. Without uttering a word mother pushed the rotten door and we slipped in. She made us sit in a corner on the eroded marble slates. It was neither cold nor hot. I felt a sweet numbness. We must have slept before long.

The sun's rays on my face woke me up. Mother was still sitting at the same place. Dina next to me was still asleep. For the first time I felt the hard floor under me and my bones ached. Mother's eyes were red from sleeplessness. She must have been crying all night. I stood up, stretched, yawned and felt the numbness dissolving slowly. I looked through a small window that had no glass or shutters and my eye was caught by a huge tree, one of the few in that area, about a hundred metres away.

'Mother,' I whispered. There must have been something in the tone of my voice for mother stood up and came to the window. She too remained silent for a while.

'Gipsies,' she said. Five or six donkeys were grazing. Under the tree men and women were moving. They lit fires and made strange gestures. I had the impression that they moved to the rhythm of a music I didn't hear.

'Pewtering,' my mother said again. 'Boilers, pans. They're making spits.' I had seen gipsies before at the village. In couples the gipsy women, wrapped in faded clothes, with big earrings and holding a bundle of spits, went round the houses of the village offering to tell fortunes, mend pots and pans. I was impressed by the black moles on their faces. Now that I make my own whenever and wherever I want I'm not impressed so easily. In the mornings they went round to all the village houses and took whatever they were given. In the afternoons they went to the coffee shops. And I heard the men's laughter unleashed in all directions. A horse breaking free in the human grazing fields. Sometimes I saw two or three running away as if hunted. Now that I am an expert on men's hands which I've studied in the night clubs I work, my eye catches even the most imperceptible movement of their fingers, when I know with mathematical accuracy what movement will follow, I know why they ran away as if hunted.

Dina woke up and came to the window too.

'Gipsies,' I said.

It must have been past eight because the sun was already high in the sky.

'Can't leave,' mother said, 'before they leave.'

The men, after their morning mobility, now looked like machines that have exhausted their fuel. The women, in twos or threes began to leave for the village. The children, holding slices of bread, began to play in the open fields without minding the sun. The men spread coloured rugs wherever it suited them and lay lifeless. We sat again in our corner. Every hour we looked through the window but the gipsies were not leaving. Mother caressed us from time to time but said nothing. We felt hungry but we dared not complain. Mother left the small window and sat in the corner. We remained there staring at them.

'Can't leave. The gipsies will see us,' mother said again. And we stayed all day. We were afraid even to move. We left the window, we sat on the bare floor, we spoke in a low tone, we went again to the window. Our movements hit on the four walls and fell lifeless on the floor. Around five in the afternoon the gipsy women began to return. Some of them carried their infants on their backs. The way they wrapped themselves in their coloured clothes left a small hollow space at the back of the waist where they popped their infants and carried them wherever they went.

I remember one day a baby was crying. The gipsy woman,

spits in hand, went round, from door to door. At last she sat at the edge of the road, took the baby from her waist and in a neutral way thrust her nipple into his mouth the way you thrust a milk bottle into the mouth of a baby to silence it or help it to sleep.

Flames began to dance under the big tree. With dusk the flames became livelier – an illuminated background on which dark shadows danced.

'Time to go,' said mother. 'They will not move from the tree.' She stood up and we tore ourselves from the window. She opened the door as noiselessly as she could and we stepped outside, and fled in the darkness as a unified mass. When we reached home, at the edge of the village, mother said: 'Father must have left again.'

The house in front of us was dark. She cast a glance at the crude stable. 'The mule has gone,' she said. She took out a key and opened the door. Then she lit a fire, took flour and baked some chapati. I don't remember ever having eaten food with such appetite. Now that I'm writing about the night at the village cemetery, this bare place discharged of all emotion – the entire emotion was dancing under the tree with the gipsies and was reflected in our eyes – I remember a story that was reported in the papers. And in spite of the fact that I came to know men it impressed me much. A group of villagers, it was said, could not sleep. They finished their last card game and they went for a stroll. Without realizing it they found themselves outside the cemetery, at the edge of the village. Under a crude shed stood the hearse. Inside the enclosure stood the village church and outside almost adjacent to the surrounding low wall the house where the priest lived. They talked in low tones, they breathed the cool night breeze when suddenly their conversation froze, it stood suspended in the air. Groans and sighs came from the hearse. They hit on the wooden sides of the hearse. The groans and the sighs continued with some dull sounds on the wooden floor.

'Let's call the priest,' whispered one of them.

The others didn't bother to answer. Finally one of them took one or two broken steps towards the hearse, dragging his fear behind him. In trepidation he pulled open the hearse door. The sounds and groaning stopped as if cut by a knife. Three naked bodies, two women with their loose hair down to their shoulders and a man leapt out and, began to run through the streets of the village. Before the men had recovered from their astonishment the three naked shadows vanished behind the first houses of the village.

'Fucking,' said one.

They looked into the hearse. They saw two dresses, two pairs of women's shoes, a military uniform and thick boots.

'The National Guard in action!'

Father disappeared from our life very suddenly. When he came back to the village Dina and I had already gone, mother walked round the villages and worked wherever she could find employment. Our home was the link from one village to another. It was a link too among us three when, every now and then, we met again and stayed together for two or three days. Father disappeared for four years; they sent him to prison, and when he came back he was a broken man. The flash had vanished from his eyes, he never raised the tone of his voice and when he was in a position to buy a drink he drank it in the little corner of the big room and only with difficulty could he keep his head upright and his eyes open. Then he buried himself at one edge of the bed and slept deeply. The mule had been sold by mother for the lawyer to be paid. And father never rode an animal again. Occasionally he worked for a day or two and thus he secured for himself a plate of food and, from time to time, some drink.

Every now and then when mother came home she cooked for him and for two or three days he ate well. When Dina and I went to the village we took him some cigarettes and a bottle of cheap cognac. He never said a thing. He only stared at us with expressionless eyes.

It was August and the heat was at its highest. Some hot winds were blowing from the south and around noon you could see flames dancing in the middle of the road or held suspended on the rocks. Behind the high mountain, Crocus, was the neighbouring village. I still remember when mother took me with her. It straddled the valley road and the houses rose up the bare hills either side, with here and there an almond or olive tree. Lower down were carob trees springing from the rocks, and I wondered, then, how they tore the rock to drink water. But in the valley there were peach trees and apple trees, and lush vines. At the fringe of the village was the flour mill. Bread was not brought by the baker's van as it is now and the mill worked almost round the year. The miller, his wife and his deaf and dumb daughter, worked and lived there. I quite well remember the ditch through which the water flowed and fell on some huge winged wheels. And the villagers ground their wheat and barley, they made their dough and baked their bread.

That morning the miller's daughter was found in a bad condition. A slim girl, of Dina's age, fourteen or fifteen years old, with big eyes and straight black hair that fell down her shoulders. She cried and laughed with her eyes. Her parents found her sitting at a corner of the yard crying, a weeping that obstinately remained imprisoned in herself. Her legs were bruised and when they undressed her they found her nipples were swollen and bitten. They sent a message to the police and two policemen came in a Land Rover and took her to the town along with the miller and his wife. The doctor said that the girl had been raped two, three or four times; he couldn't say for sure. And when with signs the policemen tried to make her say what had happened she did not react. Her eyes filled with tears and she wrapped herself even more deeply in silence. Towards the afternoon she indicated that someone had dragged her out of her room and she kicked her feet and shook her hands, and screamed with her eyes. How he pushed her into a bush and she formed with her hand a head that went up and came down on hers, and her lips trembled and then bit. But his hands were iron pincers and in between his legs was a fire that burned her. Then she withdrew into a dumb weeping and silence. They gave her a tranquilliser the doctor had given them and the girl slept deeply, although her parents remained awake the whole night. They sat without saying a word at the crude table of the yard and the oil-lamp burned all night in the small room.

Two policemen came early in the afternoon in a police car. They asked at the coffee shop for our house, they left the car in the small square and they climbed up to our house on foot. Mother was as always in the yard.

'Is this the house of Manolis the mule-driver?' one of them asked.

Mother was surprised to see them. 'Yes,' she said, 'this is it.'

'We want him.'

'He hasn't come home for three days.'

'And where is he?'

'He goes round the villages on his mule. He always does it.'

'We'll wait for him,' said one.

Mother brought them chairs and they sat outside. She washed some grapes and took them some water from the big pot. They just sat and smoked. They didn't seem to be in a hurry at all. When father entered dragging the mule after him the policemen rose.

'Good evening,' said father

'Hello. You've got to come with us to the town. The chief wants you. We'll go in the Land Rover.'

'Is it me he wants?'

'Aren't you Manolis the mule-driver? He wants you.'

'Why? What for?'

'We'll talk or rather you'll talk about it in the town.' The policemen stood up. Mother was doing her housework but she cast some furtive glances. We sat in our corner and right from the beginning we had been staring through the open door. Father did not even enter the room. He left the room to go to the stable on his own. For a moment we saw his eyes. A vague fear had settled in them. Without saying a word he followed the policemen and started descending towards the coffee shop where the policemen's car was parked.

The night of the rape father had been drinking until late in the tavern of the neighbouring village. And as he was a bit dizzy he dismounted at the edge of the village at a short distance from the mill, roped the mule to a tree, buried himself under a bush and slept till dawn. The miller's daughter and her sobs made them understand that the one who had raped her three or four times had a moustache and his hair fell over his forehead. Some villagers informed the police they had seen father that morning dragging himself out of the bush, to tighten his trousers, to mount his mule and disappear in the direction of another village. Suspicion for the rape naturally fell on him.

When father did not return to the village the next day mother took the bus into town.

She went straight to the district police station, a large, low whitewashed building with its windows and doors painted a vivid green. In the huge yard there were some cypress trees with their trunks whitewashed, and some English cannons from the First World War. Mother entered the police station feeling a bit lost.

'Yes?'

Mother told them father's name. 'Manolis. The policemen took him two days ago from the village.'

The policeman was not in a hurry. He opened a big register. He shook his head. He spoke to someone on the phone and said to my mother: 'He'll be under arrest until the trial day.'

Mother stared at him as if lost

'For the case of the miller's daughter,' the man told her. 'She was raped three nights ago.'

'And Manoli?' Mother said again.

'Woman, there is some suspicion, a reasonable one. The law, you know.'

My mother felt the snakes of anxiety writhing in her breast. They let her see him. He was sitting in a cell holding his head in his hands. He did not even move when mother entered.

'Manoli, I've come.' Mother looked at this human wreck, who used to ride his mule and vanish over the horizon, who felt a fire burning inside him, who sometimes himself became fire and burned them.

'Manoli, I've come.'

'Good, you came.'

Mother touched him lightly – she hadn't done so for years, but the emotion evaporated at the edge of her own hands, the walls of his body. 'Today I'll see a lawyer,' she told him.

Mother returned to the village in the evening. Dina and I were sitting in the yard when we saw her coming. At noon Dina had sliced a lot of tomatoes and onions, put with them a lot of black olives, squeezed a lemon over them and added a little olive oil, and we ate. The heat was intolerable. You felt the humidity immobilised, suspended in the atmosphere, and we didn't even feel like moving. At noon the rocks of the surrounding hills emitted fire. We were able to sleep one or two hours, and in the afternoon we put the house in order so as to have something to do, and mother not to be obliged to do any housework.

We ran to her. She looked so tired. Sweat streaked her face. She took both of us in her arms and we sat in the middle of the yard.

'Father?' asked Dina.

'He's okay. He won't come soon, but he will.'

We didn't ask any more questions. Now and then she caressed our head and kissed our hair. At about eight she fried some eggs, cut some slices of tomato and we ate. 'What about you mother?' Dina asked.

'Later. I'll have something later. I don't feel hungry now.'

We sat in the yard until ten, ten-thirty. The line of the heat and the humidity that had been immobilised in the atmosphere began to break. A sea breeze began to blow and penetrated this veil and caressed our foreheads. Mother kissed us once more and put us to sleep in her own bed. Every time father was absent and she put us in her bed I felt a strange sweetness numbing the limbs of my body.

'I'll come soon,' she said, and went out to the yard again.

I remember after two or three hours I woke up and didn't find her. I walked noiselessly to the door and saw her sitting in the middle of the yard, wrapped in the night and immobility. The wind that was blowing from the sea became stronger but it didn't even touch mother. For a moment she seemed so near but so far at the same time. In the morning when I woke I found her sleeping next to me. I remained wrapped in myself because I didn't want to break her sleep.

Mother went time and time again to the town. She left early in the morning and returned late in the afternoon. She always returned tired. She lost wages and food began to disappear from the house. Fortunately, a neighbour, Mrs Evangelia, brought us from her own garden some vegetables, green peppers, eggplants, parsley, tomatoes, cucumbers. Sometimes a loaf of bread and some olives. We cut the green stuff in small pieces added some olives too, got an onion if we could find one, squeezed a lemon on them and ate them without olive oil. The olive oil bottle stood empty in the kitchen. Koumis never gave us things on credit now.

One day mother made us rise early. 'We're going to the town,' she said. 'For father.'

We dared not ask any more questions. As I went out to the yard to throw a little water on my face I saw dawn breaking on the surrounding rocks and a dim light to envelope all and I felt an untold sweetness. However the thought about my father interrupted the spell. In a short while the light would become harsh and the strong sun would affect all, lifeless or alive. And the heat would creep inside us spreading a feeling of numbness everywhere. We combed our hair and followed mother to the little square in front of the coffee house. The muktar's bus was already parked in the middle of the square.

We sat in the rear seats and silently stared at the people who began to move in the harsh light. At around seven or seven-thirty the bus was half filled and the muktar sat in a grand manner at the wheel. From above, a small ikon of the Virgin Mary stared at the passengers, and there was a small mirror through which the muktar could check the interior of the bus, and a message – 'No credit'. After casting a last glance through the mirror the muktar set the engine in motion and the bus moved off taking hairpin bends down the hills. Then it rushed free into the plain and in the distance we could see the town's slim windmills.

We passed through freshly-woken roads. Everywhere there was a movement which I, a young village girl, found amazing. Now things have changed; the town is inside me and I am inside it. The muktar parked the bus in a square.

'We leave as always at five,' he said.

We climbed out and walked through the streets of the town. The court was an old building built by the English with many rooms and stairs and iron rails. Whatever could be painted was painted a vivid green colour that hurt the eyes. Just opposite a square and a street and beyond that some boulders rolled down, one upon the other, down to the sea. And in the August morning and in the distance the horizon was an immobilised blue line. It looked as a continuation of the sea. We entered a relatively big room. A wooden bench, a big desk three times bigger than that of the teacher and on the right a wooden box without a lid and inside it father was sitting with a bent head. He gave me the impression of a broken line, a human wreck with reduced reactions. His eye caught us, something stirred for a moment inside, but he lowered his head, once more buried in a strange serenity.

In a short while the lawyer came in, tall, thin and getting on in years. He greeted mother, went to father, whispered something and sat right at the front. He placed a pile of papers on the bench in front of him. Then an inner door opened, someone banged three or four times on the bench, we all rose and the judge came in. He wore a black gown like the one worn by the preacher who came from the bishopric twice a year, Christmas and Easter, to preach in the village church. He moved his hands, he blinked his eyes, his triangular thin beard pierced your breast, and he spoke a language we didn't understand. Someone pulled the chair to make room for the judge and he stood for a while at attention without saying anything. I pressed myself, without realizing it against my mother, and felt her hand caressing my head. The judge sat down, opened some papers in front of him and began to read with a flat voice, like the boy who read from the Apostle's Acts in church. I understood he was asking my father something, and he answered in a low voice. Then the lawyer stood up, his voice rose and fell, there was a tone of passion in it and for a moment he pointed to us. His voice became unusually warm and his glance lingered for a while on us. When the judge spoke father stood lifelessly, just as he had been sitting. But his presence had something intangible, he gave the impression that he was there and at the same time that he wasn't. The lawyer continued talking, he gestured right and left, and he played nervously with the file of papers. He finished as abruptly as he had started and sat down. Father kept on standing as if lost.

The judge was still silent. He was writing something with his pen. Then he spoke, but I didn't understand what he said. The two policemen came to the opening of the dock and father turned with an effort, and found himself in between the policemen. I tried to read mother's face. I thought there was a tear in the corner of her eye. The lawyer cast a glance at us forcing himself to smile.

'I'll see you in my office, later,' he said.

Mother pushed us towards father. He only touched us with the end of his fingers, he took hold of mother's hand and then following the two policemen, he disappeared through a side door with our glance following him as if lost. We stood there for some minutes and mother kept staring at the side door behind which father and the policemen had disappeared.

'Four years do not pass easily,' Mother said, and pushed us gently towards the exit.

Thus father was sentenced to four years' imprisonment for raping the deaf-mute daughter of the miller.

Now I remember that some years later, a little while after father had come out of prison, we learned that a lonely character who lived in one of the big houses of the village, one who had lost first his parents and then his grandfather, who had brought him up, and who suffered from a kind of people-phobia, and who passed most of his time in his inherited fields, had been drinking one night around eleven in the only tavern of the village. No one was now in the tavern but he did not show any signs of going. And suddenly, being drunk, he burst into a loud crying. He beat his chest and the tavern owner tried to calm him down. Amid his tears he uttered some words, he mentioned the raping under a bush. And the deaf-mute daughter of the miller. However, for the police the whole case was just a file and the file had been sealed, someone had already paid for this crime with four years' imprisonment. Now that I carry with me so many experiences I understand what the Attorney General meant the other day when he said: 'Justice should not only be administered correctly but it should appear that it is administered correctly'.

Mother sold the mule in order to pay the lawyer and made up her mind to place Dina and me as domestic servants in two homes in the town. In this way we could secure food and twelve pounds a year would be deposited in bank accounts in our names.

On my last night at the village, I felt somewhat strange, but it was not a deep feeling it only touched the surface. Deep inside me I was unmoved. I was thirteen and Dina was almost fifteen. It was about time we earned our living. Mother had already found two homes for us. She had the addresses on two pieces of paper. Deep inside I believed that a new cycle was starting and that this time things would be better.

In the evening a shadow-theatre player arrived on the bus. Every two or three months he visited the village, climbed out of the bus at the small square with all his things in two bundles. In one were the shadow-figures and the screen and in the other, his clothing. He used to start work almost immediately. He stretched and fastened the screen on two poles which he tied to two chairs in a corner of the coffee house. He placed two tables behind the screen and spread the figures on them. At one corner he erected the vezyr's palace, a multicoloured and complex structure which made a tremendous impression on us. At the other corner he set up the karagiosis' hut. It was a square structure, four straight lines with a door and without a window, just as the poor houses of the village. He brought with him an acetylene lamp, like the one miners use, and when the performance was to start, the big oil-lamp in the coffee house was blown out, he lit it up behind the screen and as we were sitting in the semi-darkness our eyes were filled with the vezyr's multicoloured palace and karagiosis' hut. The shadow theatre player was a short, stout-man with rich curly blond hair, and blue eyes. His short thick arms were full of muscles that stuck out and during the intervals he went round the spectators, naked from the waist up, passing round a small tray, and each one threw in it whatever coins he wanted; the young ones threw pennies and the older ones threepences. They rarely threw shillings. We admired the muscles that stuck out from his arms and his shoulder blades. His voice was always hoarse but it had such a depth that, I don't know, it reminded me of his blue eyes.

Anyone who came to the coffee house was obliged to order a drink. Dina and I ordered a thick rosy syrup and then we threw our pennies on the plate. The coffee shop owner gave the player food and accommodation. A short while after the performance the player drank a small bottle of ouzo, ate whatever the owner gave him and as the noises died away and the village sank into darkness, he joined two tables in a corner of the coffee house and slept until ten in the morning when the owner opened the shop. We were impressed by his name – Bartholomew. I remembered our religious instruction teacher mentioning this name, but I never remembered on what occasion.

They said Bartholomew was a Turk who had been converted to Christianity but I didn't believe it because in his talk and voice there was nothing Turkish. Nor in his blond hair and blue eyes. On a previous occasion he was accompanied by his young wife – she was around twenty-five he was about forty. This time he was alone and I had the impression he was sad. They said his wife had run away with a policeman who passed by their house on his motorcycle every evening. And the young woman liked riding the motorcycle very much and Bartholomew had no vehicle.

As long as the lamp at the coffee house was lit I was thinking of the next day when we would leave for the town. When it was blown out and the small acetylene lamp was lit behind the screen I forgot everything. An absolute silence prevailed for the moment and the hoarse voice of the shadow-theatre player enveloped us. The performance was beginning.

5

Mathias Oriol had told Ioanna that they were going to Europe for their honeymoon. This was half the truth. He had casually mentioned that among the countries they were visiting was Switzerland. This was the other half. They were going to visit a famous neurological clinic. Something had to be done about the disease of his mind. Since 1948 the disease had manifested itself and there where he sat or stood his eyes were filled with the world, always full of wonder as if seeing something for the first time, light disappeared and was enveloped in darkness which lasted as long as the crisis lasted. He had asked his mother to tell him how he was when he was in the grip of the crisis, and he sensed the sorrow under the veil of a superficial indifference in her eyes:

'You simply sleep. Nothing else happens Mathias.'

'Mother, I want the truth, the whole truth. I must know what happens to me.'

'There's nothing else, beyond what I tell you, Mathias.' When he was young, around twelve, he started being tormented by dreadful headaches. His eyes had an expression full of wonder – at least this was the impression of his teachers. Someone, sometime, had told him: 'Something is dancing in your eyes, Mathias.'

He often looked at himself in the mirror and felt that what he saw in his eyes was not wonder. He felt vaguely what the others had taken as wonder, maybe it was kind of fear, just a first taste, a fear that perches on the fringes of reason – the midnight rider. Mathias didn't know how it came to him to call it that. Maybe because the midnight riders sweep along the sleepy roads of the town with great attention making as little noise as possible. A preparation for dawn, when the uncontrolled galloping would start and the endless plains would unfold in front of him. The dreadful headaches affected his eyesight to a certain degree and the doctors suggested spectacles. Thus Mathias now saw in the mirror a pair of eyes trapped behind a pair of lenses.

At the age of fourteen he had accompanied his father and mother to Cyprus. The copper mine had started functioning fully and with the start of the war the demand for ore was great. And father rubbed his hands with satisfaction. First, it had been the zinc mines in Bolivia. Now it was the copper mines in Cyprus. They had gone by ship to South Africa, by air to Cairo, then they embarked on a ship in Alexandria for Cyprus.

The metal constructions and the rails for the wagons looked like wounds on the body of the landscape and beyond was the sea which in the distance still kept its deep blue colour. And the houses of the miners' settlement, low-roofed, all having the same design, painted in the same colours was a somewhat unnatural expansion of the metal structures and the wagons. He remembered that he used to stand at the window of his room. On one side was the sea and on the other the plain and on it, like swollen breasts, were the hills. A group of children, they must have been seven or eight years old, stood under the window and set a small wire mousetrap. They didn't even notice him. When a mouse entered the trap a boy ran towards the miners' settlement. In a short while he came back, running, carrying a pot of hot water. The others stood round – there was something horribly ritualistic in it. They poured the hot water on the mouse. It squealed and danced in agony. Then there was absolute immobility. They took the mousetrap and headed for the settlement. They didn't even notice him standing at the window.

Mother had taken him to various doctors in the town.

Everyone gave his own interpretation. They suggested various measures, proposed different drugs. One remained silent for some time and fixed his eye on the table.

'Well, doctor?'

Mathias had gone out to the waiting room. He went to have a look at the magazines that were scattered on one or two small tables.

'Madam Oriol. There are no clear-cut answers. This is the strength and weakness of the human brain. I suspect that somewhere lurks epilepsy. Only strong tranquillisers can offer some way out. Very fragile of course, but we can't do anything else.'

Thus Mathias Oriol arranged his day according to the colour of the tablets. It was green in the morning, red at noon and bluish in the evening. His eyes deep inside danced but on the surface they were still. He had few friends. His parents turned part of the garden into an exercise ground. There was a basketball court and a white wall for tennis. He played by himself but always had the illusion that, somewhere, a crowd was watching him. At night he went out with his parents – to fashionable restaurants or the theatre. They often had company. Friendly families brought their girls too. Mathias was bored – a boredom that marked his movements, his words, his eyes.

In the mornings a sort of haze reigned inside him, an indefinable something that began to dissolve gradually, and the world invaded him. On his palate there was always a bitter taste from the tablets. When he had them he felt nothing. Gradually a kind of numbness spread inside him. But in the morning it was this bitter taste that stuck on his palate, his tongue. On the table, next to his bed they always placed a flask with sweet coffee. He drank two cups and he felt the numbness dissolving, the world invading him.

Now that he had finished High School, it was time to think about college, but Mathias felt his power for concentration declining day after day. He felt trapped. One day he announced to his mother: 'No more education.'

She smiled with understanding. 'Whatever you wish,

Mathias.' In her smile there was an invisible sign of sorrow.

After the war they settled for good in Cyprus. The company built the Oriols a mansion, with pillars, verandahs and stairs, a mixture of classical and modern style, something to remind them of the American South. Oriol, who had exhausted his passion for ancient manuscripts, turned now towards archaeology. He was fascinated by the Roman times with the theatres, the villas and the mosaics. He felt that the passion for football that began to spread over the island was a poor substitute for the Roman arena. But his mansion had a touch of the Roman villa, with its colonnade, white marble, pools, the green grass, the gardens. It was set in the middle of the bare plain with the clouds of dust and noise that rose from the metal constructions as a background on one side. On the other were the hills, which climbed in a crescendo towards the peaks of Troodos. In front was the sea, an immobilised indigo at one with the sky. It was at the same time a challenge and disembodiment. A challenge, both for the people and the landscape. A disembodiment because both in the rain and the heat the villa appeared to be swinging in the atmosphere.

Once his journeys had taken him to Tripoli. At a distance of about twenty miles from the city, from the very sand there rose a mass of rocks, and on the rocks the Roman ruins rolled down to the sea. Everything had been levelled. Only the arena and the theatre continued defying time, and the stone seats of the amphitheatre. He expected the Romans to rise from time itself and drag their ships on the rocks. He saw them almost disembodied laying their seal on time itself. Only their cloaks and helmets had been replaced by costumes and cigars

'The American dream. You're inevitably American, Oriol,' someone had said. And Oriol's villa was the third stage of the American dream. The metal installations with the dust and the noise and the miners' settlement as part and parcel of them was the first stage. The flats for the administrative staff, which inside had all conveniences but outside didn't seem to breathe freely, was the second stage. His villa the third.

Mathias Oriol settled as best as he could. He woke up at

ten, took the three kinds of tablets and indifferently went round from one office to the next, signed a document from time to time, and sometimes at night played snooker in the administrative staff's club with his mother discreetly controlling his every movement.

'The tablet is our only way, and no matter how fragile it is.' This word 'fragile' of the American doctor proved a fateful one for her. It was what the ancient manuscripts and the archaeology were for her husband. She didn't know if this state of affairs was the other side of the American dream. But she was determined to keep this way out open. And from inside her room she controlled everything that concerned her son. And he appeared to enjoy both the tablets and his life. And the skinny, bosomless American women. Only towards midnight he felt a sorrow piling up inside him. A bottle of champagne was the only way out. And then his third tablet. He slept deeply from two to ten and woke with the bitter taste of the tablet and the champagne on his palate. And he drank two cups of strong coffee to drive away the taste and the drowsiness.

At the end of July they always left for America. At the beginning his mother made arrangements that Mathias should be in the States when the American universities opened for the new semester. She thought some kind of excitement would make him change his psychological state and push him to make up his mind and enter college. Once, when Mathias met a childhood friend, and she started talking about the campus, the life that rolled between books and the exit of Friday and Saturday when they found themselves whirling in a collective intoxication, something stirred inside him. But it lasted for so little. And America made him feel bored. The family house at the fringe of the town, buried amid trees, emitted a serenity that made him feel bored. He had a desire for the metal constructions which wounded the landscape, the noise and the dust, things he could lean on. In his house he felt everything disembodied with nothing to lean on. The dream of an American college lasted for Mrs Oriol for three or four years. As she saw boredom piling inside him, she became resigned to the idea that Mathias' life would unfold in between the pills and the metal constructions. But every summer they still went to the American South, and she breathed the atmosphere as deeply as she could so that she could have the strength to endure the remaining nine months. For her husband, things didn't change at all. He settled in his office with his files, his private secretary, his telephone between America and Cyprus. And Mathias carried his boredom without complaining. They had turned a room into a cinema hall and when he didn't go out he watched comedies of the silent cinema. But in this broken but endless movement he found a way out from his boredom.

In 1948 the American Mines Corporation of Cyprus was the island's biggest employer with one thousand employees. A pyramid at whose base there were hundreds of miners with higher up, fewer people, and with only one at the apex – Oriol. On the wall behind his desk, there was a diagram with red and green lines spread one on top of the other, sometimes parallel to each other, sometimes cutting each other. And the pits went increasingly deeper into the earth. 'She's crying, they take her blood impure,' thought Oriol. 'So that we can purify it and return it to people.' His eye travelled over the metal constructions which were marked on the map like huge scaffolding. And the little bay with the small railway. They were also marked on the huge diagram. The copper was washed and purified and then carried by a small railway to the tiny bay. Then it was loaded on to small cargo ships. The bay water was permanently reddish. Behind the western hill the company had bought a huge area that reached the sea. They surrounded it with poles and a thick wire fence bearing the inscription AMCOC every mile. The sand was marked on the diagram with a golden colour. The miners' settlement was also marked. Before the war the company had built around thirty houses. Now there were five hundred, or more. And all around, on the diagram, the villages were marked – the Greek in green, the Turkish in yellow. And the golf pitch was all green. He had drilled at various points of the area that belonged to the company and found plenty of water for the needs of the company.

The colonial governor came often, incognito, at weekends. Oriol sent him his Cadillac and chauffeur and the governor and his wife drove into the heart of the northern plain and then for a while along the sea and for ten minutes they vanished into the orchards of the area and then they emerged in the open space of AMCOC, with the hills and the Troodos mountain range forming a protective line in the background. Then they drove through the streets of the settlement – cement bricks and green doors and windows but the real green was from flowers in pots, a few plants and some cacti – watched by the children and adults. And then the Cadillac slid into the drive and pulled up at the entrance to the Oriols' mansion.

'You've brought the American south to northern Cyprus, Oriol.' the governor said.

'The south is yourself. Therefore, Sidney, you carry it wherever you go.' And then he added rather indifferently: 'Are we going to have troubles with the natives?'

'The natives are of different kinds,' the governor replied.

'You understand what I mean?'

'With the support of some we'll bend the opposition of the others. The war and the bloody Russians have touched the body of Cyprus. The local Communist party raises its head, it wins municipal elections, sets up trade unions everywhere and cultural associations. On the other hand it's the church. Can't see beyond its nose. Enosis. For Greece to be able to breathe we killed the Communists. Then you came. You found the way open and you gave her the other lung.'

'Are we going to have troubles, Sidney?'

'Don't know Oriol. We're ready, anyway.'

A servant brought their golf bags.

'Let's go.'

They took the bags and went over to the greens, where silence enveloped them. Beyond, the sea changed colours and dusk fell over Akamas, the virgin peninsula. The sun vanished behind the trees and gradually merged into the purple sea. When they couldn't see any more they stopped playing.

Dinner was served on the verandah. The night was dotted with the lights of the settlement and the plant's red lights were drowned in the darkness.

'Time to sleep, Oriol.'

'Good night, Sidney.'

The next day both men swam in the sea, and afterwards the two couples lunched together.

'Pity the children are not here,' Oriol said.

'We'll have them at Christmas,' the governor replied.

At five in the afternoon the yellow Cadillac pulled up at the main entrance of the mansion and the governor and his wife set out at full speed for Nicosia.

Every morning at eight Roi, a tall man of thirty, bespectacled and with well-combed hair, entered Oriol's office holding a huge file. Roi was Greek, from the south of the island and had studied mine engineering in America. He loved the mines and the sea. His father had a small shoe polish factory in Larnaca, which his eldest brother had inherited and thus Roi made a career with AMCOC. He had two sisters, one older than himself and one younger. The elder one grew very fat. She passed most of the time at their house playing the piano and eating. She was lost literally among the sounds and when she gradually emerged from them she felt an irresistible appetite for food. The younger sister left Larnaka as soon as she graduated from the lyceum. She went first to London, then moved to New York and finally settled in Athens where she married a Greek officer.

Oriol knew Roi well and his family background. He kept separate files for each member of the administrative staff. The mini CIA, he liked to think. Encased in his office there was a lot of safes. Only he knew the combinations. In one he kept the files for the administrative staff. Roi, who rarely left the mine except during his month's holiday, and seldom during a weekend, had just been appointed production manager. Oriol gave him the then huge salary of two hundred pounds a month. Every Monday at eight Roi entered Oriol's office and spread in front of him some papers with huge diagrams that covered all the stages of production. And the line, broken, advanced with difficulty upwards. It panted in the effort like the miners themselves. Oriol saw the line climbing up and his eyes shone strangely.

'No problems Roi?'

'None, Mr Oriol. Some talk about work to rule. But I've got my ears everywhere.'

'In any case Roi, we should be ready.'

'My foremen have their key men in all the villages. Greek and Turkish. With the smallest incident they become operational right away.'

'Okay boy. That's the way.' But as Roi was reaching for the door, Oriol said: 'Work to rule, you said?'

Roi felt like laughing but in the presence of Mr Oriol he did not allow himself such luxuries. 'Yes, Mr Oriol. Work to rule.'

'The bloody shit. Do we work to rule? Where would they be if we did?' When emotion began to pile in him he couldn't express himself in Greek. 'Is it the bloody commies again?'

'I suppose so, Mr Oriol.'

'Watch them. Watch them, my boy. Work to rule.' He pronounced the last words syllable after syllable. 'They've got to learn something from us. Okay boy.'

Then the personnel manager came in. He was married with two children, a boy and a girl. His hair had turned completely white at the age of thirty-five, but had not thinned the least. He also spread in front of Oriol some diagrams showing the movement of the personnel. Foremen, clerical staff, those responsible for shipping the ore, miners. They were more than one thousand.

'Very good Papadakis. Excellent. We're now heading for the two thousand mark.'

Papadakis explained to him the philosophy of the personnel department. He had a tendency towards theorising, which bored Oriol, but otherwise he felt satisfied with him, because he carried out his duties with tact. There was something English in him. Papadakis had studied industrial relations in England. He explained to him how he interchanged the surface miners with those working underground according to the informers' reports. Everyone who showed particular sensitivity to matters concerning the trade union was moved from surface work to the pits. He manipulated the miners on the basis of shifts. Midnight to eight in the morning.

'Since they're underground, what's the difference?'

'Very good, very good,' Oriol said the phrase over and over. There were also the miners' houses. Papadakis used the houses of the settlement like pawns on a gigantic chess board. The five hundred houses of the settlement couldn't accommodate the thousand miners. He evacuated or filled them on the same criteria as he transferred surface miners to the pits or manipulated the shift lists.

'Walking is good for them.'

'Clever, very clever Papadakis.'

And the active trade unionists left the houses of the settlement and had to walk three or four miles to the neighbouring villages. Papadakis knew neither Greeks nor Turks. He knew only trade unionists and non-trade unionists, activists and indifferent.

'We've got to give the chance to all to enjoy the benefits of AMCOC's general policy. No privileged or unprivileged in our case. Socialism in practice, not on paper.' He mentioned the word socialism only when talking to workers. He had never mentioned it in front of Oriol.

Tony McDonald, the American, was the sales manager; he also kept diagrams. He didn't have to go to Oriol every Monday morning. He had covered a whole wall of his office with diagrams that showed the countries they exported to and the course of the exports. Usually he gave his reports to Oriol through an internal telephone. On the diagrams the price was also marked. Lines climbed steeply one or two steps, remained motionless, proceeded horizontally and then climbed with difficulty again. They rarely climbed down a step before they started climbing up again.

Most of the exports went to The Italian Mining and Trading Corporation. Their prices did not fluctuate in the same rhythm as elsewhere. Their course was steadily horizontal. McDonald saw the line and smiled. Oriol sometimes visited him in his office.

'Everything under control, Tony?' 'Yes boss. It couldn't be otherwise.'

Oriol was lost for half an hour among the diagrams. As if they were a big city's roads. He stopped at the Italian Mining and Trading Corporation line – it was an offspring company of AMCOC, something that only Oriol and McDonald knew. They were selling to it at steady prices and realized huge profits in Italy, as a result of re-selling.

In Oriol's office a diagram showed Cyprus, Italy, USA and Bolivia. A blue line joined these countries. When Oriol was asked what that was, he answered tersely: 'Air connection.'

Oriol had in front of him the Monday edition of the *Independent*, and with his scanty Greek he read and reread the announcement prominently printed on the first page.

'An extraordinary general meeting of the Agonos trade union branch is hereby convened, at the premises of the branch in Kalo Chorio, on Monday 27th of July at 6 p.m. Subject: Approval of the demands to be put forward to the AMCOC management. Representatives of the Pancyprian Miners' Trade Union will be present. Due to the importance of the meeting the presence of everybody is imperative.'

Members of the administrative staff entered his office, Americans and Greeks. Among them Roi and Papadakis.

'The *Independent* is a Communist paper, right?'

'Yes Mr Oriol. No other paper has published the announcement. The Bishop's representatives go round the villages and speak against the trade unions,' said Papadakis. 'Some preachers threaten active unionists with excommunication.'

'At least we haven't reached the Latin American stage. Red priests. Red ribbons on their cassocks.'

'The only colour that appeals to them is blue, Mr Oriol.'

'That's bad for Sidney. Makes no difference to us. We're neutral. They hate red, that's enough for us. Did we know about the meeting?' He turned to Papadakis.

'Something was said by the surface miners.'

'They're talking about increased exports and increased profits of the company, Tony. Where do they get the information from?' Oriol asked.

'My diagrams cannot be easily read Mr Oriol. Except by some. Simply they see the ships, sailing in and out of the port. And the railway working twenty-four hours a day.'

'Well. Get the information for the press ready. So as to be ready. Statistics are part of our methods. Get them ready Tony and send them to me.' He turned to Papadakis. 'What about us, are we ready?'

'The jobs down the pit will necessarily increase Mr Oriol. And the houses must be evacuated for the summer repairs. I hope they get the message in time. At a second stage credit at the groceries will stop and the taverns will have to close, temporarily.'

'I see your point. What about us, Roi? Are we ready?'

'Our men, both in the Greek and the Turkish villages, are expecting my message. On the other hand we'll start employing temporary workers. Mainly pupils.'

'Pupils are afraid of darkness and acetylene Roi. Pen pushers. They'll work down the pits two or mostly three days. Okay. Let what we've said be known discreetly.' He stood up. 'Tony, have the statistics ready, the sooner the better.'

Oriol lifted the receiver and dialled the secret number of the governor.

'Yes,' Sidney's smooth voice said.

'Morning Sidney.'

'Oriol, good morning. I was just thinking of next weekend.'

'I'll be expecting you. It seems we're heading for trouble. The Communists put forward certain claims through the miners.'

'We'll face them. I'll send you some policemen with dogs. Just to patrol around.'

'Okay. We'll talk about it on Saturday.'

He put down the receiver. He had a feeling that a new era was beginning.

In the afternoon two Land Rovers came each carrying five

policemen and their dogs. They would pass the night at one of the new police stations recently built at various points on the island.

They erected two iron cages at the Paphos Gate police station – one of the biggest police stations built on the walls of the old Nicosia. Two policemen undertook responsibility for the dogs, they gave them food and water, they talked to them while behind the iron bars so that some kind of contact would be established. For two days they didn't let them out of the cages not even for their natural needs. It was rumoured that the dogs had been bought in Britain, for five hundred pounds each. The colonial government issued only a very brief statement through the Public Information Office: 'There have been imported from Britain two police dogs.' No word of the reasons or the price they were bought for.

After two days they led them out of the cages for a stroll in the huge yard. Everything was fine. The dogs started getting angry whenever they saw a detainee in one of the cells of the Paphos Gate police station. On the third day they decided to take them for a stroll outside. According to the experts some kind of contact had been established. They led them out through the central gate in a rather official manner. They would pass them in front of the Palace cinema then down to the Solomos statue and after completing the round of the eastern section of the moat they would bring them back to the Paphos Gate. But under the huge plane tree there slept a big, shiny carefree Cypriot dog, one of those which sprang stray on the Cypriot soil.

The police dogs sniffed its presence. And suddenly the atmosphere was filled with fierce barking. The Cypriot dog lazily opened its eyes, raised its head a bit, but did not stir from its place. Everything happened so suddenly. The police dog freed itself from the policeman's hands and rushed towards the plane tree. But the Cypriot dog shed off all its laziness and started running with all its power along the pavement. After him ran the police dog. The distance between the two was becoming narrower. The Cypriot dog's tail swung in front of the police dog's snout. Everything happened in a second. The Cypriot dog turned at a right angle, crossed the road and passed onto the little square in front of the cinema. It took the police dog a fraction of a second to correct its course, but was found head long in the middle of the asphalt under a truck's wheels.

When the policemen and their dogs started patrolling the children came out into the streets and the women stood at the doors. They looked at the policemen with their dogs. At the settlement's coffee shop a few miners sat before getting ready for the night shift.

'Anglo-American co-operation,' said a miner. 'Who's the policeman and who's the dog?' He rose lazily from his chair. 'No work for me today. I'll be at the meeting.'

The Kalo Chorio trade union headquarters was a long, narrow hall with columns of concrete and bricks brought from the town. It had been built with voluntary work and represented a first attempt to introduce elements of a new building technology. They ran out of money before the building was completed and the hall was of bare concrete and unplastered bricks. A cement stair led to the verandah. That hot July afternoon the miners began to assemble. The afternoon shift and those working on the surface had finished at four. The night shift and those occupied with loading and unloading were sending representatives. By six the hall had been filled to capacity. Some were standing outside in the small square, which was nothing more than a widened street at that point.

There were Greeks and Turks from the settlement, and the neighbouring villages. Older Turks were distinguished by the red kerchiefs they wore on their heads. The young Turks were indistinguishable by dress or speech.

'Friends,' started Zantis, secretary of the branch committee. 'Before we really start the meeting our friend, the representative of the central committee, wants to say a few words.'

The central committee representative, a short, stout miner from the asbestos mines, rose from his chair and leaned on the side of the table. 'Comrades, I bring you the greetings of the central committee. I know that you've got very serious work to do tonight. Therefore, we'll keep aside the long speeches for another occasion. Three years have passed since the anti-Fascist war, and I know that many of you fought in North Africa, Sicily, Italy, before in Greece, and that drop after drop with your blood you fed the millstones that finally crushed the Fascist monster. The time we were fighting they promised us a different world. This world will be born sometime, you can be sure about that, but until it is born, we need at least half filled stomachs, less badly affected lungs, more human conditions of work. It's necessary, my friends, for us to stand on our feet. I know that work in the Agonos area is difficult. The men of the company try to build a wall between Greeks and Turks. They say we're different. We are, the way one man is different from the other. Who can tell, down at the bottom of the shaft, the Greek from the Turk? Is the rock softer for the Turk? The wagon less full? The Greek's eyes are less burned by acetylene? Does the dust treat our lungs differently? The hunger that starts from our stomachs, whose feet does it affect and whose not? Dampness erodes whose body and whose not? You've got the answer inside you, you need nobody to tell you. I know that church preachers go round the villages, and with their talk about Bolshevics, homelands, religions and families, play the company's game in their own way. But all of them have a formidable enemy! Life. And life makes only one distinction. Between the upstairs and the downstairs. Those who are riding and those who make this riding with their blood as comfortable as possible.

'Comrades, forgive me if I've spoken rather long. I convey to you the greetings of the central committee. I'm sure that tonight you'll take the right decisions.' He sat back and from the hall, and outside, there rose a torrent of applause.

Zantis, the local secretary, took the floor again and began to talk about the problems the miners faced. The wages he described as starvation wages and, at a time when prices rose continuously, stagnant wages would mean starvation and disease.

'You all know the grocer. You know how many shillings stay

in your pockets when, on Saturday, you pay the week's debts. What do we want? To increase these shillings to feed and clothe our families.' He spoke about those who work at the bottom of the pit and those on the surface. 'The company exploits the pit and the surface to split us. Elsewhere in the world, when the miners work underground, they get higher wages. We ask the same, an allowance of sixpence a day for underground work. We also want shift allowance.'

He also spoke about the settlement houses. He said that some kind of order should be kept, they should not be pawns on the chess board of the company. 'Of course, our long-term demand is houses for all the miners. Barren land, God be blessed, there's plenty; this land has also been bought by the company.'

A Turk, rather advanced in age, took the floor. 'Me, friends, don't know much. Trade union a good thing. The boss must talk to trade union. Can't say no.'

A young man, high school graduate, who, with the unemployment that plagued the graduates of 48, was forced to work as a miner in the shafts, rose to his feet. 'Comrades, what our friend said just now is very important. The trade union represents our collective power. That's why it must be in a position to negotiate formally. The company follows a clever tactic. In some ways it recognises it, in some others it doesn't. In other words, it tries to turn the trade union into an accessory of its chessboard which it can use at will. The formal recognition of our trade union is of primary importance, it will put an end to some of the manoeuvres of Papadakis.'

Another man stood. He was around fifty, but seemed older by ten or fifteen years; tall and skinny. Toil had eroded his cheeks and the dust his lungs. Amid this general collapse only his eyes kept their strength. His cough rocked his entire body.

'Friends, I won't talk for myself, but mainly for the younger men. I was twenty when I started. Thirty years of dust and dampness have eroded my lungs, year after year, as I dug the inside of the earth. The doctors call it silicosis. The older miners dug the earth, dug their lungs too, they choked and died without the privilege of having heard of silicosis. Every visit to a doctor in the town costs a day and a half's wages. Where will this money come from?' Coughs rocked him. 'From our stomachs. I wanted to say that the company has an obligation to us. To set up a hospital, where if we can't be cured, we should be relieved from pain. If it's so difficult for us to live like human beings let them give us the chance of a quiet death.' He sat down amid a silence almost tangible. But he rose almost immediately again.

'And write it down, comrade,' he said addressing himself to the secretary of the branch, 'that a pension at sixty-five for the miner is an unnecessary luxury. You can count those who will get it on your fingers.'

One by one the claims were agreed on. The representative of the central committee would help the branch committee to compile the relevant document. The branch committee would hand it to Mr Oriol the next day.

At Oriol's office on Tuesday morning it was the same scene as that of the previous day: Oriol sitting at his huge desk with diagrams, topographical and other kinds of maps covering the wall behind him. His face had turned into a mask that froze the atmosphere and did not allow room for feelings.

'The meeting, gentlemen, was held last night. And it was a success. Greeks and Turks seem to support the union to the same extent. The bloody Marxists, the bloody socialists – a full range of bloody rebels. Neither we, nor the priests succeeded. Gentlemen, I'm not criticising your work, let's understand each other. I'm just laying my hand on certain facts. Our findings will help us to take the right decisions. At eleven,' he looked at his watch – it was a quarter to, 'I'll receive a union delegation. The branch secretary has asked for this meeting. I don't want us to be criticised for intransigence. Let no one think this means recognition of the trade union. For me a trade union should be an expression of the spirit of self help. It's only from this point of view that I recognise it. To limit drinking. To create for its members the preconditions and provide them with the necessary incentives so they become good workers. Yes, gentlemen, good workers. It could also have organised their entertainment. Up to this point I recognise it. We Americans are not one-track minded. We've gone beyond this stage long ago. It's high time Europe learns from us. However, as an organ of collective negotiations I'll never recognise the trade union. So, gentlemen, as soon as you leave here, set in action your emergency plans. Word should be sent to your men Roi. Papadakis, speed up the process of employing extras. Mark out the houses that need repairing. They should be evacuated too.' He looked at them for some time silently. He wanted to give them some time so that the essence of his words should settle inside them. He looked at his watch. It was eleven. He pressed a button.

The union delegation found themselves in Oriol's office filled still with the administrative staff – who moved over to make room for the newcomers. A silence that betrayed a certain awkwardness lasted for some seconds. Oriol stared at each member of the delegation, separately. Basically it consisted of the members of the union branch committee. Only the miner who suffered from silicosis was added. Oriol knew the case quite well.

'Gentlemen, I'm sorry that, as you can see, I can't offer you a seat. Well, I'm all ears.'

The secretary took out a piece of typed paper. 'The general meeting of the union that took place last night at Kalo Chorio authorized us to put forward these claims and ask you to satisfy them within a logical period. The union, as you know, represents the overwhelming majority of the miners.'

Oriol shook his head. He read the union's demands in silence.

Then he said: 'I might have rejected it because it's not written in English. The official correspondence of the company is in English. However, to show the goodwill of the company I won't do it. This does not mean that I accept it. I'll keep it because it gives me an idea of how you feel. But I don't negotiate with trade unions concerning claims. With individuals, yes. I never deprived anyone of his right to ask from me whatever he wants. This procedure will be followed in this case too. I'll receive five workers every day.'

'It will take ten months,' said a member of the delegation.

'What if it does. There's plenty of time. Are we in such a hurry?'

'Time is one with our life,' said the miner suffering from silicosis. 'Their reserves are being exhausted at the same time.' He wanted to cough, he felt a weight pressing on his chest, but he checked himself.

'Gentlemen, I have said my last word.' Oriol stood up, a sign that the meeting was over. The union delegation went out first and then, one after the other, the administrative staff.

On Tuesday evening a general meeting of the union branch took place. The four o'clock shifts interrupted their work and came en masse to the meeting. The miners began to assemble soon after four. They stood in groups and talked aloud. They talked about a lot of things. The war that ended, the ruffian Koutouroushis who entered sums for goods they never got in his credit books, the prices of agricultural products that refused to rise, the grapes which the vine industries refused to take this year.

The young ones talked about the Seagull nightclub, where they could listen to music, drink and dance with girls brought in from the town. They paid a shilling for a dance, and sometimes they took them outside to the beach.

And now that the townsfolk had started buying cars, they came out to Agonos and they drank and ate on the beach. And sometimes they swam in the sea in the early hours and the feast continued until dawn.

'Friends, the branch committee had a common session with representatives of the central committee of the union. We unanimously arrived at the conclusion that Oriol's attitude is tantamount to rejecting our claims. At the same time it is a provocation and a mockery. He will discuss claims with everyone separately, five each day, and conclude an agreement with each.'

'Tell it to the Marines,' shouted one from the floor.

'Comrades, to the provocation we don't answer either with irony or words. We answer with action. It's obvious that Oriol sticks to his tactic of a limited recognition of the trade union. He receives our delegation, he receives the petition with our claims but refuses to negotiate with us. In his vocabulary the term collective agreement does not exist.'

The word 'strike' was heard from various directions.

'We'll have to show the American the Cypriot stubbornness. Comrades, we're coming to the question of the strike.' He started talking about the possible consequences. The union, with its small subscription, was not able to set up a strike fund, and the strike might last for two or three months.

'We've been hungry for three years. Three months more or less wouldn't make much difference.'

'The Pancyprian Miners' Union, as a first contribution, offers one thousand pounds.' Loud applause greeted the announcement.

'Koutouroushis will stop credit for us.'

'We'll go round the villages to collect food.'

The miner who had his lungs eroded by silicosis managed to be heard through his cough: 'Comrades, the struggle is not for ourselves only. It's also for the miners who'll come. Their right to live with decency and die with decency.' The deep silence that reigned, suspending the meeting for a while, was a sign of the impression his words had made.

'The company will try to evict us from the houses.'

'We've paid for the houses with our sweat three times their value by now.'

A young man of around twenty stood up on a chair. He had graduated from the Solea High School. He had been fascinated by economics, and wanted to study in Athens or London.

'Proletarian comrades! From the quarterly *Mining Review*, that is published in two languages, English and French, and circulates in all the Mediterranean countries, I got the following data! "The American Mining Corporation, having as its centre of activities in the Mediterranean the mine of Agonos in Cyprus, realized record exports of copper last year, the value of which exceeds four million pounds. AMCO is the chief mainstay of the Cyprus economy. It leaves in

Cyprus two hundred thousand pounds in the form of workers' wages and fifty thousand pounds in the form of administrative staff's salaries. The government receives thirteen thousand pounds in the form of income tax." Two hundred thousand pounds for one thousand miners and fifty thousand for one hundred office workers! Comrades, when we take into account installation maintenance expenses, paying off annuities and so on, we'll see that there is a profit of two million pounds for AMCOC. Two million pounds from the heart of our earth, our hands, our lungs, our eyes.' He stepped down from his chair. The miners didn't understand much but they got the talk about the two hundred thousand and the two million.

'Comrades,' the secretary continued. 'Besides the company, we'll face the hostility of the government. The policemen and the police dogs. And the theologians of the diocese, who will be talking about Communists, families, motherlands and the rest.

'No word about our stomachs and lungs. Only about our souls.'

'Evkaf will also be mobilised,' the secretary said.

'We'll face them,' two or three shouted.

The committee wanted a secret ballot on strike action.

In the *Independent*, and other morning papers of the following day a three column report was published concerning the situation that prevailed in the mines. 'At last night's general meeting of the Agonos miners it was, by secret ballot, decided to authorize the committee of the local trade union branch, in co-operation with the central committee of the Pancyprian Trade Union of Miners, to declare a strike if by next Monday the efforts of the committee for a solution satisfying the miners' claims come to nothing due to intransigence on the employer's side. The latter refuses to negotiate.'

The next day the secretary of the union branch came to Oriol and informed him that the committee would be expecting the official answer of the company by the following Monday, at ten in the morning.

Oriol listened to him in silence. Then: 'You'll have it,' he spat. As soon as the secretary left he dialled the governor's private number.

'Sidney, it's Oriol here.'

'So, after all, we're not avoiding the troubles.'

'No. I want a collective arms-carrying licence for fifteen or twenty of the administrative staff.'

'I'll send you enough for thirty, in case.'

'I'll be expecting you for the weekend. Golf and discussion.'

'Okay.'

Then Oriol pressed the button for his private secretary. He gave her a piece of paper with names. 'I want to see them separately today. Tomorrow at nine the administrative staff meet at my office.'

Meanwhile Mathias Oriol continued to wake at ten, drank two cups of strong coffee and went round the various departments. At night he sat in his room with the windows open and inhaled the sea-breeze. In these hot nights of July there were times when they nailed the wind in a corner and it did not make up its mind to rise. But there were times when it started timidly playing with the surroundings and then it warmed up and rose and Mathias Oriol was standing at the illuminated window with a glass in his hand and felt it infiltrate deep inside him. He sensed that the strike was coming, and noticed the policemen with their dogs.

'Who cares,' he said. 'The hungry will always ask for something. The old man can cope by himself.' And continued the same life. During the night he saw human figures mingling with dogs' shadows and had the impression that they infiltrated everywhere noiselessly. 'The law is a sleepless guard. For us who pay.' There was an imperceptible tone of irony. 'The American dream. What happens to the Cyprus dream?'

On Monday at midnight the shift miners put down their axes, took off their metal helmets and went through the dim shafts towards the exit. They refused to clock out.

'Clock your cards, boys,' the guard kept saying.

'Next time. There's time for the cards, Constantine.'

The surface foremen exchanged furtive glances. This strange silence and the warm human presence on the surface at midnight were new experiences for them.

'Boys, it's not right.'

'We don't negotiate individually. It's Oriol and the trade union.'

6

The waggons were immobilised on their rails. The great metal constructions remained silent, nothing disturbed the serenity of the summer night. The ever present dust died with the noise. In the distance the lights of the cargo-ships in anchor continued to glimmer in the night. Banners, written by hand, in thick broken letters that spoke of bread, silicosis, hospitals, recognition of the trade unions, were ready.

Fifty miners put on picket duty stood a little distance from the entrance. The rest stood silent a few yards farther. Then they sat on the ground, in groups of four or five, opened their little parcels or their food boxes and started eating their dinner. The policemen with the dogs made their appearance. The dogs seemed a bit impatient but were held fast by their straps, at some distance from the pickets.

The branch committee met continuously through the night. Every half hour a young man riding his bicycle set out from Kalo Chorio and disappeared in the direction of Agonos. Every thirty or sixty minutes somebody arrived in the same way from the mines. He leaned his bicycle on the wall and entered the union building.

Mathias Oriol did not sleep at all that night. It was past two, his usual time for bed, but he kept standing at the window. He stared at the pickets, the policemen with the dogs, the silent installations. He drank champagne but could not get himself to go to bed.

At four-thirty the dawn began to break. The plant, an

amorphous dark mass dotted with small lights, started taking definite shape against the sky. It was strange that amid the immobility and the dim light this metal giant lost its bulky shape. Beyond, in the sea a red disc – a red palette that dripped red paint as it ascended in the sky. And the fifty pickets became a hundred and formed a human wall in front of the entrance of the mine. And the miners of the morning shift began to assemble. A van was found – someone placed it at the disposal of the union. Somewhere three huge saucepans were found and coffee with milk was made. They loaded the saucepans, the coffee and loaves of bread, and set out for Agonos. The miners filled their tins with coffee, they each got a piece of bread with some olives and went to a corner where they drank their coffee and ate their bread. The pickets were replaced by miners from the morning shift. At seven the foremen began arriving.

'No work today,' murmured one of them.

Oriol watched what was going on in front of the mine entrance. Strangely he felt no anger. He had submitted himself to a profound catharsis and left no space for sentiments he didn't control. His brain was clear as steel.

'They shall not win, it will be a beginning without end.' He glanced at the diagrams and the maps that covered the office wall. That was his area. 'I'll let no one interfere with my lines.'

Mathias Oriol, half drunk, looked at the picket and the assembled miners.

'Little soldiers they place for battle,' he thought. 'Will they mow or be mown down?' And suddenly he thought it was time he went to bed with one of those American women. His glance went to the Seagull. Of course he went on the arranged excursions to Nicosia with his two gorilla companions. Now, at the end of July, the families of the administrative staff would be arriving from the States. He emptied the half filled glass of champagne and looked at his watch. Seven-thirty; time for sleep. Feeling his head light he walked to his bed. He took two tablets and swallowed them with a little water. He fell asleep almost immediately.

To the policemen with the dogs were given two offices on

the ground floor where they installed two tables each with a telephone. The back door opened to a big yard. There they tied the dogs under the trees, put food in front of them and water, and let them sleep. The rest were yawning in the two offices. They watched the miners.

'Hunger will make you dance,' one of them thought, but he said nothing.

At nine Oriol's office was packed with the members of the administrative staff. 'Forgive me for having piled you all up here. But it's an emergency situation and if there's a certain lack of comfort it's justified by events. What's going on out there you've seen with your own eyes. They will not win. The strike and its outcome will provoke chain reactions in Cyprus. I read in the papers that the builders' union has put forward tough claims to the building contractors. Natural consequences of the war. From now on we must all be on the alert. You'll be at the company's disposal twenty-four hours a day. If need be we'll help the policemen as guards. The mine installations are sacred – we'll allow nobody to touch them. They're part of us and we're part of them.' His clear steel-like mind exercised such control on his voice that his speech was in a monotone, but harshly penetrating. 'Well gentlemen, I'm listening.'

McDonald said: 'Three cargo ships are anchored at Agonos bay, half loaded. Loading would normally have finished tomorrow. The small railway, as you see, doesn't function. To set it in motion now, with the strike, is somewhat difficult, if not impossible. However, the ships have to leave at the latest in four days. Otherwise, the company will sustain big losses. We'll set in motion the old system, waggons and barges. The foremen will work, the clerical staff and, as a last resort, the administrative staff. In any case the ships will leave in four days. We've got reserves for fifteen days. I've studied the contracts for delivery.

'Priority,' he said, and glanced at Oriol, 'is that of the Italian Mining and Trading Corporation. We'll honour them under any circumstances. As for the other trading partners, I'll send them telegrams today. Loading is suspended temporarily due to technical difficulties. I hope they will understand. Gentlemen, loading of the three ships is resumed today at two. I hope you will be ready if need be. Thank you.'

As long as McDonald was talking Roi, the production manager, was thinking that he had been planning a fifteen-day holiday at Larnaka. He would stay at the family house, with his mother and his older sister. He would be tortured a bit at the beginning by his sister's piano – this endless stream of sound that was unleashed during all the hours of day and night. Somewhere inside he had a feeling that his sister had become sound and food. He wondered what part sex could play in her life. But her massive buttocks and belly seemed to exclude any such possibility. He would accompany her, sometimes, to a dance or a restaurant, to an open air cinema. He would take his boat with him. He would load it on a trailer and drag it after his car. He would explore the coast to the east of Larnaka. He had heard of some sea caves outside Ayia Napa. And he would attempt to reach Apostolos Andreas promontory. But now with the strike . . . Roi snapped out of his reverie.

'Our men at the Greek and Turkish villages have been mobilized,' he said. 'They face, however, union terrorism. Men who, before, would have come on their knees to the mine entrance in order to be employed, now feel scared. Even to talk to our men. Terror is the only explanation.'

'You're exaggerating Roi,' Oriol said. 'But the theory of terrorism is extremely convenient.' He cast a glance at his private secretary. 'Take it down, we'll include it in the communique we're issuing later.'

'Our men,' Roi went on, 'in spite of this managed to convince fifty agricultural labourers to start work at the mines. They are ready to present themselves whenever they're needed.'

'We won't present workers tomorrow. However, they must be ready for Thursday.'

Then it was Papadakis' turn. He pushed back the white hair that fell across his forehead and shook off the drowsiness that permanently perched on his eyelids. He spoke flatly. He opened a file.

'Employment of temporary workers. The recruitment of the fifty peasants by our men to which Mr Roi referred is employment of temporary workers who can become permanent. An attempt will also be made to recruit pupils. I've got the announcements ready and this morning they will be posted outside the churches and in some coffee shops. In the meantime, some work has been done, and already fifty pupils will be employed as temporary workers.'

'Of course, down the shafts, they won't stand it for more than half a day. Anyway, they can be used as surface workers,' Oriol said.

'Subject number two. Essential repair of the settlement houses. It's necessary for maintaining and keeping the houses in top condition. It's part of the social policy of the company.' Oriol cast a glance at his secretary, as if telling her to underline that. He would need plenty of ideas for the communiques the company would feel obliged to issue regularly during the strike.

'And for the essential repairs their evacuation must be ordered right away. Previously something like that would have been done gradually. I don't see the reason now to follow this tactic.'

Oriol said the plan should be put into action in a week's time. Not before.

'Anything you decide Mr Oriol.'

A short discussion followed during which every one of the administrative staff expressed his opinion, made suggestions and demonstrated his endless devotion to the company.

'Gentlemen, thank you,' said Oriol. 'The union branch committee has not taken into account the administrative staff. My secretary has been keeping notes and a special document will be composed that will be found in a special file, both in mine and Mr McDonald's office. You can consult it whenever you want. I'll see you at two when loading of the anchored ships will be resumed. You'll carry on your normal work at your offices.'

At two in the afternoon, the whole administrative staff, with Oriol at the head, came down to the installations. Oriol had sent a note to the police officer in charge, just in case, but asked them, at present, to keep themselves at the background: The foremen were there too. Mathias Oriol crept among them and enjoyed the spectacle of his father who gave the impression of an elderly general directing his staff at the battlefield.

The picket and the other miners who were assembled at various points smiled ironically. The loading system could not be put into operation. But when they saw Papadakis, Roi and McDonald roll up their sleeves to shovel ore into the waggons, and the foremen to push them into the little bay and load the barges, with Oriol holding a big pad and noting down the waggons used, their smiles vanished. A cyclist set out for Kalon Chorio, for the union branch. It was something they had not anticipated. Loading lasted until eight when the light began to fade. Oriol gathered them all, foremen and administrative staff and proceeded towards the illuminated offices of the company. A beer and something to eat. Mathias Oriol enjoyed it immensely. In this afternoon development he found an escape route from daily routine.

Late at night the union branch committee took the decision: Loading should be stopped.

At seven in the morning the number of pickets was doubled. A wall-like line covered the entrance to the mines and a human circle surrounded the metal structures. At eight Oriol arrived with the administrative staff, the foremen and some pupils. It was very early for Mathias – normally he woke up after ten. Oriol nodded to the chief foreman. He proceeded towards the pickets.

'You must make room, for the waggons to be loaded. We don't prevent you from doing your job. We demand the same, no more, no less,'

Their silence formed a wall.

'I repeat. We must do our job.' Pushing, Oriol tried to make way between two miners. It was impossible – as if they were rooted to the ground. He made a signal to the foremen and the pupils. The latter took some steps towards the miners but were forced back. The foremen tried four or five times but the human wall held fast. Their silence didn't break either. And suddenly the policeman with the dogs appeared. The one in charge was holding a portable loudspeaker.

'Gentlemen, what you do is illegal. We won't allow it. I give you two minutes to make room for the loading of ships to continue normally.'

The miners made no movement. The dogs felt uneasy; they growled and felt their leashes tighten. The two minutes had passed and the policeman in charge began to lose his patience. He looked at his watch. Everything happened suddenly. The signal was given and the dogs rushed upon the miners. Banners were torn. Planks came down on the dogs' heads. Human flesh was bitten and cries of pain were heard. The pickets who were guarding the entrance of the mine left their positions and rushed towards the installations. The foremen rushed towards the miners but the pupils, trembling, moved away. The noise struck the settlement with unusual force and hundreds of miners gathered around the waggons. The one in charge gave the signal for retreat. Each side licked its wounds. The policemen retreated to the point where Oriol and the administrative staff were standing. Mathias Oriol opened his window and through the morning mist that reigned in his brain and eyes he saw men swimming in a vacuum like shadows. The miners were carrying their wounded to the nearest houses of the settlement. Women boiled water and washed their wounds. No cries of pain, no shouts. Anger – horizontal, persistent – covered the pain.

At ten, Land Rovers full of armed policemen arrived. They jumped out, arranged themselves as if for battle and, without warning started shooting above the miners' heads. Some of the bullets hit the iron beams and produced terrifying noise, whistled, changed course. Two or three miners fell on the ground moaning from pain. but the wall and the silence had broken. And the miners retreated towards the settlement. Silence had broken. Silence reigned again. The silence of the policemen arrayed in order of battle and that of their rifles. Around twelve, Oriol came down from the offices accompanied by some of the administrative staff. He inspected the installations, the waggons, the rails. Damage could be repaired very quickly.

'Loading must be resumed as soon as possible,' he said.

At around four, with the July sun dominating the earth and the sky, with the policemen arrayed as if for battle around the settlement, Oriol emerged again holding his files, accompanied by the administrative staff, the foremen and some pupils. And the loading of the three ships started slowly, persistently. It continued into the night for Oriol gave instructions for all the lights to be switched on, and the night became day, and the policemen changed shifts, and the wounded raved in their fever and the women dipped towels into vinegar mixed with water and placed them on their foreheads.

At five the next morning the light balanced on the edge of darkness. Movement and anti-movement, something that imperceptibly infiltrates everywhere pulling out from the inside of a temporary non-existence. Everything was still in the morning haze.

'Not bad, last night.'

'What a shift we were on. We'll have this kind of fruit from now on.'

'People have to eat, you know.'

'And work.'

'Work and not be able to eat?'

The other voice remained silent. It was as if it lost its way and felt for it in the wilderness of the morning.

'What do we care? We obey orders. The less we discuss about them the better. Even our rifles have ears.'

Now it was the other voice that had lost its way. And it didn't find it in the dim light of the morning.

The pickets took their places in front of the entrance. For a time they didn't approach the plant. And the policemen had instructions not to move against the pickets as long as there was no reason. All depended on the way things developed.

However, from the back doors of the settlement houses

there slid human shadows, one after the other was drawn against the dim background of the sea. They headed for the Seagull. They then turned left. Fifty, one hundred shadows slid in the same way. Noiselessly they arrived in front of the small port.

A policeman who had noticed two or three shadows said to himself: 'Don't bother, they're just going to the sea for their early morning piss.' And he leaned on his rifle.

The sun started rising fast. It was only seven but Oriol was already at his office. Going in he glanced at the maps and the diagrams. He felt an immense satisfaction for his immediate environment, which did not change easily.

'This is reality,' he thought. 'We won't let it be disturbed.' He looked at his watch. The hour hand had just gone past seven: 'Let them sleep a bit more . We've got time.' He sat at his desk, took a piece of paper. He started writing the first AMCOC communique concerning the strike. The right of work is inviolate . . . . He didn't like it . . . The sacred right of work, when freely exercised, should not be violated by anyone . . .

At around eight the administrative staff were at their places. The foremen were already in the yard. They all looked tired. Every new adventure, according to Oriol, has a relative cost. At eight-thirty they came down to the yard. The policemen on the night shift were replaced. Except for some scratches on the metal beams, and some empty cartridges scattered on the ground nothing else indicated what happened the previous day. The only strange thing was the immobility and the silence of this metallic giant. Ten waggons were placed on the rails, one after the other. Some pupils began to work. Now the miners were not around they did not feel so bad. The chief foremen would push the waggons towards the little bay. There they would help the bargemen. It took them one and a half hours to load the waggons. At a distance of about two hundred yards the policemen were walking their dogs around, to give them a chance to exercise and relieve themselves. Between the metal structures and the settlement stood the policemen with their helmets and their rifles. And at some distance the pickets were guarding the entrance. The waggons set out slowly and Oriol made notes in his book.

About a hundred yards from the little bay the waggons stopped. 'Stop – Ei stop – stop – st . . .' the cry moved horizontally as if taking part in a relay race.

Thirty human bodies lay across the rails and the waggons could not move. Confusion reigned for four or five minutes. Then a foreman tore himself off the line of waggons and men, and went running towards the loading area. Oriol heard the news undisturbed. He called the policeman in charge.

'The rails are the company's property. Just as the land on which they're laid. Trespassers are prosecuted. Loading shall be carried out.'

The one in charge took ten policemen and left the others staring at the settlement with their sleepy rifles in hand. When the ten arrived at the point where the waggons lay immobilised they saw the bodies lying across the rails and didn't know what to do with their rifles and helmets. The one in charge scratched his head awkwardly. He overcame that soon and gave the signal for the removal of the miners from the rails. But the bodies that lay on the rails shook violently at the human touch as if suffering an electric shock. Their hands held fast on the rails, their feet kicked violently in the air.

As a body was removed another took its place. The miners crept in between the wheels of the waggons and it was a struggle to get them out. He called the rest of the policemen and they, sweat streaming down their faces, carried the human bodies and locked them in a nearby store. Three policemen with rifles guarded the door. They were given clear instructions. Anyone trying to escape should be shot in the legs.

At noon the field was cleared and the waggons began to move slowly towards the little bay and the work continued unabated until ten at night. Oriol, all the time, made notes in his pad.

The night shift of the policemen took up their positions outside the miners' compound. All was quiet. They sat on the ground and leaned on their rifles. Two or three walked up and down.

It was past midnight and Mathias Oriol drank his champagne as always. He was staring at the sea when the night was filled with a blinding flash and a noise that made the policemen spring to their feet.

Two shadows had slid in a rubber boat to the west of the tiny bay. They tied two bundles of dynamite sticks on the rails, they unrolled the wire and left in the direction of the boat. The waggon rail was shattered. Then the compound was quiet again.

On the third day Oriol gave instructions for the three ships to sail with whatever ore they had. On Friday Oriol gave orders for the shafts to open. Those employed after the declaration of the strike would begin work. And those pupils who could stand the stress. In addition to the ordinary wages they would be paid an extra allowance that would vary according to their productivity, from sixpence to one shilling and sixpence a day.

'Exceptional loyalty allowance,' Oriol described it.

Early on Friday morning a force of eighty armed policemen and thirty foremen arrived at the entrance, and pushed aside the pickets. The policeman in charge had learned his words by heart: 'According to the law the pickets should not, physically, obstruct the free flow of labour.'

'Tell it to the Marines,' one of the pickets commented.

Those who were going down the shaft began to approach the entrance. They felt somewhat strange at the policemen's presence. And suddenly they found themselves in between the pickets. There was something naked like steel in their glances. The blacklegs pressed through, nervous but in need of wages. Then two pupils broke down and started running towards Kalo Chorio. The policemen were at a loss for a moment. A wild triumphant cry tore from the chests of the pickets. And the remaining blacklegs, almost running, went down the shafts. Oriol watched the scene from his office window. He didn't seem particularly satisfied. 'It's something anyhow. Every beginning is difficult.'

Ten armed policemen remained to guard the entrance. The rest withdrew. They went to bed. They should be back by four, the time the blacklegs would be coming out. Two or three policemen with dogs patrolled the area of the installations and the little bay. All the rest were resting, for their main responsibility had been now shifted to the night.

The same day two policemen found a rubber boat tied on some rocks which formed the entrance of a small cave. It had been stolen from a store where the administrative staff kept various recreation equipment. They loaded it on to their Land Rover and took it to the police station. From there they would take it to Nicosia for a detailed examination for fingerprints. The same night two young miners who were sitting at the small square outside the union branch were summoned for interrogation and late, at around eleven, they were sent in a police car to Nicosia.

7

On Sunday morning he came to Kalo Chorio in the Bishop's car. In spite of the morning heat he was wearing a dark costume and a black tie. His thin beard, white here and there, was carefully trimmed and his thinning grey hair was well combed. Every Sunday he went round the villages of the diocese and preached at the end of mass. The Bishop himself had given him a definite three sections line; religion, homeland, family. And the godless and the enemy of homeland and family would be his speciality. He faithfully interpreted the Bible and his interpretation left no room for doubt. Even the Bishop himself felt somewhat uneasy in his presence. After his first child the doctor warned him that his wife could not have a second without risking her life. And he started explaining to him using here and there a scientific term. The preacher did not listen to him. When the doctor finished he said: 'If it's God's will.' And his wife became pregnant a second time and died during labour since the preacher obstinately resisted every suggestion for abortion. And he published in the newspaper: 'I accept no condolence. My wife has been summoned by God to be near him.'

His food was meagre, in contrast to that of the Bishop, and he gave the impression that he ate mechanically without any trace of enjoyment. But he never said anything about the Bishop. Hierarchy was one of his laws. The first time he went to preach in a small village on the slopes of Troodos, a hermit, follower of the old calendar, came down from the neighbouring forest. His long matted hair hung over his shoulders and his fierce beard covered his naked hairy chest. His rags hung like his fierce beard. A strong smell of pine, sweat and dried urine arose from his body. But within his eyes there was a cruel serenity. The preacher refused to preach unless the church committee drove the hermit away. The latter was standing motionless at a corner of the church, carrying a crudely made wooden cross. He was wrapped in his silence, and was balanced between conscious existence and subconscious non-existence. The angry voice of the preacher touched him.

'Why?' his vocal chords sounded as if from a deep gorge since they were not often used.

'Because you ridicule Christ.'

The hermit turned his head backwards. He saw no one. He was again wrapped in his silence. An absolute silence reigned in the church. After fifteen minutes the hermit, as if waking from a deep torpor, stepped slowly out of the church and carrying his wooden cross vanished in the nearby forest.

Hierarchy, apart from being a law by itself, has its own laws. And the preacher preached his sermon. Now he does not know how many sermons he has delivered.

'Villagers,' he was standing on a big stool, the Bishop's throne as the villagers called it. 'For the first time I won't talk on a specific passage of the Gospel. Reality forces us to. No one, preachers included, can ignore facts. At the beginning it was the Word. And the Word above all meant and it still means the negation of chaos. Chaos and anarchy lead us away from God. Order and persistent discipline lead us nearer to Him. The whole area is shaken by the miners' strike. The church does not turn a deaf ear to the workers' claims and it is fully aware of the difficult conditions they live and work in. Nothing, no situation however tragic it may be, can be taken as an excuse for deviating from the lawful order and resorting to the dark forces of violence. It's even more serious when these things are done under the leadership of Communists, enemies of God, homeland and family.

He paused to look at the crowd. 'And I can't overlook the

fact that strikes like this one disorientate the people, they cut them off from the only permissible struggle, that is the struggle for the union of Cyprus with Mother Greece. And this struggle we won't be in position to carry out if we do not keep ourselves, literally and metaphorically, pure, if we turn away from the tested Greek-Christian traditions and we allow alien ideologies to infiltrate us.'

He kept on talking in this manner for more than forty minutes, and there was the strange spectacle of the preacher who progressively sank in his own emotion until he himself became an emotional cry and a congregation found it impossible to follow him and internally it remained indifferent. At the end the village priest read a short circular of the district bishop who expressed his sympathy for the workers' demands but unmistakeably condemned the strike.

With August the weather became hotter and more humid. During the day the thermometer climbed to forty and during the night it didn't fall below twenty-two. With the heat there came humidity too, a thick transparent veil hanging motionless in the atmosphere, that stuck to naked skin, and clothes. The villagers didn't dare go to bed before eleven, but there were some staying up until twelve or one and they sweated in the stillness trapped in a lake of humidity. After one, all was deserted; the last lamps were blown out and the villages around Agonos sank into absolute darkness. The mine installations became an illuminated pillar that disappeared in a dark background and the tiny lights of the Seagull twinkled dimly in the distance until two.

It was then that the miners set out in groups of twos and threes. They put on dark coloured overalls and pulled brown stockings over their faces. They slipped like shadows from various points. In their pockets was pepper and other spices, improvised combinations to mislead the dogs in case of being chased. On that first night three groups of two set out. One at Kalo Chorio, one at Lefka the Turkish village with its orchards and one at Spilia, the village that had sprung as a projection of the forest.

Hidden under their clothes each had two freshly cut branches.

The strike had entered its second week and the blacklegs neither increased nor reduced. The pickets' glances were like iron on them every morning and afternoon. Gradually, however, the blacklegs got used to the situation and went on without caring.

At exactly two-thirty, in all three villages, loud knocks on three doors were heard.

'Who is it?'

'Kouspos? The chief foreman, wants you.'

Between sleep and wakening the brain did not work, it stretched sluggishly, and pushed the body without realising it towards the door. The door half opened but four hands pushed it and on the threshold were two men in dark overalls and stocking masks.

'The American sends only to Kouspos his present.'

And the fresh sticks hissed in the night as they tore the air, mingling with human cries. And in the background there were the voices of Maria, Aishe and Areti, and somewhere deeper inside children's crying. Then the shadows vanished the same way they came and three blacklegs in Kalo Chorio, Lefka and Spilia were left sobbing on their own thresholds. Prematurely awakened neighbours found them in this state with their wives bending over them, crying woefully. After taking them inside they washed their wounds with vinegar dissolved in hot water.

Oriol wrote the communique himself: 'Last night, at two-thirty, there took place a cowardly attack carried out by masked men against workers who refuse to obey foreign instructions and continue to offer their service to the company. Repeatedly we have mentioned that we regard the right to work sacred and as a company we will do whatever we can to safeguard it. The case has already been reported to the police and the company management has appealed to the government of the colony to take the necessary measures for securing uninterrupted work in our mines. We state once more: Terrorist actions like this one will not force us to give in to unreasonable demands, which we believe do not emanate from the miners themselves but are foreign in origin. Our attitude and policy serve the well-understood interests of the workers because without a healthy company there cannot be a prosperous working class.'

The police statement gave a brief outline of the night's events, and added: 'The police are carrying out investigations'. The following night, after eleven, police dog patrols appeared in the three villages. And when he had the chance the preacher, during his Sunday service, elaborated on the commandment 'Thou shall not murder'. His main argument was that violence leads to murder and consequently to the violation of God's Word.

In Nicosia and elsewhere a strike had been declared in the building industry. The builders were the hardcore of the working class movement.

The bus was proceeding to Korno village in the direction of Limassol. The asphalt road was narrow, full of bends and pits. The light traffic consisted mainly of buses, a few private cars and many motorcycles.

The bus drove on and two motorcyclists followed it at some distance. The bends piled, one on top of the other, and the bus lost its normal rhythm. At the last bend the motorcyclist overtook the bus and forced it to stop.

From the fields on the right a third motorcyclist appeared. He held the handle bars with his left and a pistol in his right. His eyes were neutral.

'Follow the motorcycles,' he told the driver, the tone of his voice similarly neutral.

The two motorcyclists drove on and the bus started reluctantly. Behind came the third man, pistol in hand. In this way they covered a quarter of a mile when the motorcyclist turned right and followed a country road that skirted the edge of the forest. Behind a small hill, out of sight of the main road, they stopped. The bus stopped too. The driver and the passengers had been wrapped in a frozen silence. The third motorcyclist was still holding the pistol, pointed at the bus. The two motorcyclists dismounted slowly, boarded the bus and took the building contractor Pitsiaklis. He was strongly built, tall, with a huge moustache. In his youth he had been a pioneer of the builders' trade union. Now he was a pioneer of the Building Contractors' Association so that, as he put it, they should collectively face the demands of the workers. Four hands gripped him like pincers. From the time he had stopped working the stone and swimming in sweat he gradually lost the steel that was inside him, his muscles softened and his stomach bulged. He did not resist. There was a time when he would have turned the bus upside down, but now his strength was gone. The two pairs of pincers dragged him out of the bus. The third man was still holding the pistol pointed at the bus. From the bus only the disturbed breathing of the passengers broke the silence. The strange tangle of the three men moved towards the forest and vanished behind the trees. Silence for ten minutes, then the two motorcyclists tore out of the forest, mounted their machines and, with the third, disappeared in the direction of the main road. Women and children in the bus started crying loudly. The men ran towards the forest where they found Pitsiaklis rolled on the ground, smeared in blood, biting his lips in order not to shout.

'Ruffians, you'll pay for it.'

Agonos and Nicosia had joined hands at a certain point.

In the middle of the second week after the declaration of the strike, Papadakis was given the signal to put into practice his plan for repairing the settlement houses. Escorted by three foremen, he went from door to door giving a three day written warning for the evacuation of the houses. At the foot of the notice there was a note that said that the company kept for itself the right to return or not to return the houses to their present occupants. The trade union had been expecting such a development and had instructed the occupants not to evacuate them. On Monday when repairs were supposed to be starting Papadakis, escorted by the same foremen, visited all the houses. None had been emptied. He was holding lists and each time he noted something.

‘They refuse to evacuate the houses,’ he told Oriol on the phone.

‘We’ll empty the houses for them,’ Oriol said. ‘Don’t forget that the men are on strike!’ His voice was harsh. ‘Give them three days more.’

The three days passed and Oriol invited the police to help evacuate the houses. Members of the administrative staff, all the foremen, fifty policemen – some had their rifles on their shoulders – and ten police dogs gathered outside the miners’ compound. The occupants, mainly women and children, some miners who were not occupied with picket duty or collecting food for the strikers from the neighbouring villages, were staring from the windows.

The man in charge spoke through a loudspeaker. ‘I give you two hours. Take your personal possessions and leave behind whatever is the company’s property. The holding on your part of private property constitutes a criminal offence. I call your attention to the relevant law.’

For two hours the occupants, like bunches of grapes hanging in the August sun, remained gathered at the windows. They neither spoke nor laughed. They simply stared out at the administrative staff, the foremen, the policemen with their dogs and rifles.

When the two hour period expired, the man in charge instructed ten policemen to proceed to the first house. The door was closed. At the window the five or six occupants stared at the policemen. Two policemen tried to force the door but with no success. Someone produced a master key, the lock was undone but the door, being barred from inside, did not open. Ten policemen rushed against it, they fell on it with their weight. At the third attempt the door opened, and the foremen went in and they started taking out the family’s clothes, cooking utensils, a toy, some school books. They threw them indifferently in the street while, in vain, the occupants tried to prevent them. But suddenly a crowd of women and children – something like five or six hundred – gathered around the first house, the women shouting, the children crying. They tried to stop the foremen who seemed to enjoy their new activities. The men stayed behind because, lately, on the thinnest excuse the police arrested strikers and sent them in a police van to Nicosia. A lot of charges were levelled against them, disturbing public order, illegal entry to private property, and many others which the miners could not understand. They passed them through a summary trial and sentenced them to long imprisonment. Already fifty miners had been sent to the central prisons.

The policemen in front of so many women and children were momentarily at a loss. The voice of the one in charge brought them back to reality! 'Regroup!'

The fifty policemen retreated and regrouped. The ten with the dogs rushed against the crowd but at the last minute they held the dogs back. In every attack the children cried, the women were paralysed. And the policemen with the rifles began to fire in the air – and fear started the retreat. And the foremen continued, undisturbed, to empty the houses. The miners' homes were in the street and the children and women in the fields. Improvised camps were set up two hundred yards from the Agonos compound, silent and stubborn, personification and symbol of the strike struggle. Groups kept coming from the villages around, from Nicosia, from the distant villages of Pendadaktylos and Mesaoria. They brought food and solidarity messages.

The first month passed by. The thousand miners continued their struggle and Oriol his own battle. 'If they win we'll have chain reactions,' he had said to Sidney. And the Nicosia builders strike seemed to prove him right. In spite of help it was not easy to maintain two or three thousand men. Malnutrition began to make inroads without them even realising it.

The young ones made up their minds. 'We'll pay them in the same currency. We'll never give in,' said a tall, strongly built red-haired man. The Irish, as they called him. He came from a village in the heart of Akamas, a short distance from Fontana Amorosa. French, Italians and other crusaders had, during the Middle Ages, passed through these places. Knights had thrust their swords into the earth, erected their rough tents and drank the water of Fontana before carrying on to Jerusalem. Akamas and the human landscape became part of their inner selves, elements they would erect on the walls of Jerusalem as cornerstones of their existence. His blue eyes were filled with the light of the Mediterranean. He had specialised in dynamite. Wherever the job was difficult, explosions on steep hill slopes or in dark corners of the mine, he took his smiling eyes and his fire-red hair, strode over stones or felt the walls of the shaft with his hands and worked in a devilish rhythm. His hands worked with the accuracy of an electronic machine, he tied, cut, released wire. And his explosions were a work of accuracy. Some nights at the Seagull, chain explosions took place inside him, alcohol, dance, girls until dawn.

He went on into the night. It was strange how he could dissolve his six-foot figure into the darkness, to become a shadow that glided without even touching the air. Belted round him was dynamite and wire. Oriol would personally taste a dose of violence, primitive, savage, he thought. He touched the dynamite he carried fastened to his waist. He knew that sleepy policemen went on drowsy patrols with their sleepless dogs. Every now and then he scattered pepper. Noiselessly he arrived at the mansion. It was wrapped in darkness. Mathias' room was an exception. A dim light and champagne were the signs of a sleepless presence. It must be past two, Irish thought. He pressed himself in a cavity of the wall and became one with the darkness. Mathias was staring at the empty bottle of champagne and his half filled glass. Another day, he thought. He switched off the light and stood at the window. He liked to drink the last glass inhaling the seabreeze.

The shadow detached itself from the wall. Irish tore off the dynamite sticks and placed them at the base of the wall. His hands found their electronic rhythm. He unrolled some wire. He tied it carefully. He began to unroll it further.

Mathias sipped a little and inhaled fresh air.

Then Irish's hands lost their electronic rhythm. An explosion – a deafening noise tore his ears and a formidable flash blinded his eyes. And then it was absolute darkness.

Mathias had an epileptic fit. The delicate balance that had been preserved with tranquillisers and champagne was shattered in a second.

And Irish's blue eyes lost their light. In their place two expressionless cavities wrapped in absolute darkness.

Irish stayed in hospital for several weeks. His head was wrapped in bandages. When they removed the bandages the cavities which previously were his smiling blue eyes were dark as they had been after the explosion. His fire-red hair and beard had grown during this time and they caught the light like lime twigs on naked trees. It was a formidable contrast between his fiery hair and beard and the dark cavities that had been his eyes. They took him to court and the judge said he would have sentenced him to many years' imprisonment but he took into account his plight and sent him to prison for two years. After a year he was granted grace and was found in the wide world without having his eyes to lean on.

They took Mathias Oriol to the United States for treatment. His mother cared for him as if he were a small child.

The strike came to a stop at the end of its second month. Oriol gave in on some points and urged on by his wife, he set up a hospital, three miles from Agonos, in a eucalyptus wood.

Mathias Oriol after his wedding is getting ready for Switzerland. Someone had spoken to him of some clinics buried in green, with the blue of the lakes breaking the monotony of the green and the Alps in the distance to vanish behind clouds.

'We'll go Ioanna,' he said. 'I want to try.'

'We'll go Mathias.'

The following day Mathias Oriol, his wife Ioanna and their lawyer Christides left.

Irish, a blond cry, a statue of an ancient God with holes instead of eyes, with a wooden box hanging from his neck and a stick in his hand, went round the streets of Nicosia selling small things in order to fill his stomach and his empty time.

8

The three of them climbed onto the upper deck, Ioanna, Mathias and his lawyer Christides. Mathias had booked the two best cabins in first class – one next to the other.

When Mathias had asked Christides to accompany them to Switzerland in case any legal questions were raised the lawyer said: 'Yes. With three conditions – my expenses, my possibly lost profit and no plane.' Flying brought him out in a cold sweat.

Mathias agreed, but now standing on the upper deck and with a four day voyage in front of him to Venice, felt trapped.

The wind ruffled Ioanna's hair. The first time she had been on a ship was when she was sent to Beirut to learn to dance.

'Wherever you want my girl, we send you. Even to the Far East. You'll learn while working,' the boss had told her. 'And when you come back we'll still be here.' He had pushed some papers in front of her and she signed them without reading them.

Mathias liked flying. The hours in the long narrow space had a dimension not found anywhere else.

Time changed with speed and height. His brain was trying to record an equation. He couldn't find it – it was there on the fringes of self-awareness yet it always slipped him. And since he couldn't record the equation he drank.

'I'm hungry,' he said. At the first class restaurant they could dine at any time. Thus they didn't see the departure. When they climbed up to the deck again Limassol had become an amorphous mass of small lights against a dark background. They went to the first-class saloon. Mathias ordered champagne. He felt tired with the people but he said nothing. He drank his champagne silently. Ioanna sipped her own silently and enjoyed the first-class excitement. After the first glass Christides shut his eyes behind his thick lenses and his head slipped. Around twelve he stood it no more.

'Forgive me, but I'm going to bed,' he said.

'Goodnight, professor.' Mathias felt bored.

Christides rose rather awkwardly, bowed imperceptibly and went out, walking slightly unsteadily.

Mathias slowly raised his hand and signalled the barman for another bottle of champagne.

'My love,' said Ioanna taking his hand. He looked at her through his heavy eyes as if for the first time. She didn't dare say anything about the champagne. The barman brought the champagne in ice.

'Does the gentleman want anything else? I'm closing, sir.' The waiters had gone to bed. He was holding the bill in his hand. Mathias raised his hand as if he wanted a pencil. The barman gave him the bill and his pen.

'Don't forget your tip too.' He signed the paper and gave it to the barman.

Ioanna stroked his hand, he drank one or two more glasses. Ioanna just touched the glass with her lips. After one or two glasses champagne had a sour taste.

Mathias rose. The bar had closed down and the barman vanished. 'We carry on in our cabin.' He stiffened suddenly and started walking slowly as if counting his steps, Ioanna took the champagne and the ice and followed him. She didn't dare hold him by the hand.

In the cabin he threw off his coat and tie and plunged into bed the way he was. Ioanna joined him and began to caress him. Mathias had the impression that he was coming out of clouds. He made love with the feeling that he was outside the very action itself. Champagne played strange games. The culmination was something near and distant at the same time.

He slept immediately. Ioanna switched off the light and she, too, was soon fast asleep. Next day they woke at ten and shortly a steward appeared with a tray of coffee.

'Put it somewhere,' Mathias said.

The man placed the tray on the bedside table – coffee, milk, sugar and hot water. 'Anything else, sir?'

'No, thank you.'

'Good-morning love,' Ioanna whispered.

'Good morning, Ioanna.'

She rose and poured coffee for him.

He felt the coffee sliding pleasantly across his palate driving away the bitter taste.

Ioanna lit a cigarette. 'Did you sleep well, love?'

'Just vanished, for one more night.' With the champagne and the sleeping pills Mathias Oriol just vanished from this world for eight hours. He opened his bedside table and took a green tablet. Ioanna refilled his cup.

'What about you Ioanna? Did you sleep well?'

'The sea rocks me to sleep.'

'Breakfast?'

'Yes. I'm hungry.'

Christides had been on the deck for some time. He had woken up when day broke. He had looked at the sea through the cabin window, it seemed mauve, a neutral thing that fastidiously covered its abundant vitality. His head still swam with the last traces of champagne.

He climbed up to the highest point of the upper deck and watched the sea becoming alive minute after minute. Then he noticed the woman. She was wearing a red pullover and black trousers. She was clinging to the rail as if afraid she would fall.

In the dining-room they found themselves at the same table. They looked at each other without saying anything. On the table there were a small jug with milk, envelopes of sugar and tiny packets with butter on plates. The waiter placed a big coffee pot in front of them.

'Do you allow me? Christides asked.

'Please.'

'Do you like the sea?'

'No, I'm afraid of it.' And after some time she added: 'But there are other things which I'm more afraid of.'

The waiter brought eggs, bacon and toast.

'Christides. We haven't been introduced to each other.' He smiled behind his thick lenses.

'Paschali,' she said. 'Beauty salon manageress.'

'Lawyer,' said Christides. 'And, Miss, you're from ...?'

'Mrs, Mrs Paschali. I come from Nicosia.'

'Think of it. Living in the same town and not knowing each other.'

'Nicosia is becoming a city.'

Christides told her he was travelling on business, accompanying the Oriols. 'The lawyer is like a doctor. He has to go wherever he's needed. And you?'

'I'm just travelling. Must there be a definite reason?' But from her words uttered at random her story took shape – fear of earthquakes. Every time she read about earthquake tremors of the Eastern Mediterranean she was gripped by an unexplained fear. She felt the earth shaking under her feet and a tingling feeling was hovering towards all directions, as if it wanted to free itself from her body.

'Cyprus is, of course, in a zone of geological change. It's for this we've got Salamis and Amathus. Earthquakes, tidal waves and sand. But we've been excellent builders. It is said that the bell towers and the minarets swung like pendulums last time, but when the tremors came to a stop they were found still intact. You see, we've been excellent builders.'

'I don't seem to be strongly built.'

He saw her lower lip trembling slightly and fear was in her eyes. 'And how do you solve the problem by travelling?'

'Avoiding it, for the time being, is something. You know the proverb. I shall stay with friends for a month in England. After that we see. The heat wave would also have passed.'

'And your husband?'

'He is looking after the salon. He's responsible for the financial side. But there are others too, professionals and apprentices. He's never shaken by anything. No tremors for him, whether earthquake or post-earthquake.'

'Fear's a terrible thing.'

'Especially when the one who sleeps next to you is quite indifferent.'

They finished their breakfast. Christides offered her his arm and she took it and they went on deck.

'In two days we arrive in Venice.'

'I know,' she said.

The Oriols had their breakfast at eleven. Ioanna ate with a great appetite. Mathias just touched his.

'Why don't you eat my love?'

'You do and that's the same.' There was something in the tone of his voice that annoyed her. 'Come on, I was just joking. It's this compulsory immobility that gets on my nerves. Just imagine if I didn't have you.'

Ioanna was satisfied. She finished her breakfast while Mathias half ate. She drank more coffee. They lit cigarettes and for some time they smoked without talking.

'It's this uncertain expectation too,' Mathias said.

Ioanna half understood what he meant but said nothing. She took his hand and looked him deep in the eyes. 'Shall we go up?' They ascended to the deck. Half the passengers were wandering in the open spaces of the ship. The swimming pool attracted many. They were lying half naked and enjoying the autumn sun. No one went inside. The further north they headed the colder became the waters. Mathias inhaled the sea breeze and felt a strange vitality infiltrating him.

'The fucking pills,' he said. 'It's high time I gave them up.' He felt the cool sea spreading inside him. Ioanna caressed his hand.

'All will turn out the way you want.'

'When something is fucked ...' He didn't go on. The continuation frightened him, even as a thought.

They saw Christides leaning on a rail, talking to a woman.

'Minas is going to fix it,' said Mathias. Sleep, food, pure air, a little champagne. It must do something.

Noiselessly, they approached Christides and his companion, who had not seen them approaching.

'We haven't seen you since last night,' said Ioanna.

'I thought you were still asleep.'

'Past eleven Minas,' said Mathias.

'Let me introduce you. Here's Mrs Paschali. She's travelling to find somewhere to lean on.' He wanted to say to lean her fear and desire but he didn't dare. 'Mr and Mrs Mathias Oriol. Cyprus mines and the Oriols are one and the same thing.'

'You're as always exaggerating Minas.'

They shook hands rather reluctantly with Mrs Paschali. They talked about the weather, they said something about Cyprus, then they sat for a long time in the big saloon. Sometimes Mathias remained silent, something that made Ioanna feel uneasy. At once Christides suggested going for lunch.

'We had breakfast at eleven,' said Ioanna.

'I don't feel hungry,' said Mathias as if returning from somewhere distant.

'Forgive us,' said Minas. 'The sea breeze always works its miracle, it goes straight to the stomach.'

'Let's not keep you,' said Mathias.

'I'll see you in ten minutes in the dining hall,' Mrs Paschalis said, and left.

'I'm going for lunch since you don't feel hungry,' Christides said.

Christides crossed the big hall, turned right and disappeared up the first stair he came across.

Alone again, Ioanna turned to Mathias. 'You'll see, everything will be okay.'

'I'm always returning to the same point. The worst game our brain can play at our expense. We don't have any other choice Ioanna.'

At around two they rose. 'I'm hungry,' said Mathias. Ioanna, without a word held his arm and made towards the stairs that led to the dining-hall.

At night around ten they went into the bar. Mathias ordered champagne. The waiter brought it, observing the ritual to the last detail. In a short while Minas came accompanied by Mrs Paschalis. Mathias nodded to the waiter for two more glasses.

'The ship rocks us badly,' Mathias said bringing the glass to his lips. 'No way to avoid it.'

'Sea shaking is different from that of the earth,' said Mrs Paschalis. And Mathias found a chance to say what he knew about tidal waves and earthquake tremors. Once he had been fascinated by the books his father was reading in his wild hunting for ancient mines. And this wandering had brought him to the Cyclades, Cythera and the Eastern Mediterranean. He read everything that had been written or translated in English about this area. And at some stage the earthquake tremors and the tidal waves were mixed up in him. And he saw his recurring crises as tidal waves formed after certain earthquake vibrations. They started from somewhere deep in him and galloped upwards and he held fast on his feet not to fall. But when the tidal wave arrived it headed straight for the brain and his feet could not sustain the weight of his brain. The Eastern Mediterranean in micrography, Mathias thought bitterly.

At around midnight Christides and Mrs Paschalis stood up. Ioanna's eye caught their exchanged glances.

'For us it's sleep time. Wonderful company but it's already twelve.'

Mathias' clouded mind recorded vaguely what Minas said. He raised his hand and waved. 'Goodnight.'

'Goodnight.' said Ioanna. 'We're going soon, too.'

They stayed at the bar until two, then went to their cabin. Ioanna told the waiter that they didn't need champagne in their cabin. As soon as they entered the cabin Mathias switched on the light, went straight to the bedside table and took the tiny bottle with the red tablets. Ioanna stopped him before he opened it. She took it away from him and put it back on the table. She started undressing him and at the same time her tongue travelled on his chest. They made love for the second night. But Mathias fidgeted in bed until four. Ioanna's medicine didn't work this time. He fumbled for the table. He found the tiny bottle, took a tablet and swallowed it with a gulp of water, and soon he was sleeping deeply.

It was early in the morning when they entered the port of Venice. Ioanna heard the noise involved in the preparations for arrival and woke up. The sailors tried to do their job as quietly as possible but something always escaped them, a splashing that broke the early morning silence. The ship reduced speed and its engines worked lazily. She dressed in a hurry. She cast a glance at Mathias; the pill must have been at its highest effectiveness because at this time nothing could waken up Mathias. She opened the cabin door and closed it carefully. It couldn't have been later than five-thirty and the early morning light dripped like a white mist that wrapped everything.

She felt the morning breeze caressing her everywhere and threw the light overcoat she had taken with her over her shoulders. In the morning mist Venice was rather eerie with the buildings dotted with lights floating in an imaginary vacuum. Like lightning, Beirut, wrapped up in burning light and sand, crossed her mind. The minder had settled everything, their suitcases the taxi, the lodgings. At around eight in the evening he handed them over to the Beirut boss who looked at them as if he were undressing them. At around eleven he took them to the night music hall.

Ioanna remembered it so clearly. The man had said: 'No work tonight. Work and training begin tomorrow. You'll sit wherever you want, you'll drink whatever you want. If you want you may do some pinching. Or you may be pinched. No difference as far as the shop is concerned.' At midnight the shop was full, white Arab robes, military khaki, European worsted. All mixed up in an unprecedented amalgam. At around three he led them to the lodgings. He whispered something at reception. They were given the keys of their rooms. They had left reception when a man's voice was heard: 'Eh, you, the young one.' Ioanna turned back. She was not sure whom the boss was addressing. 'Yes, you. You come with me. I like to try the new stuff first.'

'Venice is something else.' Christides' voice interrupted her thoughts. Next to him it was Mrs Paschalis. 'We're disembarking at nine. What about Mathias?'

'Asleep,' said Ioanna. 'I'll wake him up soon. Did you sleep well Mrs Paschali?' The tone of her voice was innocently teasing.

'Yes, of course.' At twelve I'm catching the train for Calais. The following day I'll be in London.' She paused for a while. 'I hope we meet again in Nicosia.' And she cast a side glance at Christides.

'Of course. No doubt.'

'It'll take us some time to return,' said Ioanna. 'Then we go to the States. Mathias wants me to see his family. Ciao, for the time being.'

Mathias was not in high spirits. Ioanna woke him at eight-thirty. He drank two cups of coffee, he swallowed his green pill but his drowsiness could not be driven away. They climbed to the deck and he saw Venice covered in mist resting in the sea. His father was never interested in Venice. 'Just grocers, shopkeepers,' he had once told him. He, himself, had been fascinated by Rome. He followed step by step the Roman line of expansion. North Africa, Greece, Eastern Mediterranean. He lived one after the other the lives of the generals and the senators. The only difference being that he never carried a sword. He just had eyes and brains. The wandering lasted until he arrived in Cyprus.

Mathias cast off, with a last effort, his drowsiness. Christides stood beside them, behind his thick lenses, his briefcase under his arm.

'Just a moment,' said Mathias. He went to the cashier, paid the bill and left fifty pounds as tips.

'Everything is all right, Mr Oriol. Your luggage will be at the customs. Just as you said. I hope we have you with us again.'

Mathias had arranged for them to stay for two days in Venice, before they caught the train for Geneva. Ioanna had asked for it since there was nothing urgent about his illness. He arranged for the suitcases to be sent to their hotel and they went in a gondola. In the novels that Ioanna had read Venice was the city of the newly married and the gondola was the bridge the couple had to cross. The only difference being that they had Minas with them and Ioanna had seen so many sides of life that it would be difficult for her to discern which of them were at each edge of the bridge. She had asked for the gondola and Mathias accepted it rather passively, just as he accepted a lot of other things in his life. This attitude was becoming a rule for him, broken only when he erupted, violently and fiercely. A provocation and disdain in his sick mind.

Ioanna was wearing a broad-brimmed hat that hid her face almost to her eyes. Mathias had the respectable appearance of the American south, a grey suit, a dark brown tie and well-combed hair. Christides, as always, was entrenched behind his thick glasses; the wind got entangled in his thin hair and his tie was askew. At eleven-thirty they arrived at the hotel.

'Mathias Oriol, American from Cyprus. I reserved two rooms.'

The girl glanced through her list, took two keys. 'I understand you want them separate. They are, however, next to each other. Your suitcases have been sent there.'

'Thank you,' said Mathias.

After lunch they rested for an hour then they started exploring Venice. They went by a bus-boat to Saint Mark's Square and cruised along the Grand Canal past the sinking houses. Ioanna's eyes danced in every direction. Beirut had no canals, only streets that suddenly touched the sand. And men who fumbled your body. Near Saint Mark's Square they climbed out of the boat. They went into the cathedral. Ioanna took off her hat. The stained glass on the window formed a number of images. There was no temple with icons here. No wood on which the passions would be depicted. Statues and paintings. And stained glass that formed images. Ioanna felt lost in an eerie world. Mathias, a lapsed Catholic, dragged his feet indifferently and Christides kept silent; he never talked in churches.

When Ioanna wanted to say something she saw both of

them wrapped in themselves as if in an overcoat and she, too, kept silent. In the Doges' Palace Minas' tongue broke loose. He showed them Venice, the mistress of the sea, and somewhere at her feet Cyprus. She remembered Ecaterini Kornaro, Saint Sophia of Nicosia and Saint Nicolas of Famagusta. Surrounded now by Turks. Then he mixed up a lot of things. He talked about rococo, the gothic style, the frescoes of Michelangelo and Raphael. Ioanna listened and kept silent. Few things did she understand. Mathias didn't listen and kept silent. A protective wall surrounded him from the environment. He set it up according to will. They walked for hours through the narrow streets of Venice, Ioanna's eye caught by the profusion of tempting shops.

'Won't you buy anything, Ioanna?' In his voice there was something tender, a light that flickered at the edge of darkness.

'Later.' She liked to browse and think about what she saw before making a decision. They crossed the bridges, Venice, they sat in pizzerias and cafes, ate something and drank coffee. Exhausted they returned to the hotel at around nine. They would spend another day in Venice and Ioanna would do her shopping.

After dinner around ten-thirty, Christides rose. 'Forgive me. After the afternoon walk I prefer a horizontal pose.'

'Okay Minas, the difference being that you'll be alone tonight!'

'I'm alone every night,' said Christides.

They also rose. 'The Italian cuisine's good,' said Mathias. He asked the waiter to bring a bottle of champagne to his room. Once there he filled his glass with champagne and started sipping it. He looked at Venice's lights through the window. Outside it was hot and humid. Inside the air conditioning worked noiselessly. He switched off the light so that Ioanna might not be disturbed and sank comfortably into an armchair. In his mind a light had been switched on. It was a strange white light uninterrupted by images. He had the impression that his head covered the entire room, a room stripped of furniture or any other presence. He drank half a glass of champagne. He had a remote feeling that Ioanna was sleeping somewhere there. He picked up his red pill – he found it by switching on the bedside table lamp. Ioanna did not stir. In the naked, neutral light of his mind the table light was but a drop in the ocean. He brought the pill to his mouth and swallowed it with a little champagne. The naked light was about to be broken by the sour taste that for a moment hit his palate, and he sank once more in this vacuum, that was not a vacuum, simply naked, neutral light. Suddenly he was hit by fear. A fierce horse that hit on the walls of his brain and then rushed throughout his entire body. The naked light began to break under the impact of this fear and darkness infiltrated inside him. He couldn't stand the thought that he was to stay another day in Venice and then they would catch the train for Geneva. Geneva, for a moment, became everything. He suddenly felt that he could lean on it his fear and started sweating because of his agony springing from the idea that time was working against him. Venice and the train imprisoned sometimes him and sometimes time. He felt the sweat furrowing his face. Around five in the morning everything was done in a hurry. He took his little suitcase and went down to the reception. He settled the bill for the three of them for two days, he left money for any extra expenses to be covered and asked for a taxi to the airport. As soon as he had settled in his plane seat at around seven he felt his fear for the first time lose its intensity. It wasn't any more a trapped horse but an exhaustion that touched everything but which left his brain unmoved.

Ioanna woke at about nine. She felt pleasantly relaxed. She found her watch and saw the time. She didn't want to get up. She knew that Mathias never got up before ten. She glanced at Mathias' bed. It was untouched. Suddenly she was afraid. She jumped out of bed. There was an empty champagne bottle, but the two tiny bottles with pills were not there. She looked into the wardrobe. Mathias' suitcase was missing. She dressed in a hurry and went down to the restaurant where breakfast was being served. She discovered Christides in a corner, at a table for four, eating like a wolf. As soon as he saw her a broad smile broke on to his face. He stood and made room for her to sit. Then he saw her expression.

'Ioanna, is there anything wrong?'

'Mathias didn't sleep last night. His bed is untouched.'

Christides waved the waiter for coffee.

'His small suitcase. It's missing too'. She wanted to tell him about the pills, but checked herself at the last moment.

The waiter came with coffee.

'What breakfast will the lady have?'

She shook her head.

Christides poured a little milk in her coffee. 'Sugar?'

'Just a little,' said Ioanna absent-mindedly.

'Okay. It's not the end of the world. He must have gone somewhere. On business, perhaps.'

'You think so? He never spoke to me about something like this.'

'Oriols are not easy when talking about business. It may be a secret mission on behalf of the old man. By noon, we'll have him with us. We're not leaving for Geneva until tomorrow. Have something to eat, Ioanna.'

She smoked two cigarettes, one after the other. They left the hotel and started wandering in the streets of Venice searching for Mathias. At around one they were exhausted.

They went back to the hotel and straight to the restaurant which was packed. Mathias, however, was nowhere. Ioanna went to the reception and asked if he had left any message.

'No, madam. I'm sorry.'

'Thank you,' Ioanna whispered.

In spite of Christides' urging Ioanna didn't want to eat. In solidarity Minas didn't eat either. He held her hand to express his sympathy and Ioanna felt a strange shuddering.

At around three Minas said: 'We've got to report it to the police.'

Ioanna had sent a note to the reception informing them that if anyone asked for her she would be at the big hall. She smoked cigarettes one after the other and Minas out of solidarity tried to follow her but he felt the bad taste of nicotine in his mouth and stopped smoking for a while only to start again soon, not wanting to let Ioanna smoke alone. He rang police headquarters and asked for someone who could speak English. He told him about Mathias Oriol.

'Venice has many temptations,' the policeman said.

Christides explained patiently, that they were going to Geneva to consult eminent neurologists; that Mathias had just married.

'Okay. We'll see what we can do.'

At seven there came the first message from the police. They had been in contact with all the hospitals and police stations of Venice. Nobody knew or had heard anything about Mathias Oriol. 'I'm sorry friend,' said the Italian. 'However, we'll keep searching.'

Christides asked the reception for the bill. 'Yes, yes for all three of us.'

The cashier opened his book. 'All settled,' he said with a broad smile. 'There's even an amount of fifty pounds for any possible extras. Otherwise it'll be given as a tip to the staff.'

'And who settled the account?' asked Christides.

'Here, it's the signature of the man in charge of the night-shift. He leaves at seven in the morning.'

'He must have gone to Geneva,' he said to Ioanna. 'There's no other explanation.' He pressed her to go with him to the restaurant where he ate with his usual appetite. Ioanna chewed unwillingly, swallowing two or three mouthfuls. After lunch he took her to the bar and ordered her a double whisky. She felt better. Minas had two doubles.

'Tomorrow we leave for Geneva, as was planned,' said Minas.

'I hope we'll find him.'

It was midnight when they left the bar. They went to their rooms. When they reached them they stood for a while. 'Minas, can't you sleep in my room tonight? I'm afraid alone in this strange city.'

Minas did not answer. Protectively he put his hand round her shoulder.

'If it's to drive fear away,' he said eventually.

Ioanna turned the key in the lock. She turned the switch on. The room was flooded with light. The air conditioning made it pleasantly cool. Ioanna then turned the switch off. The room once more sank into darkness. They found themselves in each other's arms. It was Minas' hands and tongue that did the exploring.

At noon they caught the train for Geneva, leaving Venice behind them wrapped in the sea and humidity. On arrival they searched for a hotel. Mathias must have booked one but he carried everything in his suitcase, the necessary clothes, his money, his notes. They were lucky. At the first hotel the taxi took them to they found two single rooms. One next to the other. The receptionist cast a curious look at them.

Exhausted by the long journey Ioanna almost slept at once. A sleep heavy and continuous. Neither interruptions nor dreams. She woke at eight, drew the curtains and rolled up the shutters. Light hit her forcefully on the face. Down below stretched Lake Geneva and opposite the horizon was cut short by the dark green Alps.

She remembered the first dream she had in Beirut. She went around the first corner of the street where the lodgings were and found herself lost in a strange city. A multitude of unfamiliar people in their white robes, their uniforms, turbans, and thick black beards. The women were wearing long tunics, sometimes white, sometimes flowery, sometimes multi coloured. And a blood spot marking their forehead. And their Gods were found everywhere, in a vacuum that covered everything. With gigantic bodies, sitting cross legged, with a huge head. And she was inquiring about Renouar Street. She kept walking. She had the impression that the lodgings would show up at the next corner. She seemed to recognise familiar signs every now and then but at the last moment they proved deceitful and Renouar Street could not be found.

The telephone rang and brought her back to her room.

'Morning.' It was Minas' familiar voice. 'Slept well? Shall we go for breakfast?'

'Yes, I'll be ready in ten minutes.'

The waiter brought coffee. On the table there was butter, jam, cake. Minas ordered a little cheese.

'Ioanna,' started Minas. 'I've got two days at my disposal. I can't leave the office for a longer time. We've got to solve all our problems in these two days.'

'There's only one problem. To find Mathias. If there are any more we'll know later. I think two days will be enough.'

By taxi they went to the central information office. They were given a list of all the Geneva clinics, neurological or not. They went round them, one after the other and asked if Mathias Oriol had registered.

'I'm sorry, he doesn't seem to be in our clinic.' The answer was the same time after time. On the second day Christides tried one or two hospitals. 'I'm sorry. He's not in our hospital. Try another one.'

On the evening of the second day, tired and disappointed, they sat at the hotel bar. Christides ordered two whiskies. They sipped, wrapped in silence and their thoughts. Ioanna broke the silence first.

'Minas, I know you've got to go.'

'You should come with me.'

'Out of the question Minas, he couldn't have been swallowed by Switzerland. I'll find him somewhere. I owe this to Mathias.'

'I understand.'

'Minas, I'm asking a favour. Before leaving see that three thousand pounds is transferred in my name to a Geneva bank. I'll stay as long as I have to until I find him. He may need me.'

'Okay I'm leaving tomorrow night for Venice. I'll find a ship for Cyprus.' He rose and went to the reception.

'I want to send a telegram to Cyprus.' The girl gave him a form. He telegraphed his senior clerk: 'Tomorrow, I want an answer,' the telegram ended.

At noon the next day the answer reached Christides. 'Money sent Geneva bank. It'll take two or three days.' He gave it to Ioanna.

'Thank you, Minas.'

At four that afternoon they went by taxi to the railway station. The train left at five.

'Minas, thanks for everything.'

'Serving clients, my duty.'

'I'll see you in Cyprus.' She gave him her hand.

'Good luck. He can't have been swallowed by Switzerland.'

Thus Ioanna found herself alone in Geneva. She didn't feel like returning right away to the hotel. She walked out of the station and started wandering aimlessly. She found herself at the lake bank watching the anglers. She took a taxi and returned to the hotel, had dinner and went to the television room. At around eleven she went to her room and slept almost immediately.

The next day she made a plan. She got a map of the city, divided it into small squares and decided every day to walk in one. She woke up at eight and at nine she was ready. And she began to walk. A quiet, slow walking. Always on the pavement. She buried herself in the crowd in the hope she would stumble on Mathias. Sometimes she was on the point of confusing Beirut with Geneva. But here there was no room for confusion. There were no multicoloured robes nor the torrent of Arabic. Here everything was under an invisible control; the people's movements, their talk, the way they dressed. Only the fishermen along the lake reminded her somehow of Beirut. And the hotel was by no means the shop. Here was the apotheosis of control. Even the smile itself was formidably controlled.

Boredom played strange games. Like the weather. Now the sky 'opened' and the Swiss landscape was flooded with an intense light and the Alps became darker green and the Swiss themselves roamed half naked in the parks and their yards and then it became cloudy and the Alps were wrapped in mist and above Lake Geneva there hung an indefinable threat. She bought a mackintosh in case. And she walked. Sometimes it darkened inside her. Boredom pressed her to catch the first plane for Cyprus. And sometimes she felt somewhat serene. 'I'll find him. He can't have been swallowed by Europe,' she said to herself.

Systematically she covered one quarter of the city after the other. And when she covered every single one she started from the beginning. Sometimes she sat on the banks of the lake and lost herself in thought. Sometimes she watched the fishermen.

A voice next to her was asking her something in French. A woman of about fifty-five was sitting next to her. The woman asked again, in accented English: 'Where do you come from?'

'Cyprus, Chypre, Kypros.' She remembered Beirut when she had to say countless times where she came from.

'You're Greek,' said the other and a smile lit her face.

'Yes, Greek from Cyprus.'

'I too am Greek,' the woman said.

'I've been to the island two or three times,' said the woman. 'My husband loved it though we never visited it together. I carried out his unfulfilled pledge.' Her husband had been a writer, she told Ioanna. 'And you?' she asked. 'What are you doing in Geneva?'

'I like the lake. We don't have them in my country.' After a minute's silence: 'I'm trying to find my husband. He's American. He came for treatment. In Venice I lost him. He must be here somewhere. We had set out for Geneva twelve days ago.'

They agreed to have coffee at Ioanna's hotel the next afternoon. 'You'll find him,' the woman said. 'People do not get lost easily if they have somebody to search for them.'

The next afternoon at four the two women sipped their coffee in the hotel. Ioanna from Cyprus and Amalia from Greece.

'What's your husband suffering from?' Amalia asked.

Ioanna searched her mind. She remembered the word that Christides used – neurological.

'Is it the first time he's been to consult specialists?'

'His whole life was doctors. Because of the mines, you know. There was never a problem with doctors. They saw the best ones in America. Nothing. After our wedding he had the idea of coming to Switzerland. It's his last chance.'

'There are good doctors in Switzerland.'

Ioanna wanted to light a cigarette but she didn't know how Amalia would take it. The latter smelt something when she saw the packet of cigarettes in Ioanna's' bag: 'No limitations on smoking.'

Ioanna felt relief. 'When you are in unfamiliar places you've got to be more careful,' said Ioanna.

'You easily get used to Europe.'

'Where do you live?' Ioanna asked.

'I've got a permanent room in a hotel. The window opens on to the lake. I stayed at this room often with my husband. When he was not writing he liked to sit for hours at the window staring at the lake. It's some years now since he died.'

'And how do you fill the hours, here in Geneva?'

'No time to spare,' said Amalia, smiling. 'All the Greeks ask me the same question. I have very little time. Just time to read the letters and answer them. The publishers' letters require time. I've got to consult my lawyer. And it's the ordinary people from all parts of the world.'

Ioanna could not grasp that some people can have so much correspondence it fills their entire time. She had seen piles of letters arriving at the Oriols', too, but they were channelled into various offices. Letters and offices were for her one.

Amalia suddenly asked: 'Do you read?' She went on: 'There is a German writer. My husband liked him very much. They had exchanged a few letters. He wrote about a clinic near here. The affected body and the affected soul. My husband was not much interested. He was attracted more by the force of life.' She took a small card out of her bag. 'I suspect it's this clinic that the German writer had in mind. It's twenty miles outside Geneva. Try it.'

Amalia stood up. 'I have to leave you. If you have any news send me a note. Good luck. We'll have lunch together one day.'

Ioanna stared at the card for some time. She didn't understand French at all. The taxi-driver will find it, she thought.

The next morning she called for a taxi at nine. She had

breakfast, smoked two cigarettes and at nine she came out of the main hotel entrance. A taxi waited a few yards away. She climbed in and gave him the card. The driver said something in French, but she didn't understand, and they moved off. The morning traffic was heavy and the taxi made its way with difficulty. Then they were out in the green countryside. She remembered Troodos: places have their distinctive marks.

The building must have been thirty to forty years old, it was a wound on the side of the mountain. She went straight to the reception. The girl, around twenty, looked at her with eyes flooded with laughter.

'Madam?'

She didn't know what language to speak in. With her broken English Ioanna explained that she wanted to see the doctor in charge. She wanted to know if a patient, an American from Cyprus, had been admitted to the clinic.

'Have you got an appointment?'

'No, no. The American is my husband. We were travelling together but we parted in Venice.'

The young girl lifted the receiver. 'Dr Rainer will see you.'

In two minutes a nurse came to reception. She was dressed all in white, with a small white hat split into two by a blue ribbon. She made a sign asking her to follow. Rainer sat behind a huge desk, with many telephones on it. Behind him stood a huge bookcase.

The doctor spoke English with a heavy German accent. 'What's the problem?'

'My husband. I am trying to find him.'

'We're not private detectives, young lady.'

'I know, I know. I went to all the clinics and hospitals in Geneva. Everywhere I asked if my husband had been admitted.'

'What's your name?'

'Ioanna Mathias Oriol. I'm Greek. My husband's American. American who lives in Cyprus. It's the Oriol family, you know. Mine owners.'

'And what makes you believe your husband's in our clinic?

There're so many clinics in Switzerland.'

'Nothing. I'm just asking. At whatever clinic they tell me. Even hospitals. When I finish with Geneva I'll go to another town.'

'Your husband, Madam, entered our clinic ten days ago.' Ioanna felt her breast lighter 'We've made an agreement with him. Written. He won't see any members of his family for six months. We want to bring him to an absolute emotional neutrality.'

Ioanna didn't understand.

'We want to limit to the least this relationship. Or rather to neutralize it. To an absolute degree if we can.'

'I won't be able to see him?'

'Not for six months. I'll let you see him for the first and last time in three days' time. We've got to prepare him correctly for this meeting. Afterwards you and the Oriols and Cyprus must disappear from his life. It will be only Mathias and the clinic. It's part of our quest. Do you understand me?' And for the first time an indiscernible smile broke the dark line of his face.

'I understand,' whispered Ioanna. 'I'll see him in three days.' She rose and made for the door. 'Thank you,' she said. 'You're very kind.'

In five minutes she found herself heading back to Geneva. She showed the taxi driver the card of her hotel. In the afternoon she rang Amalia and told her she had found her husband.

'Come to my hotel for coffee.' Amalia said.

'I'm coming right away.' Ioanna felt the need for company.

Amalia led Ioanna to her room. 'I prefer having our coffee here instead of downstairs,' she said. Her suite was a room, a small hall and bathroom, plainly furnished but comfortable. Amalia opened the window on the lake view. 'It was here that my husband liked to sit.'

Ioanna spoke about Dr Rainer. 'For six months he has to be on his own. Cut off from everything. They'll let me see him for the first and last time in three days. It must be difficult for him.'

For two or three minutes they remained silent, looking at the lake and the Alps.

'And what will you do? I mean after you see him.'

'Don't know. I think of staying in Geneva as long as I can. I feel it like my debt to Mathias. To be somewhere he can reach me.'

'Do as you feel. It's the only way. I'm sorry I won't be in Geneva. Next week I'm leaving for America. Then I'll go to Greece. Perhaps I will see you here when I return.'

They agreed to have lunch on Saturday. Amalia was leaving on Monday. Madrid would be the first stop.

The three days passed quicker than Ioanna expected. When Friday arrived she got a taxi and went to the clinic. The receptionist welcomed her with a wide smile. She lifted the receiver and said something in French in a low tone. Ioanna thought she caught the word Oriol. In two minutes the same nurse, who had come the first time, appeared. Again without saying anything she made a sign that Ioanna should follow her. She opened a door and Ioanna found herself face to face with Mathias. He was standing in the middle of the room dressed as usual, freshly shaved, and with nicely-combed hair. She threw herself at him and started crying on his shoulder.

'Don't act like a child Ioanna.' There was something neutral in the tone of his voice. The same tone was in the entire room. The furniture was painted white, everything nicely arranged with perfect cleanliness.

When the first moments passed, she managed to utter: 'Why?'

'I was panicked at the thought that I'd be travelling for hours by train. I had to do something quickly.'

'You could have leaned on me.'

'You were fast asleep. I didn't want to disturb you.' He remained silent for a while. 'I ought to have left a note at the reception. I couldn't think rationally.'

'Now, how is it Mathias?'

'Good. As much as it can be. I still take some pills. I don't drink champagne. I can say that I sleep better.'

'Are you staying here for six months?'

'Yes, without seeing anybody. Without receiving news from anyone. It was something I owed to myself, and you, Ioanna. I try to feel and behave just as they want me to. Maybe it's the last chance.'

'Since it has to be done like that, Mathias.'

'What about you, Ioanna?'

'For the time being I'm staying in Geneva.' She gave him her hotel card. 'You can reach me there.'

'Okay. I wrote to mother explaining everything. She will write to me, but I won't be given her letter. I'll have it after six months.'

Suddenly Mathias felt tired. And the meeting ended abruptly. She had only time to kiss him.

'I'll see you in six months, Ioanna.'

'I'll be waiting for you.'

She told the hotel receptionist that she was staying indefinitely. 'I'll let you know when I'm leaving.' She went to her room and sank in an armchair. Her eyes were filled with mountains and trees but somewhere this vivid line of green broke off and somewhere there was a white spot – Mathias, she thought.

Amid the white walls, the white furniture, the white people, Mathias Oriol started slowly sinking in a neutral vacuum. The red and green pills were replaced by others. At eight he went to the dining room and had breakfast in company with others. It was a strange mixture of people. Some talked, they talked ceaselessly as if the words were compressed in their chests and had to come out, to make room for others, and for others that emerged from a dark depth to take their place. Others remained silent and listened. Sitting over a vacuum they found themselves in a state of everlasting expectation. They were literally hanging like bunches of grapes from their silence. Mathias was somewhere in the middle.

9

Prince de Samargan was rather short, fifty-one, with a Chaplin moustache, and hair cropped in American style forming a small plateau.

'From France?' Ioanna was trying to find a common language.

'From Spain. Directly from medieval Spain, Miss Ioanna.'

'Mrs,' said Ioanna.

'Miss fits like a glove in the case of some. What does it matter whether married or not?' It was their first meeting in the hotel bar.

'What are you doing in Switzerland, Miss Ioanna?'

'I'm waiting for my husband.'

'When is he arriving?'

'He's not arriving. He's coming out. From a clinic in five or six months.'

'But it's incomprehensible. A creature like you in a state of expectation. Life plays with us, Miss Ioanna. Strange games.'

'What about you, Prince Samargan?'

'I'm travelling. Someone, somewhere will be found. You see, when you come straight from the Middle Ages, when you have lived so many years, not individually but collectively, I mean, it's incomprehensible that you should be doing something specific. You understand what I mean? And travelling is the most intangible thing in the world.'

She started seeing him often, almost every day. His unchecked prattling filled her hours. He used to take her hands and kiss them. He embraced her knees and rubbed his head on them. Sometimes he kissed her cheeks, as someone kisses a child or his mother. Slowly it dawned on Ioanna that de Samargan was sexually neutral. She remembered that once a student, who was working as a waiter during a summer at the cabaret, had brought a Scandinavian friend. A sculptor, skinny, with thick glasses, untidy hair and a beard. He carved a lot of things on the stone.

'Where did you discover this fruit, Kakos?' the boss asked.

'Scandinavia. He's a sculptor.'

'Profession or whim?'

Kakos revealed that his Scandinavian friend, Toby, was sexually neutral. Nothing moved him except the stone. The boss had some difficulty in understanding this business of being neutral. But when he understood he spat through his teeth. 'What sort of man is he who neither fucks nor is fucked!'

He took his glass with the whisky and went to another corner. 'Offer him something, Kakos, though he is not a man!'

However, Ioanna found Samargan a man in spite of his neutrality. His words filled her just as his harmless kisses. One of the mornings he said: 'I'm leaving tomorrow, Ioanna. For Spain.'

'Why?'

'Is there a why? I'm returning to my base. I'm penniless.'

'Prince de Samargan. Allow me something, just a token of our friendship. Stay for a bit longer. I'll be paying your bills.'

'But it's inconceivable!'

'I beg you.'

He took both her hands and kissed them.

That night she wrote a short note to Minas Christides: 'I need three thousand pounds more.' Two months had passed since the bank sent her three thousand pounds.

In three or four days she had Mina's answer: 'What you have asked is done.' With the money there came bank statements concerning her account. She cast a quick look at them without understanding much. One thing did not escape her. Her money increased by five thousand pounds a month – it was from Mathias.

No news from Mathias arrived. The clinic had swallowed him. Sometimes she took a taxi and was driven to the clinic. She asked the driver to park somewhere out of the way and for five minutes she stared at the entrance. The driver stared at her in wonder, Ioanna felt his glance falling like a shadow on her but before he could ask her anything she made a sign to him to return to Geneva.

Boredom piled in her gradually. She no more paid attention to the mountains or the lake, they had been assimilated by her daily internal landscape. And Samargan's mannerisms no longer gave her the little satisfactions. Two or three times she rang Amalia but the answer was always the same: 'Mrs Amalia has not yet notified us when she's coming back. We're expecting her.'

So one afternoon she went to the reception, asked for the bill and asked them to book her a seat on the next day's flight to Nicosia. She looked at the calendar behind the receptionist. Three months had passed since she came to Geneva. Three months without a word, without a line from Mathias. What difference does it make whether I stay here or I am in Nicosia she thought. The same afternoon she informed Samargan about her decision.

'I knew it,' he said. 'I saw it in your eyes.' He took her hands and kissed them. 'Accustomed to snow are the mountains. It's always the case. That's why I'm travelling. You feel the change less. You become part of it. It becomes part of you.'

'And now what are you going to do my friend?'

'What I always do, my dear Ioanna. I'll return to my base. I'll spend a month or two in Madrid before I return to my den, in Catalonia. I may find a friend or you may come.' He gave her a notebook with addresses where she might find him if she ever decided to visit Spain. 'My dear Ioanna, something inside me tells me that this can't be the end of our intimacy.'

'I believe it too.'

At night she settled the bills, hers and those of Samargan. She had dinner in her room and for the first time after a long while she drank a bottle of champagne. She felt a sweet numbness spread all over her body. She slept as soon as she went to bed. She woke early in the morning, packed her suitcases and rang for a taxi.

'It's too early for the airport,' they told her. 'Won't you have breakfast?'

'No, it doesn't matter.'

In a short while she found herself in the big departure hall of the airport and felt relief. Through the glass walls she looked again at the Alps and the lake.

By taxi she went straight from the airport to Agonos. She walked to the main entrance. A maid saw her and went to her.

'Have you returned?'

'As you can see Marietta.'

'And what about Mr Mathias?'

'He hasn't. But he will. It won't take long now.'

Marietta called one of the men and asked him to take Ioanna's suitcase. 'I'll notify Madam Oriol,' she said. In ten minutes Marietta was back. 'You'll stay at the usual room. It's ready. It's always been ready.'

When the door of the room closed and she found herself alone she didn't feel any greater security. At the time when she stayed here with Mathias she rarely saw her parents-in-law. She felt an invisible wall between them. But she passed her day and part of the night with Mathias and the wall inside her was dissolved though she found it again from time to time. She had a bath and lay in bed.

At eight Marietta knocked at her door: 'Where are you dining? Here or in the dining room?'

Ioanna understood. She wouldn't see her parents-in-law. 'Here, Marietta,' she said with as much unaffectedness as she could rally. She opened the window and in the darkness she guessed the presence of the sea. October was almost out and sometimes the clouds began to gather in the direction of the sea. On the right she saw the yellow, red, green lights of the Seagull.

She stayed at Agonos for a week. Not once did she see either of Mathias' parents. Any time she tried in an indirect way to learn something from Marietta the latter repeated, rather mechanically: 'They've been far too busy lately. Guests from America all the time.' On the eighth day she broke down. She asked Marietta to find a car for her and for someone to take her suitcases down.

'Are you staying long, in Nicosia?'

'I've got some business to settle, Marietta. I don't know how long it will take. Perhaps until Mr Mathias returns.'

She asked the driver to take her to Ledra Palace, the hotel that split the capital in two, the Greek and the Turkish sector. She went to the reception. 'Madam Oriol,' she said. 'I want a suite.'

'For how long?' the receptionist asked with a professional smile.

'I don't know,' said Ioanna.

From her room she rang Christides.

'When did you return?'

'It's been a week now Minas. I was at Agonos. It seems that without Mathias Agonos is inconvenient. I'm at Ledra Palace. I want to see you tonight.'

'All right. And what about Mathias?'

'I don't know. He's at the clinic. I saw him three months ago. I'm afraid he'll stay for another three. My staying in Geneva served no purpose. We'll talk about it tonight. We dine together at ten, here.'

'Okay. I'll have all the papers with me.'

At around nine-thirty Minas, holding his briefcase, arrived at Ledra. 'We have a lot of things to discuss,' he said.

'Let's dine first Minas, relax and then we can see.'

Minas saw in her eyes what he had seen that night when they stayed in Venice without Mathias but he pretended to have seen nothing.

'A drink Minas?' She dragged him to the bar and they ordered whisky. 'And what about Nicosia, Minas?'

'Strange things happen in Nicosia. I don't know how passing all this is. When you read the papers, you'll understand.'

They went to the dining hall and Ioanna ordered French wine with their dinner. Afterwards Ioanna said: 'And now

Minas, we go to my suite, to discuss things.' She saw some embarrassment in Minas' eyes. 'Minas, you're my lawyer. Professional instructions are inviolate.'

She closed the door behind them and pushed him towards the bed.

'Ioanna?' there was an imploring tone in his voice.

'Minas, neutrality chokes me.'

They made love at a stretch just as Mathias drank his champagne. Then they sat relaxed, as if nothing had happened, to talk business. Christides opened his briefcase and took out some papers.

'Your income, Ioanna, is increasing fast. Your deposits in various banks are amounting to almost a million. Apart from your income from Agonos it's something like three per cent of the shares of the Zinc Mining Company of Bolivia and the Copper Extraction Company of Argentina. Every month the profits go to the banks. You'll have a problem in a short while.'

'Problem?' An ironic smile appeared on Ioanna's lips.

'It's so much money,' said Christides.

'We'll find a way, don't worry.'

He laid before her a lot of papers and she signed. When she finished she had the air of a very busy businessman. 'I appoint you as my representative for an indefinite period. For the banks, for anything. I only want to have reports every month. With details. You decide how much you get. I'll just sign. Cheques and documents.'

Christides said nothing. He felt some kind of change in Ioanna but she couldn't define it.

'See that you buy a good house in Paphos. For my mother and Dina. And see that the bank gives them a hundred pounds a month. Have some men look after them. They should lack nothing.'

'Whatever you say.' He picked up his papers and put them in his briefcase. He closed it and stood up. Ioanna stood up too. She pushed him to the bed.

'Ioanna?'

But Ioanna didn't have time to lose. This time their movements were rather slow, there was something ritualistic in the whole procedure. Slowly they sipped their carnal love. But there was something professional about Ioanna which Minas disliked.

It was past two when he left and before he reached his car Ioanna was fast asleep.

The days passed quickly. Ioanna knew how to fill them. She hired a teacher for three hours a day. He taught her English and French. And manners too.

'Behaviour's everything, Madam Oriol.'

'Not everything, Mr Yiannakides.'

The man sweated and dried near her, he took out his handkerchief and wiped his sweat and his thick lenses and his eyes were suddenly trapped in a momentary vacuum and there was no way to fill it. But he found his mood again and started lecturing in French and English and talked about good manners. He kissed her hand with French finesse and asked her to keep her head erect, with her chin projecting a bit.

'It gives the eye a manly expression.'

'But I'm a woman.'

'It doesn't matter, Madam Oriol. The manly look underlines your feminine sensitivity.' And he took out his handkerchief once more to wipe his sweat and his thick lenses.

Three months passed without her realizing it. She had bought a car and hired a chauffeur. He worked endless hours, but Madam Oriol paid well.

One morning the telephone rang. She had not even woken up completely.

'Ioanna, is it you?'

For a moment Ioanna could not utter a word.

'Mathias, when did you return?'

'Yesterday, I spent the night at Agonos. Today I came down to Christides.'

'I'm coming right away.'

'No, Ioanna. I've already ordered a car. In two minutes I'll be at the Ledras. It has always been my favourite hotel. In two minutes.' He rang off. Ioanna stayed another two minutes holding the receiver. Then she put it down slowly.

Their meeting had nothing explosive. Ioanna felt flooded with a strong feeling. She didn't know if it was love. Mathias had not yet completely escaped from the tentacles of neutrality.

'What about the clinic, Mathias?'

'It belongs to the past. The crises became rarer at the beginning. Then they disappeared. It's three months now, Ioanna. I have neither pills nor champagne. For some time I have been standing on my feet the way I'm standing now. They were lying, almost naked, in bed. Ioanna caressed his face gently, his chest, his genitals. He accepted all this passively at first, but soon he was aroused. It took them an hour to make love. Then he lay still and quiet. Ioanna did not dare interrupt the silence. She stared through the open window and got lost in the blue sky. Finally she broke the silence: 'Let's return to Agonos, Mathias.'

'No reason for it. We'll keep the suite at Ledras. We'll spend our weekends in Agonos. In a month or two we're leaving for America. You have to meet the rest of the family.' After a while he said: 'Ioanna, I'm hungry.'

They dressed and went down to the dining room. Minas was waiting for them at a table.

In two months a short announcement was published in the newspapers: 'Mr and Mrs Mathias Oriol have departed for the United States to visit their relatives. We are informed that the Oriols' visit to the States will last several months'.

10

The small church that carried the centuries like dust hanging from the chandeliers had become the nationalists' headquarters. The iron gate that opened to the courtyard was guarded by five impassive men who examined passes before allowing anyone to enter.

The English conqueror, who carried the rust of time in the form of a cruelty strewn with civility, said: 'There are colonies, which, because of their nature, will remain for ever colonies.' And the new Press Law demanded the depositing of a sum of five hundred pounds as a guarantee against violation of the law. Sedition was the word that began to appear in government communiques for the first time after the Second World War. And then it was everywhere. Not to express your thought. The Saxon experience over many years showed that thought without a language is a harmless intellectual exercise. 'Five-finger exercise', the Colonial Secretary had said jokingly.

And the informers, a special unit attached to the Information Service, plain clothes police sergeants, began to assemble. Two were well known, Salingaros and Poullaos. They attracted attention so that the less known could do their job better. They leaned their bicycles on the trees or the low wall opposite and vanished into the small crowd that had gathered in the square.

Salingaros' hair, thinned by time, formed tiny paths on his head while his false smile had something of a wrinkle on it, like his entire body. The other one was entirely different. Erect like a horse, muscular but always a kind of shadow in his eyes. Maybe it was that shadow the Information Service had trapped.

'To the insolent provocation of the foreign conqueror that we are for ever like brutes to carry our colonial yoke, and like brutes not allowed to look at the sun of our freedom, we shall answer with all the strength of our Greek soul.'

In the atmosphere there is electricity in a latent form. And a latent conflict. Those from Kyrenia had lost the leadership battle. 'Makarios II is dead. Long live Makarios III.' However Makarios III is not from Kyrenia. A plot is being hatched.

A struggle. Those from Kyrenia filled the void with a stream of words. The parthenons and the blue-white flags become verbal sweets. They talked about heroes and the necessity of material compensation. Money to compensate them we had. Heroes we didn't. The son of the so-called white politician from Limassol – in recent years his white hair and his unearthly appearance did justice both to his name and his real character – talks about lurking dangers, quixotic adventures in mid twentieth century. However now there are no windmills but iron birds and tanks. Shouting drowns his words. A plot was being hatched. And outside Salingaros and Poullaos, with the information unit, tried to put their fingers on something.

They dragged themselves through the fields. The Larnaka lights twinkled. Somewhere there are the palm trees, and beyond, the sea. The palm trees with imperceptible movements underline the up and down movements of feet and bodies. The glances move up and down too. Instantly they are stopped in the middle. Beyond, to the east a metal structure is sleepless in the night and through its intestines it vomits electricity which is stored in huge metal wires and transported to all the spots of the horizon. A horizontal movement, incessant. A vertical movement could stop it. To cut it as if by knife. And the electricity would be swallowed by darkness and absolute darkness would reign for three hours, and Nicosia would in vain try to stand on its feet. It would stumble in every step on the absolute darkness and would be immobilized. And the English would be running, swearing, in all directions.

They dragged along cautiously breathing the starry night with the passion of an unlawful love. They carried a reel of thick rope. They would throw it over the thick wire carrier. The short circuit would stop the flow of electricity. It should take two or three hours before they discovered the damage. In the darkness they would be at their mercy.

'Are you afraid?'

'Something is hovering inside of me. You think it's fear?'

'Maybe. With me it's the very opposite. When I'm afraid I feel nothing.'

'It's better like that. I find this hovering a bit annoying.'

'There in the middle, are those the lights of the palm trees?'

'I think so.'

They arrived at the spot that had been pointed out to them. They dropped the reel of the rope at the foot of a tree and advanced a few steps to examine the wire at the point where they would throw the rope for the short circuit. The first one glanced at his watch: two forty-five.

'We've still got ten minutes.'

The other one glanced at his watch, but said nothing. They went back to the tree and began to unroll the rope. Under the swift surface of their movements nothing could be seen. Two fifty. The instructions were clear: at two fifty Cyprus would sink into darkness, especially Nicosia. Two fifty-two. The rope had been unrolled.

'Don't leave the tree until there is deep darkness. Then you vanish. We'll meet at the Virgin Mary of the Vines. On the little mound. To the west of the village. From then on everything will be easy. Ready?'

'Ready.'

The rope is dragging through the green grass of April. The previous evening he had fastened a lead counterweight on one side. And suddenly there was darkness.

And there was light: from his childhood this phrase had stuck in his mind. The scene changed: and there was darkness. He vanished in the night. He has two hours in front of him. He has until five o'clock to be at the Virgin Mary of the Vines. At times he felt the morning dew stroking his legs. His trousers got caught on the thorns. He didn't care.

This time the palm trees suffered from a heavy immobility, seemingly nailed on the night itself. His mind, however, stumbled on his feet. He breathed heavily – the fucking smoking. From time to time he cast a glance in the direction of Larnaka. Darkness swallowed it. Headlights of a delayed car or maybe one on an early morning errand lanced the darkness – beams of steam – then at a bend were swallowed by the hills. He moved on. He knew where he was heading. At four-thirty he arrived at the little church.

'Yiannis?' No reply. He looked at his watch. There was half an hour. He sank into a corner and lit a cigarette. Anxiety began to rise inside of him. From the beginning it had been something undefinable. He lit a second cigarette. Every five minutes he looked at his watch. His chest reflected his quick breathing. Had Yiannis fallen somewhere?

The Land Rover stopped. It is four forty-five.

'Must be somewhere here,' the Englishman shouted. He jumped down from the Land Rover. The headlights were on. Their light, cool and lifeless, moved reluctantly on a horizontal line. With his torch, the Englishman examined the wire. Then he tripped on the thick rope: 'Sabotage,' he shouted to those in the Land Rover.

They all jumped down, torches in hand. They saw the thick rope riding the wire and touching the soil, caressing it. Three yards away the beams fell on a human body. The muscles were contracted, the face buried amid a thicket of thorns.

'Rascal. Since you don't know the job, why did you get involved?' He bends over him.

'Dead. Dead as a piece of wood.'

It was five fifteen and Yiannis hadn't come yet. In a little while, in the dim twilight, a flashlight flickered somewhere from the carob tree opposite. And Yiannis? He hesitated. In the twilight they called him. What about Yiannis? He proceeded cautiously toward the carob tree. Their Jeep was hidden among the bushes with its engine running. He stepped towards the driver. 'Yiannis hasn't come.'

'Jump in.' He climbed in mechanically and, with its lights off, the Jeep moved off, vanishing in a second. At the main road, the driver switched on the lights. 'Can't rouse either curiosity nor suspicion,' the driver said. He wanted to say – And Yiannis? But he kept silent.

There was an extremely tall antenna in the middle of a vast enclosed space. It gave the impression of a creature that climbs towards the sky. A reddish-yellow light marked its edge. Every evening he walked through the fields and stared at it. He had marked everything, the antenna, the studios, the offices, the iron gate, shut one minute after midnight, and the nightwatchman who strolled around. At three different points, there were clocks in wooden boxes. Big clocks. The nightwatchman opened one box after another and clocked his card. His mind had recorded all of this in every detail. At five minutes past three he entered a wooden shed to drink coffee. At three fifty-five he went on his stroll again. He carried on until six when the day watchman arrived.

Afxentis stood in the middle of the room. The other three sat like pupils staring at the wall. A map was pinned to the wall. It covered the entire area of CYBC.

'We still have the luxury of talking in rooms. Tomorrow we may not have even that. We limit our own personal freedom for the sake of others. To be free as an individual transforms you inside. To be free as a people transforms your country. This is what counts today.'

The others listened without saying anything. He moved toward the map.

'CYBC must be silenced for a few hours. And it will be silenced. We want it to be known here and elsewhere that our struggle begins on April the first. It is not a lie, at two fifty-five there will be an electricity failure. Nicosia will sink into darkness. We shall be hidden in the bushes, to the east. When the lights go off we start to move toward the wire fence. We'll cut it with our pincers. We have had ample training. Right?'

The others simply nodded.

'You,' he addressed the first one, 'will proceed to the small wooden shed. You'll be responsible for the nightwatchman. He will have no coffee tonight. What can we do? It's a small sacrifice for the homeland. I'll take care of the antenna.' He pointed to the second one. 'You will take care of the studios, and you of the offices,' he nodded to the third. 'At nine minutes past three we'll be right at the point where we entered. The three bundles will be set off simultaneously.' His hands moved smoothly over the map. 'Here we split. From four different paths we will make our way to the Athalassa forests. Any questions?'

'No, we're ready.'

The pincers bite the wire fence. No time for chewing it. They cut it right away. The opening widened like the ripples in water after a stone has been thrown. It was dark. The four moved sure-footedly through the blackness. The nightwatchman was trapped in the small wooden shed. His eyes filled with darkness and fear.

'My friend, I must ask you to forgive me, but you see we've no alternative.'

He felt the cold iron in his back and shuddered. 'I've got children.' The second man tied him up with cocksure, abrupt movements.

'I have to gag you, otherwise you'll be in trouble.'

The whole operation was finished in two minutes. He locked the shed carefully. As he moved away he had the impression that it was a coffin instead of a simple wooden shed, but he drove the thought away and his mind became crystal clear.

The four of them met again at their starting spot. Afxentis shone a tiny torch on his watch. Three minutes after three. He waited for a few seconds. The silence was loaded with expectation. Now. The dynamite sticks blew, flames leapt in all directions. Stones and pieces of wood were thrown everywhere. The men scrambled in to the Jeep and tore off, past the sleepy lights of a police station and into the narrow streets of Aglanjia. Human shadows appeared for a second only to disappear the next. The town continued its sleep. The noise had been swallowed by the night and there was silence. The reaction came slowly like a yawning crescendo. And then the yawning was cut short, as if by a knife. Cars drove at a devilish speed. Their headlights pierced the darkness and the roar of their engines broke the silence. In the Jeep a smile spread. Wide enough to cover five faces, the four of them and the driver's. They disappeared in the narrow streets of Nicosia. In a while they themselves were swallowed by the night and the silence.

11

Before leaving for the United States, with Mathias's consent, Ioanna had appointed someone to be responsible for their public relations. Christides had found him. He was a freelance journalist always reading or jotting something down. He fastened his glasses on the bridge of his nose in a way that if he were to bend down a little, he would run the risk of letting them drop, and every now and then he had to push them back in position. He was ageless, with his frail physique he could be anywhere between forty and fifty. Manos – everybody called him by this name and it was hard to tell whether this was his surname or his first – represented Greek newspapers, one Athenian, one in northern Greece, and one from Patras. He was often to be found circulating about, covering the distance between the Colonial Secretary's office and the Archbishop's palace on foot. He was comfortable in all sorts of corridors.

In semi-darkness he breathed easily, he believed that big news could be found in dim corridors. Even with his rather poor English, he tried to elicit news from the English clerks of the Colonial Secretary. The atmosphere was becoming charged with electricity and Manos vaguely felt that now the most significant period of his life had started. He neither smoked nor drank. He took coffee in the morning at eleven in the Court Square, in the heart of the Turkish sector. Sometimes around twelve he liked to visit the neighbouring brothel which was hidden in a narrow street, about fifty yards away.

He knew that at twelve the Turkish girls came out of the hamam. It's a different story to eat bread just taken out of the oven. Once he had fallen in love with a fifteen-year-old Turkish girl who crossed the Court Square every morning to take her finished work to her Greek boss in the Greek sector. The angel, Manos called her, although houri was more like it, since she was Turkish.

The angel, he could accept no objections. Her face had permanently settled in his eyes. A rosy face with downcast eyes. Manos followed her, sometimes with his eyes, sometimes with his feet.

He followed her from a distance of three or four yards, watched her body swaying imperceptibly. Now and then he adjusted his glasses because he had the impression that he did not see well.

'Twenty pounds a month,' Christides had told him in the presence of Ioanna and Mathias Oriol. 'You'll be responsible for the public relations of the Oriol couple.'

A confused feeling of wonder and satisfaction took the form of a lump in his throat, but he dared not clear it away. It felt like a foreign body!

'A great honour for me,' he dared to whisper.

'We shall tentatively appoint you for a year. Your duty is to publicize the activities of the Oriol couple. It's also your duty to keep the Oriol couple informed about the situation in Cyprus, sending them detailed reports.'

Mechanically, he took a notepad out of his pocket. 'To publicize their activities and to keep them informed is our business. Everything will be done at a professional level.' He began to feel more comfortable. 'Publicity will not be limited only to Cyprus, it will embrace Greece as well. I have connections with foreign newspapers – mainly English and American.'

Ioanna and Mathias had listened without speaking. Ioanna wondered what this frail figure might be able to do.

'What do you think Mathias?'

'Me? Nothing. I agree.'

'Since it is the wish of my husband, I too accept your proposals, Mr Christides.'

Ioanna signed the contract. 'Will you sign Mathias?'

'One signature is enough.'

On arrival in America Mathias and Ioanna took a taxi to the Oriol mansion. It was designed in the neo-classical style; with a colonnade which imitated a pediment. Buried in green, it was located in one of the rich suburbs relatively near the city, only half an hour by car, but at the same time far enough so that the city's pollution did not reach it. The atmosphere was refined, literally and metaphorically.

The house was a magnet for all branches of the family. Children and grandchildren felt the need to spend one or two months a year with Mrs Oriol, a woman of eighty-five who, in the company of her servants, lived in the house permanently. Mathias's parents came here almost every year – leaving Agonos for one or two months to breathe the American climate. Mrs Oriol had a clarity surprising for her age. Her agility, spiritual and bodily, was unexpected. She had split the mansion into four wings, three for her children and their families and one for herself. Although she was the only permanent resident, she was rarely alone. She often sat on her verandah in an old rocking chair with her eyes fixed on the lawn and her mind on the memories of some eighty years.

The taxi pulled up at the entrance. There was something about the place that reminded Ioanna of Agonos. Two servants came out of the front door, wide smiles on their faces.

'Like snow, Mr Mathias?'

'What can we do Al?'

They shook hands. 'Ioanna, my wife,' said Mathias.

'Welcome.'

'How is Granny?'

'Fine. She counts the months waiting for you to come.'

The two servants took the suitcases and Mathias and Ioanna walked toward the door.

'You'll find her at her usual place,' Al shouted.

Mathias walked along a long, rather dark corridor, and Ioanna followed him. A feeling, something like insecurity or fear numbed him. The corridor led to a small room and immediately they found themselves on a big verandah, where they came face to face with Mrs Oriol.

'We missed you lately, Mathias.'

'There are things, Granny, that I can't control.'

'What can we do? Welcome home.'

Mathias sank in her arms and she stroked his hair as if he were a small child. Ioanna suddenly felt superfluous. In a while Mathias turned to her.

'Granny, this is Ioanna, my wife.'

The old woman looked at Ioanna. She stretched out her hand without saying anything. Ioanna took it and with a shudder felt how lifeless it was.

'I'm delighted, Mrs Oriol.'

'No one enters easily into our family. Welcome.' There followed an embarrassing silence.

'Granny we'll go to our room for a rest.'

'We'll dine together tonight,' Mrs Oriol said. She started rocking her chair, gradually sinking into her own world.

At eight o'clock in the evening the three of them sat in the spacious dining room, Mrs Oriol at the head of the table. Al served the first course and filled the glasses with wine. Before they started eating, the old woman sank into a silence that lasted about a minute. Her lips opened and closed as she said a prayer to herself. Then she raised her glass and brought it to her lips. 'To your health Mathias. Welcome.' Her glance passed through Ioanna without touching her. Mathias was looking with some embarrassment at Ioanna. They both raised their glasses.

'Glad we found you well, Granny.'

They finished the first course, and Al served the second. Mathias had not had a drink for nine months and found the taste of the wine strangely pleasant. Proclivities do not disappear so easily, he thought.

'And where did you go into hiding, Mathias, these last few months?'

'I went to Switzerland to be cured, Granny.' Her face darkened and her upper lip trembled.

'It wasn't a big thing Granny. Just drying out.'

Mathias's illness was a wound inside her, a foreign growth on the Oriol body.

'The Europeans have their ways . . .' But she did not finish. Sometimes she adopted this manner, leaving thoughts unfinished so that listeners could interpret or complete them as they wished.

'We Americans need them sometimes, Granny.'

They finished the second dish. Mathias and Ioanna drank a second glass of wine. The silence was disturbing for Ioanna.

'And you Ioanna, what was your profession before marrying?' Granny broke the silence.

'Artist, Mrs Oriol.'

'That is?'

'Ballet dancer?'

'Not exactly. I danced,' she searched for another word instead of cabaret, 'in a music hall.'

'In Cyprus, music halls are still in operation, slightly decayed, though modern, Granny,' said Mathias.

'You mean they're not full of whores and drug addicts?'

It was the first time Mathias heard his grandmother use such harsh language. He felt the shudder passing through Ioanna's body.

'People, Mrs Oriol, are sometimes forced to earn their living.'

For some time now Ioanna had noticed she was casting away a certain natural timidity, brushing aside any signs of an inferiority complex. She acted and spoke in a way that would have been unthinkable only two years ago.

Mrs Oriol looked at Ioanna. 'The way is part and parcel of the effort.'

Ioanna did not know whether the tone of her voice was critical or not. They finished the third dish. Mrs Oriol stood up.

'Forgive me Mathias. I have to retire now. You will have coffee by yourselves.'

'It's okay Granny. We'll go for a ride and have coffee out somewhere.'

Mrs Oriol, leaning on her stick, went away slowly. Mathias

thought about rising to help her, but decided not to.

In a little while Al appeared. 'Your coffee, where shall it be served, Mr Mathias?'

'Forget it for tonight Al. Just get the car out of the garage. We'll take a drive.'

Mathias's father kept his own car in the family house; he hated change and he wanted the two months he stayed at the mansion to be passed with familiar faces and familiar objects. He felt the need to carry something of his own with him so that he could breathe more comfortably.

'Anything you say, Mr Mathias. It will be ready in five minutes.'

They smoked their cigarettes at the table.

'Let's go Ioanna. I'll show you the town, or show the town to you.'

'Mathias are you sure, I mean you don't feel tired?' Rarely had she seen Mathias drive a car. There was always a chauffeur waiting. The truth was that she was afraid of an epileptic crisis and the chauffeurs and the crises had become different sides of the same coin.

'I hate the chauffeurs in America,' said Mathias. 'In Cyprus it's different.' He took her by the hand and led her to the door. The car – a black Buick – was already parked at the front door.

Al emerged from the darkness to open the door for Ioanna. 'The switch is just there, Mr Mathias.'

'You never forget anything, Al.'

Al was at Mathias's door but Mathias had already settled into the driver's seat. 'With the end of spring traffic increases somewhat, Mr Mathias.'

'Don't bother Al, we haven't forgotten America.'

They swallowed up the streets one after another and the city's lights flickered in an irregular pattern, giving the impression of a gigantic electronic toy. At a bend in the road, Mathias reduced the speed, turned off the road into a huge space, and parked the car beside other cars. Without saying anything, he got out of the car and disappeared among the parked cars. In five minutes he was back carrying ice cream and coffee. 'I wanted to relive my old days for a few minutes,' he said.

They ate their ice cream first and drank the coffee afterwards. Mathias switched on the engine and set out for the family house. May had suddenly become warm and the cool nights made a striking contrast to the warm days.

It must have been after eleven when they went to bed. Mathias kissed her. 'Welcome to America.'

'Thank you, Mathias.'

During the night he felt his way around. His hands faltered on the corners of the bedside table, advance, fall, climb up again, and fall again. He felt the drops of sweat on his forehead; between sleeping and waking, he was confused for the moment. He didn't know where he was, somewhere between Cyprus, Switzerland and America. Awareness of reality came in a tormentingly slow manner, from a great distance. He did not want to disturb Ioanna. The awareness of reality, a tiny spot at the beginning, widened increasingly and spread chaos through him, and fear. He did not want to switch on the lights; he was amazed he could still reason things out. He rose and felt his way to the door.

After closing the door behind him he felt a sense of relief, but his fear crystallized in drops of sweat. He knew where to go. Somewhere in a corner of the dining room there was a tray holding bottles of alcohol. He opened a bottle of wine and filled a glass. He drank almost all of it in one gulp. His tension lessened. He filled the glass again and sank into an armchair. Fear had retreated for good to the dark corners of his soul. He took the bottle and returned to his room. Ioanna was asleep. He finished his third glass, then slept.

12

Ioanna searched the papers she received with the morning mail. Al brought them in on a silver tray. In contrast to the old woman, Al treated her like a lady. Professional intuition, Ioanna begins to think, but does not continue.

> FROM: Manos to Oriol
> FROM: Cyprus to USA
> SUBJECT: Information
> The Greeks have plowed the seas from the time of Argo and Jason. Since then there has been no return. Somewhere there must have been a golden fleece. Since water can't be plowed, or rather since your traces vanish as soon as they are formed, you have to fight continuously. Otherwise, you lose the sea and if you're Greek you get lost too. (Forgive me for the short introduction but, without the first it's difficult to go to the second.)

Ioanna tried to understand. She found it difficult to grasp the meaning of the last sentence.

> A short distance outside Paphos is Hloraka. The shadow of Ayios Neophytos' monastery falls on it like time. It cultivates its tasty cucumbers and supplies not only Paphos, but the whole of Cyprus, including Nicosia. It seems that for some time

> Greek caiques, with very small crews so as not to arouse suspicion, set out from the Greek islands carrying arms. From Petra tou Romiou to Akama. No one knows for sure, we suspect much. But the English have their hunting dogs. Could they be in all continents if they didn't have their hunting dogs? Salingaros and Poullaos are only the window.

Ioanna searched her mind. She remembered them now, descending the basement stairs into the cabaret and staring around for a while standing on the bottom step. There was an air of expectancy in the atmosphere of the cabaret. The boss lost that eagle look of his! 'Drinks for the boys,' he said, and brushed aside chairs and girls. He accompanied them while they sat, making them as comfortable as he could. Whiskies appeared; one, then a second and a third.

'And what did you do for a living before marrying?'

'Artist.' The word whore is fermenting, but why? Ioanna Manoleon. She's gone now. Ioanna Oriol. Mathias brought her to America to meet his relatives. But the old woman pierced her with her eye as if she was being undressed.

Sometimes Salingaros and Poullaos disappeared into the private rooms, with girls. Though it had not happened to her, Ioanna knew it happened.

Manos' report went on:

> At midnight they descended from the surrounding hills. They caught them when they piled the boxes on land. There was no possibility for a battle. There were only four of them and there were many of the others. The caique and the arms were captured. But it's not the end. It's not even the beginning. Not many details are known so far. It is rumoured that the leader of this mission was an ex-leader of a peasant organization (definitely not a leftist one). They're all under arrest in the Central Prisons where security measures have been intensified.

> Only recently, the barbed wire fence that surrounds the area has been strengthened. There is a possibility that electrically-charged wires may be used. No one knows. We enter the era of guessing. One thing is certain. The searchlights on the thick walls of the prison have been strengthened – they turn night into day. The garrison has also been fortified. Double guard every night.

Ioanna remembered the Central Prisons. Sometimes she went there with the other girls out of a sense of professional solidarity. Foreign artists were obliged to secure permission to stay from the Aliens Office. There in the corridors Salingaros and Poullaos often wandered around. Sometimes the permission to stay ended because the agent arbitrarily failed to renew it. But the girl continued to work at the cabaret. Sometimes the police arrived in the early morning hours and in the discreet presence of Salingaros and Poullaos they piled the girls into the police Land Rovers and led them to the Central Prisons, until their agent managed to renew their permits or the Aliens Office deported them. Along with the other girls, Ioanna visited to comfort them. Whores and drug addicts – the words of Granny Oriol came to her mind. Not whores. Girls who earned their living in a certain way.

The report added:

> In spite of the security measures of the English, the struggle began. With proclamations, compulsory curfews, and explosions. The leaflets were signed by Dhigenis. There are many rumours concerning the identity of Dhigenis. Perhaps he is a known Greek officer of Cypriot origin. However, we can't proceed beyond guessing. The colonial government reacted right away. Flying the Greek flag and singing the National Anthem are prohibited. The Governor's house has been surrounded by English soldiers and huge searchlights. The Pedieos river

> bed, passing just below the Governor's house, has been turned into an illuminated line that creeps along the earth. Along with the police, an auxiliary body has been set up to patrol on a shift basis at night. Mainly Turks are enrolled, but some Greeks too. They appear everywhere.

Sometimes she rented a room at Fatma's. It was a big house straggling along the ground. But gradually they trimmed the yard and built rooms. They even had a small Turkish hamam. Bread, hot from the oven, that's the thing. Fatma was almost permanently seated on a chair and it struggled to hold her body which overflowed in all directions. Fatma with her three daughters. Business and sex. Sex sold on a temporary basis, Lily used to say.

Mr Fatmas, in sharp contrast to his wife, could be blown away by the wind. Each morning at six he left for his business, the cafes of the harbour, where he worked at whatever he could find. Sometimes he earned enough for his lunch and sometimes he didn't. He always came back at seven and buried himself in a small room at the far end of the house where Fatma delivered a plate of food to him, along with a half bottle of wine.

He passed the night by listening to Turkish songs on a small radio. The customers were mainly Turks with moustaches and greasy hair. They'd wait for hours in the front room, staring at Fatma's daughters. They undressed them with their eyes, one after another before proceeding into action. Ioanna saw them all; late birds who spent the night there and didn't want to leave before three in the morning when she came back from the cabaret, others who were in a hurry and arrived before Ioanna set out for work.

'Auxiliary body.' Ioanna reread Manos' phrase.

> In the whole situation there is a dose of irrationality that borders on the ridiculous. There are Turks who are well-known in the Greek quarter where they either sell such oriental delicacies as Koupes,

> yogurt, and baked eggs, or set up small shops at a point where the Greek sector enters the Turkish or vice versa. They begin business at four o'clock in the morning selling, especially in winter, hot tsorvi. Suddenly, when the signal is given, they are transformed into auxiliary policemen, they put on khaki uniforms and blue caps, like those worn by the pupils in a private school. They hold clubs in their hands and they pour onto the streets. I am not sure whether they have been given pistols as well. During the night they patrol the streets in groups of four. The one in charge of the area goes around in a Land Rover, and swells from pride when he sees how many patrols he has under his control. The Governor has been replaced. He left suddenly by sea for the United Kingdom.

The emergency situation required 'emergency people'. This phrase stuck in her mind. For some time now she had felt very different about herself – especially every time Minas Christides sent her a report on her bank accounts. Through Christides she gave instructions to an architect to draw up some preliminary plans for a new house. She wanted a house to command a view of Nicosia, just as the Oriol mansion commanded a view of Agonos, with a high wall and tall iron gates. Deep in her subconscious there was a big house that commanded a view of the sea, which an Englishman had built for his sick wife. There was a tall wall which, as a child, she used to climb with her sister Dina and from a distance they watched the ex-Turkish policeman taking care of the Englishman's dogs.

It was an atmosphere of mystery. Emergency situation. Tall iron rails to go deep inside the wall and to lance the sky. One time she had read a book about Catherine the Great. She used to return from the cabaret around three in the morning, and when sleep eluded her, she took a book. She remembered Catherine's blonde hair, her piercing eyes, her full bosom. She remembered the rail, the mansion, the stairs, and the tiny balconies. What a woman Catherine was.

Mathias, too, cast a glance at Manos' report. 'We're heading for trouble in Cyprus,' he said.

'You think so?' Sometimes so much naivete is concentrated in a word or phrase.

'I hope that Agonos won't be affected.'

In the morning, after breakfast, he took her to the city where the buildings were vertical stabs. They seemed to lance the sky. Her eye ascended eighty floors. It hangs for a fraction of a second on every floor and then remains suspended in the vacuum.

A shuddering that springs from somewhere inside her follows closely her glance and in the end it stays suspended in between the building and the sky. They leave her behind down on earth.

'You manipulated him quite easily?' Ioanna had not understood whether the old woman was addressing the question to her. She spoke while rocking on her chair.

Ioanna did not know what to answer.

'I mean you must be very smart. Young men like Mathias are not easily caught. You don't find an Oriol in every street of the town.'

'Madam, it all happened so accidentally.'

'And in a calculated manner.'

'I don't understand what you mean.'

'However you, yourself, can see the result. See that you don't harm the Oriols.'

'Madam!'

'Men are harmed too. Just like houses, my girl.' She stopped rocking abruptly. She rose with difficulty. Ioanna did not dare offer her help. She leaned on her stick and began to proceed with difficulty. From somewhere Al emerged. His glance embraced Mrs Oriol protectively as she advanced slowly. This glance did not even touch Ioanna. The old woman crossed the room hitting the floor now and then with her stick and Al followed from some distance, noiselessly, like a shadow. And Ioanna stood suspended, somewhere between the building and the sky.

'It's not easy for Granny to like a man,' Mathias told her.

'How long are we still staying?'

'We've hardly come.'

Sometimes they dined with Mrs Oriol. It was part of the family ritual. The old lady always sits at the head of the table, she makes Mathias sit opposite her. Ioanna sat at the corner next to Mathias. The old lady eats in an irritatingly slow manner. Her glance is a straight line – it never goes astray, it usually leans on Mathias, it sometimes goes beyond him but it never deviates to the right or to the left. And Ioanna usually sits on the left of Mathias. Al comes and goes with a smile – a crack that splits his face in two. He is holding a white napkin and fills the glasses with water. In the presence of Granny, alcohol is never served. Alcohol exists only in Al's movements. The way he is holding the bottle of water half-wrapped in the napkin he gives the impression that he is serving champagne. Champagne is a vertical incision in the horizontal glance of Mrs Oriol. And Al is such a muscular type. This neutral smile of his is in sharp contrast with his muscles. Ioanna doesn't know how but she has the impression that male muscles neither laugh nor smile. Mathias eats rather reluctantly like Granny – in his eyes there begins to dawn dimly a strange vacuum. Ioanna does not feel comfortable since her appetite is not under control.

'The first man killed . . . a few miles outside Agonos,' Manos wrote. Mathias' eye flickered. He filled his glass with wine. When Grandmother was not present Mathias drank. Al saw that there was always a bottle of old Spanish wine.

'The military truck brushed the foot of the naked hill. In the unexpected heat it dragged itself roaring. The sentinel hiding on a tree sent a signal waving a white handkerchief. And the shock unit waited behind the bushes. The truck moves on. Five soldiers holding their guns sit uncomfortably at the back. Next to the driver a skinny English officer. He is staring in front of him without saying anything. At the hairpin bend the driver reduced speed, almost to zero. The one in charge gave the signal. The bullets tore the air. They didn't touch the truck. The English jumped from the truck and began to fire at the bushes. The duel of the bullets continued for some minutes. And the bushes were suddenly silenced. The English officer who was sitting almost motionless at his place jumped off the truck and advanced to the edge of the road, revolver in hand. And he saw the young man bending over his gun. It seems it had been blocked. Two or three shots came from the bushes.

'And the English officer fired at the young man. He didn't miss. The other three of the shock unit escaped through the bushes to the forest of Psokas Cross.'

Mathias did not easily catch the details. But the main events didn't escape him: 'We're heading for trouble,' he said. 'Worse than those with the miners.' And he filled his glass once more. He felt his eyelids heavy and his mind darkened. Fear like a bat spreads its wings over a dark vacuum. Wine drove the bat away but left the vacuum intact. In that vacuum Mathias lost himself.

Ioanna could not sleep. But Mathias was wrapped in his own vacuum. She jumped on him. She caressed him. Her legs become two huge pincers. They opened they compressed. But still she was restless. At that certain moment Al ceased being a shadow. No smile split his face into two any more. Every particle of his lived this moment. And life found a way of expressing itself into a series of chain reactions.

'Yes, madam. My pleasure.'

Once more he became Al the shadow. Where did the man in him retreat? As he went away he said, causally: 'Anytime.'

Ioanna's mind was wrapped in a sweet numbness. It refused obstinately to record the changes.

All morning they drove through the town. Ioanna tried to understand what was happening to him. She felt his eyes two pieces of glowing coal. His glance – two parallel iron beams, solid and irremovable. His hands held the steering wheel fast.

'Mathias, is it not time to return home?' Ioanna said timidly.

He did not hear. He followed the road that led to the top

of the hill that commanded the road. The trees piled one upon the other. And below, the city spread endlessly. A huge cross seemed suspended at the top of the hill. Without wanting to, she remembered Troodos' radar. That was not suspended. It squeezed on the earth like a leech on a human body. And then the trees were filled with crosses. Some white crosses that unfolded themselves in a row, one after the other. She didn't dare ask Mathias. At the top they stopped. Mathias opened the car door and walked to the cafe. Behind the cafe a steep rock rose, and on its top a tower. A funicular car climbed lazily up and down. Ioanna left the car too. Mathias bought a bottle of wine, and sat at a table.

'Aren't we having something to eat?' asked Ioanna.

'I'm thirsty,' said Mathias. 'If you're hungry have something.' Ioanna ate a sandwich without appetite. Mathias drank the first glass at a stretch. He felt relief. He filled the glass again. The relief was short-lived. In his eyes were the flames of dark forces set free inside him.

'Shall we go back, Mathias?'

'Soon.' He bought a second bottle. He drank it silently. Suddenly he stood up, threw down a five dollar bill for the girl who cleaned the tables, and walked to the car. Ioanna followed behind. Mathias switched on and began to descend the hill. Suddenly he accelerated round the bends and fear swept through Ioanna. He drove faster and faster. Speed began to pile up and this piling now and then caused an explosion. Sparks beamed from Mathias' eyes and the hill disappeared inside them. His eyes and the car had become one. Ioanna didn't dare speak. She held on to her seat as tightly as possible, she felt for the safety belt, but didn't have the strength to fasten it. At the foot of the hill the speed decreased and Ioanna sighed with relief.

They arrived home, at last. Mathias, without saying a word or even glancing at Ioanna, climbed out slamming the door behind him. Ioanna followed in silence. They crossed the long corridor, they entered the big sitting room.

'Are we having coffee?' Ioanna asked.

'Al will make one for you.' He took a bottle from the bar

and went to their room. He put the bottle on the floor and began to undress. Naked, he began to walk up and down. He looked at the bottle on the floor and walked in circles around it as if it was part of a ritual. All the time Ioanna, sunk in an armchair, did not dare either to speak or look. Suddenly Mathias stopped over the bottle. He stayed for some seconds terribly motionless. Then he grasped the bottle with a broken movement, opened the door and walked to the bathroom. Ioanna followed. The door was closed and she didn't dare open it. She went back to her room and pressed the service button. Al came in.

'What can I do for you?'

'Just coffee Al.'

The minutes passed but Mathias did not return. Ioanna smoked three cigarettes, one after the other. Suddenly voices and noise tore the silence. Ioanna opened the window and saw Mathias running naked among the trees. Running after him were Al and two servants. They disappeared behind the trees and Ioanna remained motionless at the window. In the evening Al informed her that Mathias had been temporarily admitted to a psychiatric clinic.

'Al, when can I see him?'

'Not for three days.'

Ioanna stared at him. She felt a fire burning slowly between her legs and its reflections danced in her eyes.

'Tonight at midnight,' Al said.

'Tonight at midnight,' said Ioanna mechanically.

After three days they let Ioanna see Mathias. He was calm. He ran towards her. 'Ioanna, I must get out of here before I'm driven mad. If I'm branded insane they will take all my property. What they need is an insanity certificate. If I'm placed under guardianship, fuck everything.'

A nurse was sitting at the corner. Silent, motionless he seemed to record with his eyes everything that was said and done in this room.

'What does he want here?' Ioanna asked Mathias.

'I don't know. Didn't even bother to tell me.'

Ioanna left Mathias and went over to the nurse. 'When I

see my husband I want to be alone.'

'My orders, lady.'

'Whose orders?'

'The management.'

'Go and bring the management here, right away.'

'My instructions are to sit here as long as this meeting lasts.'

Ioanna said nothing. She went back to Mathias. His forehead was marked by drops of sweat. She took his hands and started stroking them.

'We'll go to Europe. And then to Cyprus.'

'Anywhere and any way you want Ioanna.' His eyes had turned into a kneeling supplication. That harshness that always accompanied alcohol had evaporated. Now his glance had turned loose – like the sweat that stumbled in drops on his forehead.

On leaving the room Ioanna decided to see the management. 'First on the left, third door on the right,' said the nurse. She knocked on the door and without waiting for an answer, went in. A doctor of around fifty was sitting at a desk. He raised his eyes questioningly.

'I'm Mrs Oriol. Number three.'

'And in what way can I be useful?'

'I demand you free my husband at once.'

'Your husband has undergone a crisis – the result of alcohol, psycho-neurotic disorders, I'm not sure. On the other hand I've got the signature of the family for him to stay here.'

'Have you got mine? I'm his family.' She left, and took a taxi home. At the house she paid the driver and stood silent outside the entrance. She stared at the facade and felt, for the first time, a strange kind of relief. She started walking towards the entrance but changed her mind and started walking along the road. At the end of the road she turned left. She saw the small restaurant of Pat the Greek. 'Kalymnos – souvlaki – yiros'. Sometimes they went at night and ate souvlaki and drank a glass of retsina.

Pat stood as always behind the bar, in front of a huge charcoal grill. 'What shall I get you, Mrs Oriol?' he asked smiling.

'A lawyer,' said Ioanna.

Pat didn't understand. 'Are you pulling my leg?'

'No, Pat. I need a lawyer right away. It's a question of life and death. Not for me. For Mathias.'

Pat put some cognac in a glass. 'Sit down and drink it. It's Greek. It'll do you good.'

Ioanna sipped a little and lit a cigarette. Pat dialled various numbers. By the time she had finished her cognac Pat came to her. He was holding a small piece of paper. 'Murphy, my lawyer, will see you whenever you wish. Here's the address.'

Ioanna took the paper and opened her bag. 'How much the cognac, Pat?'

Pat pushed her gently. 'You've no time to lose. Good luck.'

She took the first taxi she found and gave the driver the note Pat had given her. In fifteen minutes she found herself in front of a huge block of offices. She climbed to the third floor, found the office, mentioned her name to his secretary and that of Pat the Greek. She lifted the receiver, said something and then turned to her: 'Mr Murphy will see you right away. Go in.' She pointed to a door that led to the lawyer's office.

Murphy stretched out his hand and smiled. 'Have a seat. I'm all ears.'

In five minutes Ioanna gave him the basic information concerning Mathias' case. 'I must get him out of there, tomorrow if we can.'

Murphy listened carefully without saying anything. From time to time he entered something in his notebook.

'We need our own doctor, cut off from financial interests,' said Ioanna. 'To care about Mathias as a human being not as a financial unit.'

Murphy remained silent for two or three minutes.

'I can pay,' Ioanna said. 'My husband has deposited enough money, in my name, at the American Bank.'

Murphy lifted the receiver: 'Give me external line, Bianca. Dr Austin, good morning. Murphy here.' In a few words he explained the crux of the matter. When he put down the receiver he looked at Ioanna. 'Madam, I'll be expecting you tomorrow at nine. We'll go, the three of us, to the clinic.'

'Thank you,' said Ioanna and stood up. 'You don't know what a weight you have lifted from me.'

Murphy smiled: 'Our job.'

At the house she found an envelope waiting for her. Manos does his job well, she thought. She went straight to her room, threw off her clothes and sank naked into an armchair. She liked from time to time to embrace her body with her eyes. She discovered something masculine in her glance and felt somewhere deep in herself an indefinable shudder . . .

'The churchyard was full of people,' Manos had written. 'They had buried their first dead. The laurel wreaths were piling up . . . You could easily distinguish those of the leaders. They were double the normal size. They had been placed one next to the other – they covered all the others. Every celebration was a chance for a speech – the Archbishop commented on events in his own way. EOKA commented in leaflets. And the churchyard was packed. Policemen were scattered among them. In plain clothes. It was a mystery who had brought the leader's wreath. On the road army and police trucks and groups of five or ten soldiers, with weapons. Groups of policemen with clubs. The others in plain clothes had infiltrated everywhere. And suddenly a shot was heard. The policeman in plain clothes was shot dead.'

Ioanna read but her brain found it difficult to comprehend the meaning. She looked at her naked body. In this position Al found her at midnight.

At about one Ioanna asked for coffee. All day she had had nothing. She drank the cup of hot coffee and slept. 'The policeman in plain clothes was shot dead. The people pretended to have seen nothing. And the policemen and the soldiers tore into the crowd.'

Ioanna rose at seven in the morning. Al brought her breakfast to her room. She ate, and smoked two cigarettes. She left the house and started walking. The morning traffic was at its busiest. At eight-thirty she took a taxi and at nine she entered Murphy's office. He was expecting her. Next to him was a slim, fair-haired man of around forty-five.

Murphy stood up 'Dr Austin. Mrs Oriol.'

'Number three,' said Ioanna. 'There are two others.'

'My pleasure,' said Dr Austin.

'Can we offer you something?' asked Murphy.

'I had just coffee. Thank you.'

'Then let's not waste time.'

In half an hour the three entered the neurological clinic. Murphy had fixed an appointment for ten. The director received them at his office; his movements betrayed some nervousness. Murphy talked quickly – to an extent that Ioanna found it difficult to follow him. He referred to the constitution, to the rights of the individual, what the legal interpretation of the term family was and finished: 'Your patient can't be here without the signed consent of his wife. His closest relative after his marriage is Ioanna Oriol. She is legally closer to Mathias Oriol than his mother or his grandmother. If you do not object we would like Dr Austin to examine him.'

The director coughed. He felt his position was difficult. He chose his words with great care: 'Of course I can't prevent Mrs Mathias Oriol from making use of the services of a doctor of her own choice. You understand that they brought Mathias Oriol to us, as an extremely urgent case. His family wanted his immediate admission to the clinic. Until yesterday morning we had no idea of the existence of a wife.' He pressed a button and a nurse came in.

'Please, take Dr Austin to Mathias Oriol.'

Dr Austin came back in half an hour. Without sitting he said: 'There's no doubt that the patient's state is serious, however, I believe that here we have a peculiar case. A neurological clinic would be right in other cases but not in this one. At least for the time being. Treatment would be more effective in a familiar environment. His psychosomatic state would vastly improve.'

Murphy stood up. Ioanna followed. The director remained seated. He said: 'We'll notify you of our decision at four this afternoon.' He stared rather harshly at Murphy. He avoided looking at Dr Austin.

At six o'clock Ioanna was in a taxi outside the clinic.

Mathias walked slowly towards the car. He smiled rather weakly at Ioanna: 'Book a hotel, my love,' he said.

Thus Mathias and Ioanna Oriol left the Oriols' mansion. When they found themselves alone in the room Ioanna threw her arms round Mathias. She seated him on the huge bed. He reacted mechanically – his will power had been completely eroded. Ioanna pressed a button and switched off the air-conditioning. Then she started undressing Mathias as if in a ritual. He stared at her in a rather wondering manner – while in his eyes there began to dawn a suspicion of hope. Ioanna undressed herself too. She began to embrace him with hands and legs. Her tongue, her lips, her breast, her hands and legs had become part of a tight unit that worked with the accuracy of a clock. Slowly, Mathias' body began to wake from its torpor. In his eyes the suspicion of hope became a suspicion of desire. Ioanna's body shone anointed with sweat. All the sensitive spots of Mathias' body were caressed by the entire body of Ioanna. And slowly his particles began being activated like particles suddenly exposed to a fierce bombardment of strange radiation. His feet, his hands, his lips, his tongue, his eyes began to live. Just like water is suddenly rippled under the caress of a light wind, and minute after minute the ripples surge and a weak wave is raised, thus Mathias' body started being rippled at the beginning and then it started being furrowed. Then a huge wave covered them. Then the two naked bodies were wrapped by an absolute immobility. And Mathias slept for the first time since ages without tranquillisers.

The next day they were visited by Dr Austin. He cast a questioning look at Ioanna and from the way she looked at him he understood that things were being set in a kind of order. Dr Austin examined Mathias once more. He wrote a prescription with various pills.

'These'll do the job for the time being. Later I may give something else.'

In the afternoon Al came and brought their suitcases.

'Everything okay at home, Al?' Mathias asked.

'The old lady is a bit annoyed. Otherwise it's as usual.'

'The others are coming to her soon Al. We have to leave soon.'

The pills caused a kind of drowsiness in Mathias. Ioanna brought him all sorts of papers. He concentrated for ten minutes but then reading tired him.

For the first time he noticed how thick the window glass was. Trapped in the walls, not moving either right or left, neither upwards nor downwards, it looked like an instrument of trapping harder than the wall because the wall did not let the eye roam while the glass gave the eye all the freedom of movement. His eye settled for a while on the road islets, human or not. Islets that changed shape and appearance every minute. But it stopped nowhere. It was a ceaseless movement the difference being that it was the eye that determined the rhythm and the brain followed while in the case of the newspaper it was the opposite.

Half-naked Ioanna wandered into the room and touched him, and caressed him from time to time, and it was the only time that, for a short while, his eye and brain relaxed.

They had all their meals in their room. When darkness began to fall and the traffic became less Ioanna dragged him out and they walked slowly for an hour while Mathias breathed the evening air and felt a relief.

They made love for a second time. Ioanna remained in bed. Mathias rose and searched his pockets for a notebook. He went through it, found something, noted a number on hotel paper and gave it to Ioanna.

'It's my local manager, arrange that he should see us at ten, tomorrow.'

'But it's almost midnight,' said Ioanna.

'He is on call twenty-four hours a day. That's why he is paid.'

Without saying anything else Ioanna got him on the phone. 'Yes, Mrs Oriol?'

The manager was a small man with thick, black hair. He appeared younger than his fifty years. Ioanna had seen him on two other occasions. She wondered how he managed in bed with a woman of normal height. If he adopted the usual horizontal position his head would nestle in the woman's breasts. She started wondering what might happen if he settled his head on a pillow next to hers, but she did not finish her thought.

At ten there was a knock on the door and the manager came in carrying a big briefcase: it was marked with big capital letters, Mathias Oriol. 'Good morning to you.' He stood still for a while. 'I see you are fine, both of you. It's good for one to relax, if one can afford it.'

'Dmitrik, have a seat,' Mathias said.

Ioanna rose to offer him a chair but before she could do so the manager settled in front of a small table and placed his briefcase on it. He opened it. 'We've got much information to give Mr Mathias. Your bank deposit account . . .'

Mathias waved his hand and stopped him: 'Leave the briefing for another time. You send everything in the afternoon, in writing. Now listen to what I want and note it down. Four per cent of my shares in Bolivia mines, six per cent of my shares in the copper mines of Brazil, seven per cent of my shares in the slaughter houses of Argentina and ten per cent of my money in the American Bank should be transferred today, in the name of Ioanna Mathias Oriol, of 37 George Iacovides Street, Lycavitos, Nicosia.'

Dmitrik stared. 'That is an irrevocable and unconditional transfer,' he whispered.

'Too many words Dmitrik. Did you note what I said?'

'But, it's a lot of money. We've got to study it, to discuss it . . .'

'I've already studied and discussed it, Dmitrik. I've called you so we can put it into practice. This afternoon I want the relevant documents here. Send them with Souzan. Smart girl, worthy of your office, Dmitrik.' Mathias rose and went towards Dmitrik. He closed the latter's briefcase. 'And don't get me on the phone. We'll have nothing to say on this. For other things, you know. You can ring me up any time.'

Dmitrik rose. For a moment he felt a kind of dizziness, but suddenly he saw the whole thing from a professional angle, one side of his brain set the other side in order as well as his nervous system. He smiled professionally. 'Whatever you say,

Mr Oriol. You know, my office has never said no to you, and never will.'

'But that's why I trust you, Dmitrik.'

In the afternoon, at exactly four, the documents arrived. Souzan left them in a sealed envelope at reception and they sent them right away in his room. Mathias opened the envelope and cast a glance at the documents. 'Yours Ioanna. From now on you have no financial problem.' He paused for a while. 'Book seats for Geneva. We're leaving tomorrow. America has tired me.'

'I didn't have any problem before,' Ioanna said. She telephoned reception: 'Book two seats for us for Geneva. Which company? Any would do. Pan American? Of course, and send us the bill.'

In a while the telephone rang again. It was to inform them that they were leaving at seven in the morning for Geneva.

'Why has America tired you?' She asked him.

'I don't know,' said Mathias. 'I feel thirsty.'

'Mineral,' said Ioanna. She picked up the telephone and ordered a bottle of ice-cold mineral water.

'It's the fucking tablets,' Mathias said, and lay in bed. As soon as he was asleep Ioanna lifted the receiver and asked to be connected with Cyprus.

'Mr Minas, it's Ioanna Oriol here. Yes, yes, do you hear me? We're returning to Cyprus. For sure, I'm returning. Maybe a paid ad? Okay. I'll see you in Nicosia.'

She looked at Mathias. He was fast asleep – the fucking pills.

13

At Geneva Ioanna had a feeling that she was returning to familiar places. She remembered Amalia and Prince de Samargan. From the airport they went straight to the hotel. The eight-hour flight made them feel tired. Towards the end she saw he was uneasy. Drops of sweat appeared on his forehead. She kept stroking his hand, made him stand up and walk to the lavatory. He threw a little water on his face, breathed deeply and the fear was pushed somewhere deeper, his chest became lighter and this made him feel safe for the next half hour.

'I'm dead tired,' said Ioanna as soon as they entered the room. Mathias kept silent. They were undressing slowly as if taking part in a ritual. Ioanna did not even remember when she finished. She buried herself under the covers and slept almost at once. When she woke she saw Mathias' empty bed. On the bedside table there was an empty whisky bottle. She leapt up. His pyjamas were scattered on the floor. On the table she found a note.

'Ioanna, as you see, I've made some progress. I don't disappear the way I did last time. I leave traces behind me. Even a Mathias can slowly become mature. I'm going straight to the clinic. It's as if I enter my old room. In America everything was so different. I had to leave or I would never have done it. From time to time I feel choked inside me. I must purify myself before I get lost in the labyrinth of alcohol and disease. We'll soon be together. I kiss you, Mathias.'

She rang the clinic immediately. They put her through to a doctor in charge.

'Yes I know, I know. The need for detoxification. How long will he stay? Three months the maximum you said? When can I see him? Okay. In three days.'

How differently she felt this time. She touched her bag without realizing it. She could lean with confidence on her cheque book. She started dressing slowly. She had three days in front of her which she had to fill in one way or another.

She went down to the dining room for breakfast. She had tried to phone Amalia but the latter didn't answer. She must be away, thought Ioanna. And she remembered that Amalia had to travel often to arrange publication of her husband's books in other countries. Last time Amalia had informed her that some of his books were being translated in Chinese. At the dining room a pleasant surprise was in store for her. She was walking towards a corner wrapped in her thoughts when someone blocked the way.

'Madam Oriol,' and he took her hand and brought it to his lips.

'My prince!' Her voice was full of joy and surprise.

'I always said that it would be in Geneva that we were going to meet again. Since you never honoured us with your presence in Spain.'

'It was in my programme my prince, but things turned out differently. Next time Spain won't escape me.'

'Will you have breakfast with us?' And without waiting for her answer he led her to his table.

'Let me introduce you. My closest male friend Simon. My closest female friend, Ioanna.'

Simon was a young man, six foot tall, fair-haired with blue eyes.

'Simon is English, he's working as a teacher of English in Madrid. Now he's accompanying me for a short or long time on my travels.'

Ioanna noticed that Samargan, while talking, spontaneously touched Simon's hands and legs.

'And Ioanna is a queen from Cyprus.' He took her hands

again and brought them to his lips.

'He said from Cyprus?' Simon asked.

'He said married?' Simon asked again.

'Unfortunately yes,' answered Samargan. 'We won't have the chance.'

'And your husband?'

'He's fixing some health problems.'

'A very businesslike mind,' remarked Simon, but Ioanna didn't understand what he meant. The waiter brought another cup and saucer.

'Breakfast?' he asked.

'Yes,' nodded Ioanna. 'English breakfast, please.'

'In spite of the situation that prevails in Cyprus?' Simon asked.

'We don't hate everything English,' said Ioanna and cast him an enigmatic glance. 'Do you know Cyprus?'

'Yes, my father is there, Ryan Jonathan.'

'Does he work for the government?'

'He's a military man.'

She looked at his broad shoulders. Above his left eyebrow he had a scar, like a faint line drawn with a pencil. And this line gave a particular tone to his glance and smile.

'It's not the right situation for army people, now in Cyprus,' Ioanna said.

'Army people do not choose the situations. The situations choose them,' said Simon.

The waiter served breakfast. Ioanna had only touched the meal they gave her on the plane and had slept uninterruptedly for ten whole hours. She ate with appetite, drank two cups of coffee and lit a cigarette.

'You shouldn't smoke, our queen. Haven't you read the latest articles in medical magazines?' Samargan said.

'I'll think about it after the age of fifty, my prince. Now it's too early.' Without realizing it she cast another enigmatic glance at Simon.

The clock on the opposite wall showed nine. She had nothing to do for three whole days. Leisure and inertia.

'What's your programme for today, our queen?'

'No programme for today.'

'Then, you're coming with us. We're climbing the Alps. Isn't that so, Simon?'

'It will be a chance for us to know each other better.' Ioanna felt his glance.

Samargan rose. 'We've no time to waste. It's already nine.'

At the entrance a car waited for them. Simon sat next to the driver and the two of them sat at the back. Ioanna had a problem about how to classify Samargan. The way he touched her showed that his male particles hid somewhere in a corner a small flame. She felt them activated from time to time but the chain reactions that took place inside were not enough to lead to a culmination, at least in her direction. She stared at Simon's broad shoulders. Did the prince lean in a different direction? Her thought remained suspended.

The motorway was a four-lane one. On one side it was a stab into the inside of the mountain, marked with a nightmarish insistence. On the other it hung over the lake – some huge cement pillars carried it on their back. And suddenly the lake disappeared. And the road became narrow. And it acquired the snaky body of a female dancer. And it climbed up panting, and the mountain was erect like a girlish breast. The trees became rarer and steep rocks rose. In their hollow spaces patches of snow began to appear. They left the main road and after the first bend the hotel appeared, built at the edge of the gorge. The snow was now thicker.

They climbed out of the car and went straight to the verandah. Simon leaned on the rails and admired the view. Samargan followed behind with Ioanna.

'I often come here with company. I like the human presence amid the wildness of the mountain. It's strange how relaxed I feel.'

Ioanna did not talk. She absorbed the landscape with her entire body.

'What are your plans?' Samargan interrupted the spell.

'I'm leaving for Cyprus in three days.'

'Pity. We're leaving soon for Africa. Safari. Me and Simon.

We'll be a big company in Kenya. Hunting fills me with satisfaction.' A short silence followed. 'And your husband?'

'Getting rid of his toxins,' Ioanna answered.

'Just like the other time?' She didn't understand whether it was a question or a remark.

'He needs it, from time to time.'

'There's trouble in Cyprus.'

'Yes, with the English,' Ioanna answered.

'Soon, others will be added,' Samargan added enigmatically.

The snow-covered gorge lay in front of them. The trees gave the impression of having just wakened, half-wrapped in a sheet, and trapped in the immobility of the first wakening.

Simon tore himself from the rails. 'Shall we walk?'

They wandered for two hours. They breathed the clean air of the mountain and felt a strange vigour. It was already past two when Simon said he was hungry. They went back to the hotel and straight to the restaurant. They drank three bottles of German wine and retired to their rooms for an afternoon siesta.

Closing the door behind her Ioanna felt an excitement starting out from somewhere deep inside her. Her interior had been transformed into a shapeless landscape from which emerged something like a male Aphrodite: Simon. And she was dancing. Where? She didn't know. Salome with the seven veils. This effort tired her, and she slept deeply for two hours.

At around seven they got into the car for Geneva.

The image of Simon came repeatedly to her mind. She always remembered the picture of Aphrodite rising from inside a blue empty space. It was the picture of an erect, mutilated Aphrodite which often appeared in cheap advertising leaflets. Even on wrapping paper or packets of the Turkish delight. This shapeless landscape or the blue empty space slowly took a more concrete form and she felt him rising from inside her.

They passed the whole night at the bar of the hotel. They drank plenty of French wine and ate one or two sandwiches. Towards the end Samargan's sense of balance became weaker and he couldn't fully control his feet and hands. Sometimes they touched Simon and sometimes Ioanna. And Ioanna felt some chain explosions taking place inside him. And his tongue was trapped inside these explosions. He was talking incessantly.

At around two in the morning they went to their rooms. Samargan was now a broken line. He was literally hanging on Simon and followed him like his broken shadow. This strange entanglement was imprinted on Ioanna's mind and kept her company until she slept. It was a deep sleep, uninterrupted, that allowed no room for either dream or figures to come to the surface, concrete or shapeless.

It must have been noon when she woke. She had a feeling that she was being watched by Mathias' grandmother – in her rocking chair. She brushed aside the picture as best as she could.

Under the door she found a note. 'Dear Ioanna, we had been waiting in vain for you, for breakfast. You didn't come. Something unexpected happened and we had to catch the plane for Kenya, at once. I hope we meet again. In Spain this time. Always yours, Samargan.' She almost felt his touch on her body but she did not even shudder. She went down to the restaurant, settled at a corner and ate something without much appetite. At the reception they gave her a small envelope. Inside it there was a note written on the hotel paper. 'I'll be carrying you inside me, Simon.' She shuddered, as if a whole naked body infiltrated into hers.

The third day she visited Mathias at the clinic. They met in a small room, almost empty. A table and two chairs at a corner. Plain curtains at the window. Mathias stared at her calmly. She felt a strange emotion.

'You have to go to Cyprus, Ioanna. I can't think of you in Geneva. Anyhow, we aren't going to meet again before three months. I feel so tired.'

'I'll be waiting for you, Mathias.'

'I never had any doubt. I must, however, relax.'

Their meeting lasted only for a few minutes. Ioanna kissed him on the cheek but he did not react at all.

She left at midnight with Swiss Air. It was dawn when she arrived. The small prefabricated rooms of Nicosia International Airport looked like a neglected village hidden in the heart of the Mesaoria plain. She noticed the change. Next to each civilian employee there stood a soldier. He seemed to be doing nothing. He simply stood speechless and almost motionless. He did his job with his eyes. She took a taxi and crossed the empty streets of the capital. With relief she felt the door of her flat closing behind her. She opened a window, drank coffee and went straight to bed. She slept until late in the afternoon.

In her letterbox she found a bundle of newspapers and a note from Manos. The newspapers were full of photographs of children who demonstrated in the streets and clashed with the police. Policemen wearing helmets, holding clubs.

She read: 'There where the Kykko forest ends, a short distance outside Kampos and Tsakistra, the guerilla group lay in ambush for two army trucks. They fired on them at the bend of the road. The fight lasted for two hours. Members of the shock unit hit and then retreated into the forest. Two more army trucks were added. Suddenly the forest caught fire. Fierce flames were fanned by a strong wind. A total area of eight square miles of government forest was burnt. It is not known whether there were any victims.'

The leader was dressed in a thick green military uniform and carried a pistol fastened on his belt. He loathed the crossed cartridge belt and the rifles since the time of the German occupation of Greece. His order was laconic but clear. 'You'll be wearing your cartridges on a belt around your waist.'

He had a separate chain of hideouts, from Limassol to Kyperounta, from Tsakistra to Nicosia, from Kokkinotrimithia to Trikomo. And a series of bodyguards who changed according to the area, even to the hideouts. Except the first one. He was the unique one.

The line of the bodyguards should be adapted according to circumstances. And to be interrupted according to circumstances. A line always leads somewhere. There's an end at the edge. If you can't interrupt it at the right moment then you're lost.

Vasilis remained silent. They wanted him as deputy leader. And the Leader didn't like his silence, charged with emotion. A thought passed through his mind like an electric wave. He didn't let it arrive anywhere.

'The five crept amid the bushes,' Manos' report continued. 'With their Kalashnikov rifles and belts of hand grenades. When the trucks appeared at the bend the one in charge gave the signal. And five hand grenades were thrown at once. And the explosions followed one after another in a matter of fractions of a second. The two trucks were immobilised. The tyres of one caught fire. There was an uproar. And the English soldiers jumped out from the back, from the sides. And the Kalashnikovs spat, and the echo came back. The English machine-guns began to fire. And the guerillas moved from bush to bush and there were bullets everywhere. And the English were delayed. From tree to tree, from bush to bush. The wireless was set behind an old pine tree. The English called for reinforcements. One of the two trucks began to burn in the middle of the road. The guerilla group showed no signs of retreating. They moved from place to place with the speed of a roe-deer. From bush to bush, from tree to tree, the English moved like a well-wound mechanism. After two hours they heard the roar of three trucks on the forest road that led to the Kykko monastery.

'When the three trucks unloaded their human cargo, the signal for the retreat was given. But the five of them were spotted. "To Aniftos' oak tree," shouted the guerilla in charge. "Don't fire during retreat. Unless you're signalled to." And the Kalashnikovs were silenced. And gradually the English machine-guns were silenced too. And a strange silence spread through the forest. And the five of the shock unit moved noiselessly. And the English followed deployed at a distance of half a mile. From time to time a surprised, disturbed shot. Until the unit was spotted once more. And then the barrage of machine-guns began. But the shock unit escaped again; they slid through the trees and bushes and the bullets brushed past them but touched nobody.

'The one in charge of the English gave the order for them to stop. And the order was passed from mouth to mouth, like a relay race. The English began to assemble where their officer stood. He belted his revolver. "The bloody bastards. They move with the wind," he said. He raised a small cloud of dust with his stick. "We'll burn them with the wind. We'll set their part of the forest on fire."

'The flame-thrower belched and flames leapt, timid at first, then wild, like young dancing girls in a disco.

'Every pine tree turned into a torch. And the wind pushed the flames with frenzy in the direction the guerilla group had vanished. The one in charge gave the signal for retreat, and they moved backwards, with weapons ready.

'Then the wind changed direction, without any warning. The flames paused for a while, then rushed with new strength in the opposite direction. The flames had been unleashed to a wild dance at the music of the wind. And the men ran and the flames danced. Then they began coming out on to the road one after the other. Their faces were blackened by smoke and their eyes shone strangely. The fear of the haunted beast had entered in them.

'It was not known,' Manos wrote, 'how many were burnt in the Kykko forest. They must have been many.'

Ioanna went back to the years of her childhood. To the north, a little outside the village, Kykko forest started. She carried the picture inside her, the pine trees moving up and down wavewise when the wind blew through them, creating a feeling of endlessness. She stayed rooted on the ground, only her eyes travelled.

The hideout was in the heart of the forest, three miles from the monastery. The leader had chosen it to confuse the English.

'Antonis, the secret is to be everywhere and nowhere.'

'You're a maitre in this, Chief.'

'Man is capable of learning continuously. Our organisation during the occupation was my big step – I mean the other occupation, that of the Germans.'

Somebody sent a signal by whistling. Antonis leapt out, fear and determination in his eyes, life mingled with death.

'The English have set the forest on fire. It seems they're chasing the shock unit. I saw the smoke, two miles away.'

Antonis said nothing. He went back to the hideout.

'We're moving, Chief. The English set the forest on fire.'

'Old tactics Antonis. I see they make no progress.' He belted his pistol round his waist and put on his beret. He had not taken off his rough boots. 'Where to Antonis?'

'I don't know Chief. We'll stop somewhere on the way. According to the information we get we'll act. We won't stop, before we cover seven miles, Chief.'

The signal-whistle was heard again and soon the guard's head appeared. 'You're late. The smoke thickens.'

'Okay. You're staying here. At the hideout. Whatever happens.' Antonis leapt out of the hideout. The leader followed. The first one paved the way with his body and the second followed.

In the newspaper reports of the Tsakistra battle and the burning Kykko forest there was the latest piece of information: 'It is persistently rumoured that in one of the hideouts of the area was the leader, who escaped at the last moment from the human and flaming cordon.'

The next day Ioanna rang Manos. 'I require domestic staff,' she said. The Oriols must live in style.

Manos published an advertisement in all the papers: 'Domestic staff required'.

Ioanna, seated in an armchair, received one after the other the candidates with half closed eyes. Her memories were at the point of being involved in a dance, but she persistently brushed them aside. 'You have to control your memories. Otherwise, your personality's in danger.' She sometimes wondered at the acrobatics of her thoughts. In the end she hired a butler who would have the overall responsibility, a cook and a maid-servant for general duties.

'For the time being, until our house is built you will be day staff,' she told them. 'In turn one will have to stay until eleven at night. The other two can leave at seven.'

The butler took charge. 'I'll make the list. Everything will be perfectly organised,' he said.

Ioanna liked his look. She also liked the way he talked. He stressed every word, and seemed to dominate the others, like a sergeant his soldiers.

That afternoon, she was relaxing in her armchair reading a cheap love story. Her body rebelled at what she read but somewhere deep in her she found a secret satisfaction. In the rebellion of her body she found her own self as it had been shaped day after day, night after night and in her secret satisfaction some dreams that had been perching in some corners of her subconscious mind.

The butler approached her discreetly.

'Someone wants to see you. He insists.'

'What does he want?'

'I don't know, madam.'

'Okay, send him in.'

The man who entered looked tired and resigned. He appeared broken. Triantafyllos, the butler, went away noiselessly.

'Have a seat,' said Ioanna. 'What can I do for you?'

The man sat with an effort. 'I'm facing a terrible problem. My children were in the car that was burnt outside Limassol. One died. The other one suffered third degree burns. He has to undergo very expensive plastic surgery, that cannot be done in Cyprus, and I have no money. That's why I've come to you.' He remained silent again.

'What about your wife?'

'I don't know where she is. After the inquiry she vanished. She may have gone abroad.'

His story began to take a certain shape. In Cyprus he had been working as a builder – whenever he found work. He and his wife and two children lived in rented rooms at four pounds a month. Sometimes he managed the rent, sometimes not. His wife was twenty-four. He had married her when she was twenty. She was thirsty for fun, and before the children were born they went to dances on Saturday nights. They drank cheap brandy and danced till three in the morning and then returned home to make love and sleep.

All this stopped with the birth of the children. The rooms they rented became their entire world, and their life a struggle to cover the expenses. His wife became bitter. The explosion of the building industry began suddenly to subside and he found himself working only two or three days a week. He was forced to go and work for the English at Suez. Half of the money went to his wife.

Then his wife began to leave the children alone in the rooms at night. She dropped a little brandy in their milk, and did not return until midnight. The children did not wake up during the night. She stayed in bed until nine or ten in the morning. The children woke at around eight, they drank their milk from the fridge, ate what they found. Sometimes they quarrelled. They started crying, especially the young one, but she didn't stir before nine.

Ioanna remembered. It was a cutting from a newspaper that Minas had sent to America. Sometimes he sent her newspapers or cuttings – so that she could maintain, as he said, a lively contact with Cyprus.

At the edge of the Acrotiri forest, a few miles outside Limassol, a car was burnt with two children inside. One of the children died. The other was saved, but badly burned. She remembered the face of the young mother. It was a beautiful face, with eyes like burning coal.

The young woman felt a fire burning in her legs day and night. At the beginning she joked about the whole thing. But the fire was there. She found it at night, she found it in the morning when she woke up, she found it at noon while having lunch, she found it in the afternoon as her glance roamed above the roofs. The English started imposing curfews. Every time a soldier was killed in a narrow street in the castle area the curfew came down like a gigantic hand and the roads were deserted after six, and then it turned into a huge curtain that covered the houses. But the curfew did not extinguish her fire. On the contrary it became stronger, this compulsory isolation became a wild wind which blew in between her legs and fanned the fire. And he worked at Suez and half his money came to her regularly.

The first time the curfew lasted three nights from six in the evening until seven in the morning. What happened on the fourth night can hardly be described. The whole town crept along the streets, it obstinately refused to get into the houses. It walked with fear in one hand and laughter in the other, like a long-distance traveller who carries his bundles.

She put the children to bed at nine and went out on a night when there was no curfew. She had no idea where she was going and that's why she started walking along the streets. She stared at the lights, she heard the frightened laughter inside her, she stared at the stars. What direction is Suez?

He accosted her discreetly. 'Alone?'

'I'm busy.'

He asked her to go for a drink.

'Who knows, tomorrow we may have a curfew.'

She followed him into a dimly-lit bar where he ordered whisky. She felt a pleasant numbness spreading to her limbs. But she still felt the fire burning in her legs. The numbness did not even touch it. They drank a second one and her head began to float. They drank it slowly and he talked continuously. He jumped from one topic to the other, about the various bars that began to multiply around the Heroes' Square, the old power station that stopped functioning. She listened, heard his voice which sounded like a folk song, long-drawn and monotonous. She liked folk songs, she told him.

'Tomorrow or the day after, we'll go to a bar where there was a popular singer,' he said. And he kept on talking. About the curfew and the fucking British. And all the time his hands and legs touched her, quite accidentally. He did it in such a natural manner. She didn't say anything about her children or her husband.

After the third drink she felt her head floating. 'Shall we go?' he said. She stood up and followed him as if hypnotised.

In the street he put his arm round her and they began to walk, two shadows in the night. Suddenly they found themselves by the sea.

'We're very far from my rooms,' she said.

'Doesn't matter. I'll take you.'

Opposite the sea was the dark structure of a half built cinema. He dragged her inside the building. The street lights entered through various openings. The scaffolding climbed up to the unfinished roof, forming some peculiar squares that give a feeling of cubist painting. He led her into a small dark room, took off her clothes, one piece after another. She lay on the bare cement floor and they made love. She felt a strange, numbing pleasure. Back home, she slept until ten and could not even hear that the children had been shouting since seven.

The following night they met again at ten. He walked her to the sea, to a small dockyard. The half finished caiques and the rotting boats that they dragged out of the water, to let them die naturally were caught in a formidable immobility. There, where life and death mixed, there was always this immobility which under its surface hid two contrasting directions. He took out a small bottle of whisky and offered her a drink. She sipped some and gave it back. He dragged her into a half-finished caique took off her clothes again, and made love to her on the wooden floor.

For two nights they did not meet. She found a note under her door. 'I'm working on a night shift tonight and tomorrow night.' The day his shift work finished she occupied herself with various small jobs, anticipating their meeting that night. But at one the radio announced the imposition of a three-day curfew. Something froze inside her. She put the children to bed at eight and threw herself on a chair, her body itching and her mind numbed. In this position a strange sleep took over her.

A light but persistent knock on the window made her jump from her chair. 'Who is it?'

'It's me, don't be afraid.' She felt the panting in his voice. 'They've called me urgently for work. I'll be waiting for you at two in the afternoon at the northern side of the square.'

'What about the curfew?'

'No curfews in the afternoons.'

He disappeared in the night and she wasn't sure whether he had heard the good night she said. She kept sitting until four in the morning and then slept deeply until ten.

At two in the afternoon she took the children and went to the square. She found him waiting in a parked car. It was an old Ford, green, that was strangely cut at the back.

'My UFO,' he said, smiling. He opened the passenger door, pushed back the seat to allow the children into the back and she sat in front next to him.

'Didn't have anywhere to leave the children,' she said.

'It's okay. We'll go to the Akrotiri forest. They'll stay in the car.'

They drove slowly through the crowded Limassol streets. Every time a curfew was imposed all the immobility of the night piled up and found a way out in an explosive mobility during daytime. People were trying to feed themselves with movement, to pile up inside them plenty of reserves so as to be able to pass their nights caught in the tentacles of immobility without having their emotional balance disturbed. They drove panting out of the town, passing the area with the the Indian fig trees, with the wine factories that blocked the view to the sea, their empty barrels piled outside, one on top of the other to form a wall that emitted a strange sense of life, with the sea trapped at the end of long narrow streets and the *hanoums* (Turkish women) wandering at the edge of an incomplete emancipation. The veils and the black or dark-coloured mantles crept along, sleeveless dresses or bare-footed children that left a cloud of dust behind them in the unasphalted side streets where they played football using a ball made of tightly tied rags.

The landscape changed from one moment to the next. The big trees and the vegetable gardens of Zakaki, the clay-brick houses, the reddish soil that advanced unimpeded towards the blue sea, succeeded each other and started again from the beginning for about one and a half miles until they were lost in endless vineyards. The children enjoyed the car drive. They sat in the back and looked full of wonder at the changing landscape. It was a revelation to them after the barren rooms which until then had been their entire world. They left behind the inhabited areas and the Ford proceeded slowly along a country road that girded the Acrotiri forest. They covered another mile and suddenly the Ford stopped.

'Here,' he said. 'We'll go a few yards inside the forest.'

'The children will stay in the car.' He didn't understand whether it was a question.

'I'll lock it,' he said.

They got out, he locked the car carefully and they went into the forest. Behind some bushes, he began to take off her clothes, one piece after another. The two naked bodies rolled on the grass, they became a strange tangle which continuously moved about, and the wind fanned the fire that burned in their bodies. And suddenly the cries of children were heard. The two naked bodies stiffened. The cries became louder. And a thin cloud of smoke filled the air. They threw on their clothes and ran towards the car which turned quickly into a roaring inferno. He managed to open the back door and the bodies of the two children were dragged out. She fainted and fell on the ground a few yards away.

The father stared at Ioanna Oriol, mute sorrow in his eyes.

'The young one died,' he said. 'They buried him before I came from Suez. The other one came out of the hospital after three months. He has to undergo plastic surgery. They work miracles abroad. That's why I've come.'

Ioanna rose. She felt choked. 'I'll undertake it. I'll send him either to Geneva or the USA. Wherever it's necessary.' She called Triantafyllos. 'Have all the necessary information from this man and send a note to Manos.'

The next day all the papers published the photograph of Ioanna next to the father and the injured child. 'Mrs Ioanna Oriol sees that the young victim is sent to America for a series of operations. She and her husband, Mathias Oriol, will cover all the expenses,' the caption read.

Ioanna liked the photograph. Tall, erect, distinguished. Her flat became a kind of refuge. Everyone who had a problem went there and asked to see her. Triantafyllos became a kind of private secretary-butler. Sometimes he tried to give her advice. She cast a rather strange glance at him and cut him short: 'I know, I know.'

And Manos found now a new kind of occupation – in charge of public relations. Every week or so a photograph appeared in the newspapers. She held the same erect position, she handed cheques. The only thing that annoyed her was that Mrs they stuck to her name.

'Mano, I don't like that Mrs.'

'It's very Greek, Madam Oriol.'

'All are Mrs. I'm the one.'

In the new photographs the Mrs was replaced by Madam. And for some time she enjoyed people coming to her flat and asking Triantafyllos for Mrs Madam. After a while she got fed up with it too.

'Manos, the thing has become stale.'

'How are we going to go about it?'

She cut him short with a strange look.

'Okay, okay. I'll take care of it. It'll take me some time. But I'll fix it.'

Manos saw that she got all the newspapers. One report read: 'A special Mass was held in the Holy Church of Our Saviour. Special prayers were said for the Cypriot people. Well known personalities were present, including the Bishop of Paphos, the abbots of St. Neophytos and Chrysorogiatissa, the priests of the district and Madam Oriol.' The photograph showed her with her hair done in Cleopatra style. The camera had caught her holding her dark glasses with the edge of the frame to her lips. Her glance was fixed on some point in the distance. The special Mass was held to mark the arrival of the caique Saint George, under the nose of the English. And in the special prayer in favour of the sick and suffering, there was added the fighters and those feeling sympathy for the struggle.

Her parents-in-law never met her, even once, since she had returned to Cyprus; she had been waiting day after day for their invitation but it never came. They stayed at the Agonos mansion. Mr Oriol was on good terms with both the Governor and the Bishop of Kyrenia. He had never forgotten the role the bishopric had played during the miners' strike.

'I'm the new generation of the Oriols,' she said. She looked at the photograph and felt a hedonistic shudder. Manos was doing a good job. She went to her study, and picked up a file. She had not increased his salary for six months. She wrote a note to her accountant: 'An increase of twenty pounds a month to Manos.'

The next day an unknown young man knocked at her door. She opened the door herself.

'Madam Oriol?'

'Yes.'

He gave her an ordinary envelope, mounted his bicycle and rode away down the hill. In the envelope there was a short note: 'Your national feelings are particularly appreciated. I hope we meet sometimes. The Leader.'

Manos, she thought, does an excellent job. She went on a lightning trip to Athens. Part of her cash was in Greek banks. Her accountant sent regular reports but sometimes her personal intervention was needed for a question to be settled. She reached her hotel at around eight in the evening. She went straight to the bath, came out and went to the dressing table. She stood in front of the mirror. The years seemed not to have touched her body. She smiled with obvious satisfaction. But in the mirror she saw that somebody had pushed a note under the door. She walked to the door and took it up. She read it: 'I welcome you to Athens. I'll be waiting for you tonight at nine-thirty at the hall. I'll be wearing a green costume and a hat. Dark glasses too. The Leader.'

She felt filled with a strange emotion. She hadn't expected to meet the leader in an aristocratic hotel in Athens. She went back to the dressing-table and began to fix her hair. She dressed, made herself comfortable in a chair and leafed through some magazines. Photographs of the snow-covered

Alps caught her eye, forty degrees below zero in Russia, forty-five in America. 'It's as if we are on safari in Kenya,' she thought in the warmth of the hotel. She suddenly remembered Simon. The snow-covered Alps disappeared in the tropical vegetation of central Africa. 'I should send a card now that the holidays are approaching. I'll send it to Spain. From there they'll find him. Samargan's nets must be spread everywhere.'

At nine twenty-five she rose. She cast a last glance at the mirror, satisfied with her deep red dress. She went down to the hall. She saw him sitting at a table, approached him and gave him her hand: 'Madam Oriol.'

He stood up, took her hand and held it for a while. 'Shall we sit.'

Discreetly the waiter approached.

'What will you have?' he asked her.

'Anything.'

'Shall I offer you a Metaxa cognac?'

She nodded.

'For me too,' he told the waiter. 'With ice.'

As soon as the waiter moved away he spoke very fast, spitting out the words: 'I'm not, you know, the leader. I'm acting on his behalf. He's in Cyprus. I'm Loizos Savvides. In charge of arms. I mean the supply. The leader esteems you deeply. Your work too. I hope you'll soon have the chance to meet him.'

'My appreciation for the leader knows no bounds. I am anxious to meet him. My deeds are inspired by his work, military and political.'

The waiter brought the two cognacs.

'Madam Oriol, in the international market there are many weapons – more than one can imagine. You only have to have money. And we don't want to involve, obviously or not, the Greek public. At a certain stage we may not be able to avoid it. Until then we'll be working on our own. Finding the arms and purchasing them is our first job, sending them to Cyprus is our second. In spite of the relevant difficulties we manage to solve these problems satisfactorily.'

She understood. She took out her cheque book and wrote

a cheque for twenty thousand dollars.

'In whose name?'

'Loizos Savvides.'

'Twenty thousand dollars as first instalment. And convey to the leader my boundless appreciation and admiration.'

'Your national work is deeply appreciated, madam.' He took the cheque and put it in the inside pocket of his coat and made a movement as if going to stand up.

'Are you not joining me for dinner?'

'I would like to, but I have too many obligations.' He stretched his hand. 'I hope we meet in Cyprus under entirely different conditions.'

He fixed his glasses, put on his hat and headed for the exit. She ordered another cognac and sipped it slowly looking at the various hotel clients. She took a piece of paper, wrote her name and the number of her room and gave it to the waiter: 'Send me dinner in a quarter of an hour.' She stood up, took the lift to her floor. She wanted to eat, to watch television and sleep. Before going to bed she wrote to Simon: 'You emerge continuously from my inside like Aphrodite'. She put it in an envelope, wrote Samargan's address on it and left it on the bedside table. In the morning she would leave it at reception, to be mailed.

The morning of the second day, at ten, she settled her account and left by taxi for the airport. She had seen her banker and made arrangements for part of her deposited money to be invested. At one thirty in the afternoon she arrived in Nicosia.

The man responsible for passport control held her passport for a while. 'Forty-eight hour visit to Athens?'

'What's holding you?' shouted the English soldier who was sitting next to him.

'Can we learn the reason of your visit to Athens?'

Ioanna looked at him condescendingly. 'The Oriols deal with banks in a dozen countries,' she said. 'I went to Athens to fix some of my bank affairs there.'

The English soldier nodded and the clerk stamped the passport.

'Here it is madam. Please forgive us.'

She took her passport and put it in her bag and gave instructions to a porter to carry her suitcase. She proceeded to the exit without looking either right or left – under her glasses her eyes tried to catch as much as they could. At the exit Manos was waiting for her.

'Everything under control Manos?'

'As far as it can be, Madam Oriol.' Among the crowd was the photographer Manos had hired. He took two or three photographs while Ioanna was walking towards the car. A strong westerly wind was blowing and pushed her hair back but her glasses gave her the feeling of a protective wall.

14

His mother, they said, wrote poems and sent them almost every week to the papers of the capital. Myrto G. Pantelidou. She always signed them like that and they talked about golden afternoons in the orange orchards of Famagusta or the purple ones swimming in the sea of Varoshia. For delayed loves that were doomed by reality to flourish only in one direction. He, they said, came to the capital at the age of twenty and worked as a journalist – a freelance. He had inherited something from his mother's talent as a writer and the nerve of his father. He didn't know quite what this nerve was – the broken movement of his body, the theatrical abrupt movement of his hands, the spasmodic, shaking of his head. Now he combined the job of the executor and photojournalist.

The two English soldiers were walking on the pavement gazing idly in the direction of the moat – their glance stopped at the huge stones of the Venetian walls. Traffic started piling up. He came on his motorcycle, his camera on his shoulder. He stopped near the pavement and discreetly someone else took the machine and disappeared. He remained standing at the edge of the road. He looked at the moving crowd and the other English soldiers.

'Lesly, behind the wall there the old town starts.'

'Can't we go?'

'Only if there are at least ten of us. The fucking streets are too narrow and in them half the army of the Empire is digested.'

'And the prostitutes, where are they?'

'To the east of the old town.'

A car came to the edge of the road; it brushed the pavement. At the front was the driver and at the back, Helen, with her black hair twisted into a knot, and her big, curved nose. Pantelides was on the pavement.

'The Middle East prostitutes are different from our own?'

'They lack finesse. And they are out of bounds.'

The car cut off the horizon for him. Helen opened the door and took out the gun from under her dress. 'We'll drive round the statue. In four minutes we'll be here.'

The car was driven off.

'Out of bounds. And how do we get fixed?'

'With our fucking five fingers. Unless we fall upon something extra, male or female.'

'Bloody shit.'

Pantelides slowly crossed the road. He glanced at his watch. Two and a half minutes had passed. He lingered a bit at the edge of the road and saw Helen's car at the roundabout. He pulled the pistol out. Two shots were heard, two dry sounds and the two bodies spread on the pavement. Frightened, the pedestrians started running in every direction. The car brushed lightly the pavement once more. Helen opened the door and Pantelides hurled himself in the rear. The car accelerated, turned left and vanished in the side streets of the old town.

In a few minutes the streets were crowded with soldiers wearing helmets and holding their guns. They spread out in groups of ten, they set up roadblocks, they hit out at anyone who proved difficult. They forced everyone to stand against the wall with their hands raised above their heads, and they searched them. Windows and doors closed noisily. Crying children buried themselves in their mothers' dresses. A town was putting on its fear and remained motionless in a pose of expectation.

The car almost touched the crudely set up roadblock and stopped. Pantelides and Helen were in the back, embracing each other. Against her flesh that piece of iron continued to remind her of its presence. And her fear had become a piece of iron inside her. She felt cold, like the pistol that rested against her flesh. Pantelides felt a strange calm, it spread inside. Two soldiers searched the engine and two the boot of the car. Another searched the driver's seat. The last one opened the back door and saw them in each other's arms.

'Bloody fucking sorry.'

The one in charge gave the signal: they slammed the bonnet and the boot and let the car pass the roadblock. It crept along the side streets of old Nicosia until it disappeared in the fringes of the Turkish sector.

Tommy raised his gun. In his village, somewhere in the south of England the houses were surrounded by woods. Squirrels and the wild rabbits reacted strangely to human noises. Sometimes they remained literally rooted at the fringes of a formidable immobility – their spines turned into pieces of iron – only their eyes shone strangely and their lower lips trembled ceaselessly, so that the delicate balance between mobility and immobility might not be disturbed. Something moved at the window and Tommy pressed the trigger. The child received the bullet in the head.

The delicate balance between mobility and immobility was for ever shattered. One squirrel or wild rabbit less, what does it matter?

'Bloody shit!'

The mother screamed. Her screams hit the window and then remained suspended, lifeless, lingering. In the evening, after half a case of beer Tommy had a weeping fit. He uttered some incomprehensible cries about wild rabbits and squirrels. They wrapped him in a blanket and threw him in his bed.

Another group forced the children against the wall. They raised their guns. An execution scene. The children froze. And they received a rain of blows at their backsides. The town stared at its wounds but didn't have time even to lick them.

The doors and the windows were noisily slammed one after the other, as if a huge hand closed the venetian blinds, the latter showing a little, impotent resistance and then closing with a liberated noise. And the town started timidly licking its wounds, behind the noise and the silence.

It was only yesterday that he played in the streets of Islington, then he found himself in Cyprus. He fixed the blanket for Tommy. He lived with his father and aunt in a decaying flat on the second floor, the old wood smelt of mould and the gas on the wall neutralised everything in his room. His mother had left when he was six. His drunken father was eternally wrapped in his dirty overcoat, his aunt in her dark dresses and her green hat.

Tommy's head shook – a sob and a sigh. Once more he fixed the blanket. He remembered his mother – her long black hair, her warm body where he took refuge. And he found himself serving as a sentry on the hills round Nicosia or patrolling the streets with gun in hand.

They had taken them swimming to the east of Kyrenia. They were loaded like sardines on a military truck. A Jeep at the front and one at the back. Swimming under military escort. Not even the Queen. On the truck floor the arms were piled. In case. 'We can't take chances.'

They drove through the Turkish villages with the small clay-brick houses. The children were barefooted, half-naked. The women wrapped up in their sheets – of deep blue colour – stood motionless in the formidable heat, small minarets in the human landscape.

The truck unloaded them two yards from the sea. Tommy's first experience of the sea was at Hastings. His father was holding him by the hand and his mother was dressed in summer clothes and the wind ruffled her hair. And he saw the sea retreating and vanishing leaving behind it an endless sandy beach with some starfish motionless to break the monotonous grey colour of the sand. 'The sea will return,' his father told him. Mother left and never came back, the starfish remained motionless for ever inside him.

They jumped into the water. But suddenly electrically charged wires hit the water and the soldiers leapt in the air and ran for the sand. The guards took up their arms but they didn't know where to turn them. Sand hills closed the visual range.

Tommy was now sleeping calmly. It was now Bryan who writhed on the beach – like fish caught in an invisible net. The taxi stopped at the first roadblock. Manos was sitting beside the driver and Ioanna in the back. Four soldiers surrounded the car.

'Out,' said the sergeant in a tone that left no room for doubt. 'And your papers.'

The driver gave him his driving licence and Manos his Press card. Ioanna took out her passport. The sergeant examined them carefully. The soldiers combed the car from the engine to the luggage boot. Nothing.

'Sorry for the trouble,' said the sergeant.

They got in the taxi and the driver drove off. At the same time the radio announced the imposition of a curfew. It would begin in half an hour. 'Two English soldiers were shot in the back in Homer's Avenue. The search for the assassins continues.'

'What you sensed is right,' said Ioanna.

The driver accelerated. Neither Manos nor Ioanna spoke. In ten minutes she found herself outside her flat. She put a two pound note in the driver's hand without asking how much the trip cost.

'What about you, Manos?'

'He'll take me home. It's only five minutes. We still have time.'

She opened the door and went in. The flat was silent and dimly lit. She looked at the walls, the furniture, as if she expected something different. Then she went to bed and slept until two or three in the afternoon.

The town remained sleepless in the curfew. However, its sleeplessness hung from behind closed windows and closed doors, something like torn curtains shaken by the wind. And the empty roads had a peculiar continuity. And it was a vicious circle, the empty streets of the town. The one ended and the other began. And the soldiers patrolled holding their weapons. Silence and the streets swallowed them. Their voices and their steps were like shadows in a huge lit screen. Some shadows that were drowned in light, a light that was drowned in transparent darkness. And the streets were cut off at the centre of the old city. As if by a knife.

It must have been past midnight when Ioanna woke up. She walked to the window and drew the curtains. Arasta street linked the Greek with the Turkish sector. It was a narrow street under the shadow of Saint Sophia's minarets and some very old palm trees that opened like firework mushrooms. The planks of the shops' huge wooden doors were tied together by iron bars. There were small attic windows high up on the opposite wall. Merchandise was piled up on the pavement. Shoes, slippers, sandals all tied on long strings hung from the wooden doors. Sometimes a copper bowl – its tinned interior in bright contrast to the dark copper of its exterior. Cloths of every kind. The rolls piled up to the height of the door. Pullovers, shirts, pants hung from wooden hangers. And at the goldsmith's the craftsman worked on his bench and piled his treasure in small shop windows. And the traders competed in variety the merchandise. The one tall and slim stands in the middle of the open door amid shoes and slippers and the second one walking nervously up and down holding an iron yard measure and caressing the cloth rolls as if they were a woman's legs, and the third one sitting with swollen belly amid cooking utensils, sucking his narghile pipe.

Reflections of fire leapt up suddenly. A mob holding flaming torches ran through the street. Flames danced, and they broke doors and the crowd grasped whatever they could. Then children took it from their hands and disappeared in the side streets sometimes towards Saint Sophia and sometimes towards the Serai. And then came the reflections. In the night the smoke was dissolved, it was swallowed by darkness, only the smell of the burnt leather and cloth, of the burnt wood, of the molten metal crept along the side streets and hit the closed doors and the closed windows. And the reflections. To break the silence in a strange way. They also hit the closed doors and the closed windows. And the screams of the mob to dissolve in the reflections of the fire, to hit the edges of the town that was under curfew. A church bell went astray – how can church bells go astray.

For some minutes a church bell tore the night and silence. From time to time a surprised shot. And after that the monotonous voice of the muezzin. Colourless, abrupt, professional.

Ioanna, standing by the window, had become an antenna that caught everything, the fear, the reflections the swollen silence, the bell, the surprised shot, the muezzin's voice. She wrapped herself tightly and felt somewhat better. But silence was still in her eyes, just as a vague fear.

Suddenly there was a knock on the door. 'Who is it?' she called.

'Triantafyllos, madam. I came to see if you need anything.'

She opened the door for him.

'But it's past two.'

'That's why I came, madam. I thought that with all that's happening outside you might need me. The Turks are burning the shops at the edge of the Greek sector. The English put the Greeks under curfew and let the Turks free.'

'What about the curfew?'

'There's always a way, madam.'

'And if you received a bullet?'

'There's always a risk, madam. It all depends on what you want.'

As if hypnotised she took one or two steps towards him and put her head on his shoulder. 'Thanks for coming.'

He stroked her hair. He led her to a chair and poured two whiskies. 'Drink it,' he said. 'We need it.'

Ioanna drank it almost at a stretch and felt her fear lessen.

'Time for bed,' he said.

'I won't sleep, in case of an emergency.' Ioanna let herself be led by him. She felt a sweet numbness. They entered her bedroom. And while he turned down the bed she threw off her fur coat and dragged him on to the bed.

15

Nobody knew why they called him the Jordanian. It might have been his rich curly hair or his thick fleshy lips or his strongly defined features. However, when they were children and he was wearing some short trousers from which his big legs brimmed over and he had difficulty keeping them under control holding a cane like a spear, it was Jordanian that they called him. And none knew who had first called him that. He put his cane down at the edge of the field and awkwardly ran a lap for warming up.

'Are we going towards the Turks?'

'No. When we decide to go you should have your spears too.'

And he cast a glance at his cane, at the edge of the field. War needs weapons.

'We're going to play football.'

It was a ball of rags tightly rolled. And they used two big stones for goal posts. There was an uproar every time the rag ball passed through the two stones. Sometimes Turkish boys came. And they ran passionately after the ball. But they always ended in a row because, as the Jordanian said, they had spat on Athanasios Diakos.

'We'll spit on him again.'

The Greeks stood on one side swishing their canes and the Turks stood on the other side loaded with stones. Most of the time the teams stared at each other for hours without saying anything. Then they put down the canes and the stones and once more they chased the rag ball and then, exhausted, sat down in a round and talked until it started getting dark and their mothers' voices were heard and the Turkish boys left for the Turkish sector.

When did the Jordanian grow up? This was one of the mysteries too. He overflowed from his clothes, his hair, curly and black, covered half his forehead. He was an apprentice carpenter. He held an axe and a hammer and split wood all day long or made wooden cases for oranges on grapefruit. When November and December arrived he exhausted himself at work. He had a bull's stamina and his boss watched him with awe.

'How's everything Jordanian?'

'You don't have any complaint do you?'

'Me? Who spoke about complaints? The wooden cases leave in time. The Fasouri Jews are pleased.'

'A clever race.' His eyes became slits, but his hand went up and down with the accuracy of a watch mechanism. 'A clever race. And we never learn.' He could pile the wooden cases until they reached the height of the door, even a little higher. Then the Jews asked for more cases, for the grapes, and as the Jordanian said, his July and August were fucked off.

He worked almost half-naked. He was wearing short khaki trousers and a pair of sandals. At about five he went to the Jews' wharf, took off his trousers and dived into the sea. For an hour he enjoyed its saltiness and afternoon coolness. Only when he reached the open sea and looked back his eyes opened widely to see the town that lay lazily in the windless afternoon and felt inside him the landscape wounded by the vertical line of the minaret.

He started filling his nights the way he had filled his days. At the beginning he came down to the square at eight, he sat on a chair, drank his coffee and smoked. He watched the prostitutes – pieces of flesh in cheap dresses who left their halls to get cigarettes or an ice-cold Coca-Cola from the kiosk. The lights of the night clubs were reflected in his eyes. One night he went into the club. He found himself in Tolyras' group. They appreciated his physique and asked him to stand at the entrance of the club, Attic Nights, to prevent dirty tricks by Princessa, the second music hall. They had pointed out Kourouyiannos to him, boss of the other place.

The Jordanian's physique stopped provocation and dirty tricks. He became a power in the square. He left the square around three in the morning. He slept deeply until ten and started work at eleven and worked ceaselessly until five or six in the afternoon. The planks passed mechanically through his hands and were transformed into boxes.

It was six in the afternoon. He had swum for an hour. This time he felt it a stab inside him. He began swimming fast, he struck out forcefully and climbed onto the wharf where he lay for twenty minutes. He put on his trousers, threw on a vest, pushed his feet into his sandals and set out for home. At the edge of the wharf Souliotis fell upon him. He was a short man, a candle merchant.

'You Jordanian. You are a real wild beast,' he said.

'What about you, what about Kokos?'

They had been classmates and sometimes Kokis came to the field and played with them, but as he was delicate he was knocked out in half an hour. On one occasion the teacher had got angry with the whole class. He gave vent to his anger on Souliotis who, when caught, stuttered his words one by one, as if he were pulling out rusty nails from a thick wooden box. And the teacher ordered him to leave the class, but as he was passing in front of the teacher's desk the latter caught him in his huge hands and lifted his thick stick. But the first blow fell on to something soft; faeces fell from his short trousers. The class sat frozen, unable to laugh or cry.

'Souliotis in name but not in stuff,' Jordanian had sometimes told him. But he regretted it the same moment and he placed his huge hands on his shoulders.

'You're still making boxes?' asked Souliotis.

'And you? Are you still busy with candles?'

'Family business,' answered the other. They walked towards the church of St Antonios. 'Jordanian I'll talk openly because I know you. The organisation needs hands, big hands, whatever it can find.' He kept silent for a while as if trying to calculate his words' weight. 'Tomorrow we'll be fighting against the Turks.' A new pause. 'We know your night life. However, it's the Princessa that's the den of the police. Not the Attic Nights. (Jordanian had some suspicions about Kourouyiannos who had often talked to policemen and informers.)

'I come straight to the crux of the matter. Would you become a member of the organisation?'

This wound of the minaret inside him became more painful.

'Souliotis, you're now both name and stuff.'

The other one clasped his hand and left. Thus Jordanian joined the ranks of the organisation.

This morning the message came to him. The fires at the fringe of the Greek quarter had died out, but smoke still rose from the looted shops. A half-burnt roll of linen cloth, a sandal still hanging from the wall had escaped the general destruction. They had taken him out of Limassol in a van that carried greens. He sat uncomfortably amid big baskets and boxes and the van shook him thoroughly every now and then but he only stroked the piece of iron hidden in his pocket. He felt the penetrating cold but his thought was on the police inspector he was to kill soon after. He didn't give a damn for those he was going to kill. They had told him his name – Demetrakis. In his case they were using the diminutive as a reaction to his well-developed physique. His weight was distributed evenly and he had a head with a Roman profile and rich brown hair. With the end of the war he had joined the police and risen spectacularly through the ranks; corporal in three months sergeant in six, lieutenant in a year. He was sent on a scholarship to a college in England. Formally he was known as Mr Odysseos. But the policemen knew him by his first name, Demetrakis. He was the first Cypriot officer who had been directly appointed by the Colonial Office, and his salary as well as the other terms of service were fixed centrally, from London. He could also be transferred to any colony. Or even to England itself. Just before reaching fifty-five he had married a Catholic girl with fiery blonde hair. Now she had given birth to a child in a private clinic and Odysseos visited her every morning before going to headquarters.

At the Athalassa wood another car was waiting for the Jordanian. It was still dark. They had a long wait in front of them. Someone took out a sketch map and spread it on his knees.

Jordanian stared persistently, he gave you the impression that he was thinking of something – but inside him everything was neutral. It was a protective mantle that was thrown over his mind before he carried out an execution. Theseos was a big street, thin movement of pedestrians thick traffic. It brushes past the old cemetery and the police station. Jordanian's mind recorded the details mechanically. He marked a square with his pencil.

'I'll let you out of the car at the back of the clinic. Here's the back door. You'll enter through here. At the front the police Land Rover will be parked. It will be waiting for Demetrakis. Today they'll have to wait. Just at the point I'll let you out I'll be waiting for you. Any questions?'

'When do we leave?'

'In an hour.'

'Okay. I'll relax a bit.' He leaned back and was soon sleeping.

The curfew ended at seven in the morning. A minute before seven the car set out from Athalassa wood.

It travelled along cart paths and after a while left the trees behind it and joined the main road. The driver glanced at his watch. 'Five past seven. We've got ten minutes more.'

'Traffic will delay us,' said Jordanian.

'It moves in the opposite direction. It doesn't obstruct us. At eight the English will impose a curfew again but you'll be on your way to Limassol.'

'Wooden boxes are waiting for me,' said the Jordanian. This absolute indifference was a kind or protective mechanism that his subconscious mind had devised to secure the necessary balance.

Behind Kasos street was Naxos Street. The driver entered Naxos street. He glanced at his watch. It was seven fourteen. He parked the car by the pavement and pointed at the back door of the clinic. There was a big yard, some palm trees, a chicken coop and a small vegetable garden. The Jordanian walked as calmly as if he were entering the Limassol carpenter's shop. He felt the cold iron, but his reaction was as if he were holding a carpenter's axe and a hammer. Without them boxes can't be made.

He pushed open the door and found himself in a dark corridor. He had been shown many photographs of Odysseos. He would be wearing his police uniform. At seven-seventeen he came out of the room where his wife was and followed the corridor that led to the exit. For a second or two he passed in front of the corridor leading to the back door. It was at this point that the Jordanian shot him. As he saw him falling he turned and walked quickly to the back door. He heard the screams begin but he had already reached the door. He opened it ran through the yard and got into the car. The engine was already running. Thc driver accelerated and in ten minutes they were entering Athalassa wood. At eight Jordanian was in the same van sitting comfortably amid big baskets full of green stuff and was on his way to Limassol. At the same time the radio announced the imposition in Nicosia of a curfew until further notice.

16

She stretched her hands slowly, brought them above her head. Her eyes blinked many times until they found the strength they lacked and remained open. She tried to guess the time, but the light did not easily penetrate the thick curtains. Suddenly she remembered, cast a look at her side; Triantafyllos had vanished. He had left while she slept. She stretched lazily, she felt all her limbs warm and relaxed. It was past nine. Now she remembered last night's flames. It must have been past one when they went to bed. She pressed a button. The door opened and Triantafyllos appeared with a cup of coffee.

' I thought it's just the thing.' He put the cup on her bedside table. 'Shall I prepare breakfast?'

'No. We're breakfasting in the dining room. When do the rest of the staff return?'

'They're not coming today either,' said Triantafyllos. 'The English have imposed a new curfew that started at eight. A police officer has been killed.'

'Okay, I'll be ready in half an hour.' She lit a cigarette, sat up in her bed and started sipping her coffee. She dressed and went down to the dining room. Triantafyllos had already laid the table with orange juice, eggs, buttered toast, cheese.

'So we're not having the staff today.'

'They didn't have time to go out of the house,' said Triantafyllos.

Ioanna sat at the table. Triantafyllos stood motionless. 'Sit,'

Ioanna said. She looked at him; there was something harsh in her eyes. It was something left over from her former life. In a corner inside her there was Ioanna Manoleon and the semi-dark hall of the cabaret. After the third whisky most of them wanted to lower their pants in that very hall. And to fuck her on the floor. They didn't give a damn penny about her.

Triantafyllos sat, a bit reluctantly. He felt strange being treated as her equal. He ate without appetite.

'Are you eating,' said Ioanna. 'Our choice is limited. Curfew, you said?'

'Yes, since eight. The previous one had been lifted for only two hours.' She didn't care about numbers – she never did. The calculations either. This was the tactic she had been following since young. Her instinct functioned better than her reason. A kind of flash passed through her eyes.

She drank another cup of coffee and lit a cigarette. Triantafyllos did the same. Food always made him feel relaxed.

'Please fetch me the plans for the house.'

Triantafyllos brought a bundle of papers from the front hall. Terms, specifications, the language of the architects and civil engineers which Ioanna neither understood nor cared about. Triantafyllos understood Ioanna's wish. He took away plates and cups and unfolded the roll in front of Ioanna.

'Agonos number two,' said Ioanna.

A mansion with elements of byzantine and gothic style, some thick straight lines mounted and cut by curves, arches and windows which ended in the shape of a half-open rose, the doors heavy as those of a church. Around it were iron railings. Ioanna did not want a wall round the house. She remembered the English house outside her village in Paphos, with the dogs and the ex-policeman guarding it. Climbing the wall with Dina they were trying to catch a glimpse of the blonde Englishwoman who was ill, but the only thing they saw was Ikkis with the dogs.

Railings as in Petersburg, she had told the architect. She had read somewhere that in Petersburg every mansion had its own railings. None was like another.

'This is what I want,' she said to the architect. 'To be unique in Nicosia. Find a craftsman who treats the iron as something living. He should be able to breathe life into it. The expenses you said? Who cares about the expenses.' Did she know where the money came from? She had a vague idea but the details escaped her – in reality she didn't care. She lay back. The house perched like a legendary bird on the top of the hill, and rose erect at the fringe of Nicosia – something in between a girl's breast and a clenched fist.

She remained staring at it for some time. Triantafyllos didn't dare to move, not even breathe deeply lest he should interrupt her. Suddenly Ioanna shook her head and let her hair fall on her shoulders. She glanced at Triantafyllos: 'Ring up Manos. I want him to invite tenders.'

'Won't you wait for Mr Oriol's return?'

'Mr Oriol will like it immensely.'

Then Ioanna leapt up and walked towards the window. She drew the curtains and looked at the deserted streets. 'We've got a curfew again, you said?'

'Yes. They killed a police officer. They gave no details. It will last at least twenty-four hours.'

She started undressing slowly, her eyes on Triantafyllos 'Here on the floor.' There was something coarse in her voice.

After some time she said: 'You'll submit your resignation. Today. You'll enter this house not as a personnel manager any more, but as an adviser and friend. We'll find some other business.'

'But it's you I want to serve.'

She closed his mouth with her hand, 'You'll serve me, don't worry. From another position. Ring Manos about the tenders.'

The eight workers from Dikomo had started work at seven-thirty. The rural bus had brought them to the half-built house at a quarter to seven. They changed their shoes, they put on old ones splashed with lime and cement, they put on patched trousers. Someone lit a fire and started roasting a smoked herring. The smoke mingled with the smell of the herring and lingered temptingly in the air. Someone else was trying to make coffee over a crude alcohol lamp. At seven-thirty the contractor came and they started work. Someone set in motion the concrete machine and the noise mingled with burnt petrol. At eight the curfew started and work stopped.

'Wages've been fucked today too.'

The contractor cursed Christ and Virgin. 'The soldiers – whether fucked or not – are on the safe side. Their wages are safe. Policemen too. Tomorrow the owner will start shouting because the house is not finished.'

The eight workers gathered in one of the inner rooms. In a petrol tin cut in two they lit a fire, they made coffee, they put some paper cement sacks on the floor and sat down to drink coffee and smoke cigarettes.

'Can't spend the whole day here.'

'I'll see what can be done,' said the contractor. He felt in the back pocket of his trousers, found his pass and jumped into his old car. 'I'm going to the police. To get permission for you to go home.'

After stopping at two or three roadblocks he managed to reach the police station of Paphos Gate. To the north of Paphos Street traffic still flowed. As a rule the curfews didn't reach the Turkish quarter. There was still the smell of burning in the air. The contractor went in and stood in front of a police sergeant who was sitting behind a tall bench. He told him his problem. 'They'll catch pneumonia if they stay there tonight,' he said.

'Take them blankets,' answered the sergeant.

'Where can I find blankets for eight people?'

'What can I do?'

'Get them a pass so they can leave for their village.'

'It doesn't depend on me.' He lifted the receiver and spoke to the town's police-chief. He replaced the receiver.

'At three there will be a half-hour break of the curfew. Before half past three they have to be outside Nicosia.'

The contractor passed by the house and told the workers about the half an hour break. 'When I go home I'll send a message to the bus driver. I'll ring up the Saint Antonios inn. In the meantime make yourselves as comfortable as you can. I'm going home for the call.' The old car disappeared noisily at the bend of the road.

At three the curfew was interrupted for half an hour. The radio had been announcing the break every half hour since one. It interrupted its musical programme to make this laconic announcement. And at three the immobilized vitality of a whole town stretched itself timidly as if yawning, then it neighed like a horse which sniffs freedom and then unleashed itself into a wild gallop – the only difference being that here were houses and streets, and it hit right and left, stopped for a bit, panted, listened and once more found its way to carry on.

At five past three the bus was outside the half-finished house. There were no other passengers. Within three minutes all eight of them were settled comfortably on seats.

'We'll travel like royalty today, Georgi.'

'Curfew has its good aspects too,' he answered.

The bus shook wildly, roared in a strange way and then accelerated into the freed traffic. It must have been twenty past three when they arrived at Ledra Palace and followed the road along the moat that brought them to the Kyrenia Gate.

At exactly three-thirty they passed through the Kyrenia Gate and, in theory, were outside Nicosia. The bus now accelerated, freed from the fetters of the town, and started running between fields that stretched to right and left, with some solitary charob or olive trees breaking the line.

Children, boys and girls bare-footed with patched trousers and torn dresses, Turkish women with thick boots and crudely made dresses, ploughed the fields. And the men sat for hours in the cafes or in front of their small shops staring at the road, suspended between sleeping and waking.

The bus took the last bend before the village and started creeping in front of the Turkish cafes. The road was narrow in the village and the driver was obliged to reduce speed. On the other hand there was fear that with the roaring of the cars the clay brick walls might fall or those mosaic structures that took the place of doors might fall into pieces. Every time they passed through Kioneli the passengers remained silent lest anything might be taken as a provocation. This lasted for a few minutes until the bus left the village and accelerated. The workers breathed more freely, and relaxed.

The shots that came from some reeds took them by surprise. The bus shook for a while and then landed on its four flat tyres.

'Have we been stranded by a flat tyre?' a voice asked.

A new flurry of shots gave them the answer.

'We've fallen into a trap,' shouted the driver.

When the bus doors opened, they leapt out and started running in the direction of the village. They were running without thinking, it was a wild, blind kind of running. And the shots came like lashes of the whip; they tore the air and brushed past the men without touching them . But when they reached half way up the hill and their breathing was laboured, the Turks appeared. They were split into groups. In fives or in sixes. Armed with knives, axes, thick pieces of wood, iron bars. And behind them the shots. They followed them closely without touching them. The group suddenly lost its thrusting movement, it remained for a while suspended half way up the hill, and then lost its cohesion, a nucleus broken to its particles whirling in every direction, to be trapped by their own fear, to be suddenly freed with an ultimate effort. And to find themselves at the edge of an abyss and to have no way to jump over it or retreat, their only choice was to run on a taut rope.

'Giaour pezeveng!' When did they shake the cafes off them?

'Pezeveng Giaour – now you pay'. When did they tear themselves from the narghile?

'One is Allah and Mohammet his prophet.'

And the trapped horse which gallops hits on the walls of its trap, dresses and undresses its fear at the same moment, it hits on wild faces, sweating, it hits on eyes which suddenly fill with hatred and blood, it hits on knives, axes, iron bars, pieces of wood, and the dance of shot sounds like a strange requiem.

'Giaour pezeveng!'

Broken necks, hands that remained suspended, heads thrust into a tiny savory bush, and a bus stranded in the middle of the road. No shots, no screams. Just bodies, no fierce faces. And the hill embracing with its volume the bodies and the darkness infiltrating timidly at the beginning, more daringly later. And behind the hill, at the opposite side of the valley, a whole village remains sleepless. The silent men changed shifts at the edge of the village lighting one cigarette after the other. The women, silent behind closed shutters, put the children to bed.

The same evening the English arrived in trucks. They had not brought even an ambulance.

'The bloody Greeks. Got what they deserved.'

But at the hospital one of the nine bodies was found breathing. And the doctors operated all night and the man was saved.

The following day the English lifted the curfew, with the same ease as a curtain is drawn and a window opens and in comes life and movement. This movement that piled up for twenty-four hours behind closed windows and doors, in semi-darkness and an unnatural silence, that started from the inside of the town itself, was suddenly freed.

Ioanna stretched lazily. She had overslept. A sun ray struggled to squeeze through a crack in the curtain. She glanced at her watch. Quarter to ten. A discreet knock at the door.

'Coffee, madam.'

The staff must have returned, she thought. 'Open,' she almost shouted.

The door opened and in came her personal maid with coffee.

'Come back to work, Maria?'

'We all are at our places.' She put the coffee on the bedside table and drew the curtains. Strong light rushed into the room.

'Okay Maria.'

Maria withdrew as noiselessly as she had entered.

Ioanna lit a cigarette and sipped her coffee. Suddenly she felt hungry.

She stood for a while in front of the mirror, dressed casually and went to the dining room. Maria had the table already laid. She ate with appetite.

Triantafyllos came in discreetly. He went to stand by her side waiting for instructions.

'Sit down Stiv.' She called Maria and asked her to bring another cup of coffee. Triantafyllos sat rather awkwardly.

'I wanted some things discussed . . .'

She cut him short. 'I'm a woman of action, Stiv.' She took her pen from her bag. She took out the cheque book and wrote a cheque in the name of Triantafyllos for six thousand dollars.

'Take this, and whatever else is needed, here we are.'

He took her hands and held them in his.

'No emotional outbreaks, Stiv.'

'There's a petrol station. . . .'

'Details are your problem. Mine are the essential things.'

Maria came to announce Manos. He came in carrying a bundle of newspapers. On their front pages were horrific photographs of the slaughter at the foot of Pentadactylos.

'The advertisement inviting tenders for the house is published in all the papers. In a month we'll have them,' said Manos.

She cast a glance at the ad Manos was pointing at. 'Excellent. In two years we'll have the mansion.'

Manos began to gather the papers. 'Do you need me for anything else?'

'Manos, as from today I want you to take up the duties of the one in charge of the staff. You don't have to be here all day. One or two hours in the mornings. You'll fix the hours of work, their time off, when they're going out and anything else.'

'Whatever you say, madam.' Somewhat timidly he asked: 'And what about Stavros?'

‘He’s on his own,’ was Ioanna’s laconic answer.

Manos took the newspapers and went to meet the staff.

‘I don’t want to keep you any more,’ said Ioanna. She looked him deep in the eyes. ‘Tonight at eleven.’

17

She was holding the telegram in her hands. Saw the words, but could make no sense of them. 'Simon was killed in a hunting accident – Samargan.' Her first reaction was an absolute neutrality, just as the meaning infiltrated it remained trapped in her subconscious mind. 'I feel you rising from inside me like a male Aphrodite.' They had drunk two or three whiskies at the bar and Samargan was somewhat uncontrolled in his movements. He led them to a table at the corner and signalled the waiter to bring their drinks there. And his hands worked under the table. But his eyes were divided between Simon and Ioanna. Somewhere inside him the male ego was struggling to stand on its feet. But after the sixth whisky Samargan went flat like a punctured balloon, his hands lost their movement as if someone had suddenly cut off electricity supply. He stood up and after touching first the one and then the other had said: 'I'm going to bed. You carry on.' They drank another whisky and ordered coffee in Ioanna's room.

She glanced at the telegram once more. She lit a cigarette and her eyes wandered towards Pentadactylos. It was an exercise she often did when she wanted to overcome the initial stage of emotion. No matter how momentarily she could escape from herself she found again and again Simon erect inside her. She wanted to cry but couldn't. She looked at the address of the telegram sender: Madrid, Spain.

She remained seated for hours at the window holding the

telegram. She wanted neither food nor coffee. She smoked from time to time and stared at Pendadactylos. In the afternoon she asked Manos to arrange an air ticket for Madrid. She would leave as soon as possible

Ioanna disappeared from Nicosia for two weeks – she had no contact with either Manos or Triantafyllos. With Ioanna's dollars Triantafyllos bought an old petrol station and was trying to redecorate it, to attract new customers.

Manos came to the flat every day at eight to see the staff.

'And what are we doing today, Mr Manos?' asked Maria.

'Food for four and clean the house. Until Madam Oriol returns.'

Manos went through the rooms, to justify his presence there, and sat in the office, and they brought him coffee. He made several calls to keep himself informed of the events of the day and then left to prepare his reports for some Athenian newspapers. In two weeks he received a telegram: 'I'm coming tomorrow. Countess Ioanna Oriol-Samargan. He looked at the place of origin: Geneva.

Then his eye stopped at the Countess. The name of Samargan rang a bell. He must have heard the word from Ioanna. He couldn't find an explanation and he didn't care. He wrote a brief announcement and sent it to the papers.

'Countess Ioanna Oriol-Samargan arrives by air tomorrow from her trip to Europe.'

Ioanna passed the first night in Madrid at the hotel. It was rather late when she arrived and ordered whisky and dinner in her room. From the seventh floor she could see the whole town. She had visited Madrid twice before and they stayed at the same hotel. Once there had been a meeting of the main shareholders of their mines in Bolivia and in spite of the possible objections of Madam Oriol Mathias insisted that Ioanna should be with him.

The next day, at around ten, she rang Samargan.

'Where are you calling from?'

She told him her hotel.

'Coming right now.'

In half an hour Samargan was at the hotel. He took her in

his arms and kissed her on the cheek. She had the impression that Samargan had suddenly become bigger. They drank coffee together, Ioanna smoked one cigarette after another. Samargan was a non-smoker. All of a sudden he took the packet of cigarettes and her lighter and put them in her bag. 'You'll hurt yourself. It was just an accident Ioanna. One of those that happen once in a million.' He paused suddenly. And then: 'What happened at that second has been recorded by time, it assumed the dimensions of time. It cannot be undone.'

They ordered whisky. Ioanna wanted to hear about Simon, but Samargan avoided the subject. It was as if a curtain of his brain had been drawn.

For two weeks he spent all his time with her. He came at ten in the morning and left at one or two after midnight. He took her round Madrid and the outskirts. He took her to folk fiestas and Ioanna remembered the time she had seen the great Spanish dancer Antonio in London. She remembered the Nicosia cabaret where she worked before her marriage to Mathias: 'And now Miss Orly in a Spanish dance.' Once or twice he took her to the theatre but she knew no Spanish and felt bored. He took her to a bullfight but she was cold and indifferent. They dined at the most fashionable restaurants, they drank whisky at night clubs, and Ioanna enjoyed Spanish music and dance. But in all this there was no room for Simon. Samargan embraced her and kissed her at ten in the morning and then again at two the next morning and the time in between was filled with their talks, the fiestas, the restaurants, the night clubs, the whisky.

And one morning Samargan took her hands and looked her in the eyes: 'Ioanna we must make our relationship official. It would be some kind of substitute for our relationship with Simon, but naturally at an entirely different level.' And before Ioanna understood Samargan added: 'I'll adopt you Ioanna. You'll lawfully carry my title, our relationship and Simon. You'll come to see me from time to time.'

For some seconds Ioanna could neither think nor speak. And afterwards her thoughts bolted like frightened horses in every direction – her village, her father, her mother, her first employer, the cabaret and finally Madam Oriol. Without saying anything she took Samargan's head in her two hands and kissed him – a kiss without a trace of eroticism.

'Thank you Ioanna, it's more for me than for you.'

Next day at a registrar's office in Madrid the formalities for the adoption were completed. Samargan was dressed in black and Ioanna was wearing a plain white dress. In half an hour the whole thing was finished, they had signed some documents and Ioanna was given her adoption certificate: Countess Ioanna Oriol de Samargan. They celebrated with an excursion outside Madrid. They felt the need for open space.

In the evening she booked a seat to leave the next day for Cyprus via Geneva. She was going to see Mathias for some hours. She wrote a cheque for ten thousand dollars and sent it with a note to Samargan: 'In the memory of Simon. Use it as you wish. Ioanna.'

She arrived in Cyprus early in the morning – but the sun was already high in the sky. Hiding behind her huge black glasses she had a feeling of protection, a security that she could lean on. Manos was waiting for her. He had looked up all arrivals from Geneva, directly or via Athens. This was the third time he had gone to the airport. Behind him stood the photographer. With a sign from Manos he took two or three photographs of her alone and then two or three with Manos next to her. Manos kept his own archive.

'Everything okay Manos?'

'As far as it can be, Countess.'

Ioanna looked at him with a triumphant smile in her eyes. She would have liked to say something, but kept it for herself. At around five in the afternoon they arrived home. Manos had piled a lot of newspaper cuttings about the situation in Cyprus on her desk. Ioanna liked to read these cuttings, especially when she returned from abroad. She had a warm bath then lost herself in reading. On such occasions the staff withdrew discreetly. Manos had left some hours before.

The first story started taking shape in front of her eyes.

The newspapers reported the essential details without comment. He was a veteran of the Second World War, he had taken part in the Tobrouk battle and later had been a mule driver in the battle of Casino, in Italy. Ioanna had seen photographs of the monastery, a projection of the rock commanding the plain. When he returned from the war he gathered about ten veterans and exercised pressure so that they might be given government land to set up a collective farm. He had seen the Jews of Palestine setting up their Kibbutz. The white soil began to turn green, carob and olive trees started climbing on the rocks. The collective farm was called The Kasino. The landowners of the area looked askance at the whole project.

This struggle against the land lasted eight years. Then one after the other the veterans left for the town. The government found a chance to dissolve the collective farm. It appointed a civil servant in charge and sent government workers under the direct supervision of the agricultural department to do the work. The continuity broke once and for all. New workers came to replace the old ones. Of the old collective farm workers only Menikos remained at the village with his wife and three children. He worked in the building industry and in his free time he was trying to reclaim some barren land he had inherited from his father. Then he was tied to the trunk of an old plane tree a little outside the village.

From early in the morning some youngsters with a portable loudspeaker went round the village. The leader ordered everybody to shut themselves up in their houses until the following morning: curfew by the English, curfew by the Organisation. But he didn't dare express his thoughts openly. They got hold of him as soon as he came down in the rural bus. The rest they ordered to be shut in their homes.

'Whose order?'

'The leader's.' He pulled up his shirt and showed his pistol.

They took him and tied him to the plane tree. From among the trees and the white rocks at the foot of the mountain young people began to emerge.

They put two with a sten to cover the village. The man in charge took out a piece of paper and read it fast: 'After a trial in front of a revolutionary court and with the leader's consent you are condemned to death through stoning on the charge of acts of treason. Have you got anything to say?' But before he could utter a word there was a volley of stones and his face had become a mass of blood.

'Have you got anything to say?'

The lips opened and closed but the words remained imprisoned in his chest and the stones continued to rain on him. His eyes were filled with blood. The teeth and the jaws broke, one after the other, piece by piece. The squad had a breathing space but then they re-armed and the volleys continued with renewed force.

'Send the message to Kruschev,' shouted someone. 'And don't forget Papis, otherwise he'll grumble.'

The one in charge raised his hand. He took out the piece of paper and looked at it. He went towards the plane tree. 'The doctor,' he shouted.

He was a specialist in ascertaining death, he had been a medical student and in the organisation he was known as the 'doctor'. He bent his ear to the stoned man's chest. The one in charge spat on the ground. The men of the squad sat on the ground, between the plane tree and the village. All of them were silent as if the night weighed heavily on them.

When it became completely dark the man in charge rose. 'Let the village know,' he said.

Two shadows tore themselves from the body of the group, they stood in the middle of the only village road and began to fire shots in the air. In the morning they found Menikos' broken body tied to the plane tree, and lamentation rose up in his house, a sharp contrast to the silence sprayed with fear that reigned elsewhere.

Ioanna looked for an explanation. The first one was given with a dose of naivete in right wing papers. One of Menikos' children had quarrelled with the son of a local right wing boss. The village was known for its nationalistic purity. Menikos hit the other child. The boss reported the incident.

Two or three days passed. Finally the leader found the chance to give a lesson of true nationalism and at the same time increase an already impressive percentage.

The second one was served in doses, timidly, in left-wing papers that circulated from hand to hand. The Americans had a finger in it, indirectly of course. In the climate of anti-Communist hysteria that McCarthyism had created any act in the 'right' direction assumed the dimensions of a symbolism the importance of which few could foresee.

The two weeks in Spain became suddenly a moment in the otherwise unbroken Cypriot continuity. The second one was a love story sprayed with death.

He was, they said, a member of a shock group. Their hiding place was at the edge of the forest. The group consisted of five people. During the day four of them went on marches, one kept guard, sitting on a rock where he could survey the area. During the night the guard was at the same spot the difference now being that his eyes peered in the darkness, searching for light signals, and his ears listened in the thick silence for strange noises. The other four rested or cleaned their guns until their turn came to march or guard. Sometimes they cooked but most of the time they ate what the food supply service sent them. Sometimes they received messages to strike. Then all five of them left their hiding place, belted their bullets and hand grenades, took their guns and set out through the forest for the pre-arranged spot.

Lately Mikos had been wrapped in a strange silence. Sometimes he had gone down to the village for work. He had to meet the man who was their liaison. He shaved, put on a pair of fake glasses, took some writing pads to look like a sales promoter and went down to the village.

There was a path through the forest but when they wanted to go to the village quickly they leapt from rock to rock.

Two men in the village knew about the hiding place, the liaison man and the one responsible for their food. The latter had never visited it. He left the food at the foot of the rock. He pretended he was going to his vineyard to work.

Mikos saw Ariadne passing outside the cafe. For some reason she had not had children and her husband got fed up with the village and became a sailor. Her only contact with him for four, five or even six months was the allowance which the shipping company sent to her at the end of every month. Often at the end of five months he came to the village and stayed for two or three weeks. He ate, he drank, he slept, he made love to her whenever he wanted, day or night. After three weeks he was like a deflated balloon. When he reached this state he got a small suitcase and went on foot to a nearby village where there was a regular bus service. From there he travelled to Limassol, boarded a ship and disappeared for another four or five months.

But these three weeks lit fires in Ariadne's legs. She opened the windows, no matter what the time was, and breathed heavily. Thus, gradually, shadows began to slip to her house. They entered through the windows.

Mikos became a shadow and slipped in the night over her wall into an interior yard. He carefully pulled open an unfastened window and jumped like a deer into Ariadne's room. He never told her who he was but Ariadne sensed something. Many times she caught herself staring at the mountain, there where the forest stopped abruptly and the rocks started with the bushes climbing up like wild goats.

Mikos was appointed by the group as a counter liaison disguised as a bespectacled sales promoter. He pretended to leave the village but returned at ten and slipped into Ariadne's house. There were also nights when he tore himself off the foot of a rock and devised a thousand and one ways of cheating the guard and going to the village.

Ariadne did not fare badly, because Mikos was only one of the shadows, and the fire she had in her legs needed a fire extinguisher. Continuity without interruption. And Mikos, no matter how taut a chord he was, all strength and nerve, did not offer continuity.

Mikos had not seen Ariadne for fifteen days, the group moved continuously by night, they had to carry out reconnoitering somewhere, they had to strike somewhere else – all this left no room. But electricity piled inside him, every particle of his body was charged.

He was serving as the guard that night, with gun in hand, with the bullets on a string hanging from his belt and two hand grenades in his pockets. His comrades were asleep. Nothing broke the forest continuity; the small noises were part of its continuity. He felt the electric charge inside him assume gigantic proportions, he brought his hand to his forehead which burnt. The night chill did not even touch him. He struck a match and looked at his watch. It was eleven. Until five he had six hours. He did not even know when he started climbing down from rock to rock. Darkness had disappeared, it was swallowed by the fire that burnt inside him. With the gun in hand, with the bullets hanging from his belt and the hand grenades in his pockets he descended with the certainty of the wind.

The village slept quietly. He rushed into the only street of the village, he turned at the first narrow path and jumped over Ariadne's wall. He went straight to the window but found it closed. He pulled at it with force. The bolt had been pushed home on the inside and it was a strong one. The lamp emitted a dim light which hardly touched darkness. Ariadne wanted this light. In semi-darkness everything acquired an existence of its own. In darkness everything disappeared. In strong light things acquired harsh dimensions.

He pulled at the window but in vain. He knocked, but heard nothing. There was silence for some seconds.

Then: 'Who is it?'

'Mikos, Ariadne. Open.'

'I can't. I'll tell you later.'

'Ariadne I can't. I've got only five hours.'

'It can't be done Mikos.'

He started knocking at the window again and pulling at it with all his strength.

'Mikos! Have you gone crazy? You'll wake up the whole village.'

But Mikos was now hitting hard at the window. He felt it

give in but simultaneously the lights of the neighbouring houses were switched on and voices were heard: 'It's midnight, you hear. What an itching you've got!'

Something exploded inside Mikos. He felt trapped – on one side was the closed window and Ariadne and on the other the lighted windows and male voices. The crying of a baby was heard too. He climbed the wall and threw himself into the empty space. As he hit the hard flagstones the grenades went off and his body split into three.

The same night they picked him up and buried him before the English knew anything. The guerilla hiding place was dismantled and moved five miles to the west. Ariadne was dressed in black inside her and her eye often wandered where the guerila hiding place had been once.

Ioanna poured some whisky into her glass. Always, love stories left an echo inside her. Not for long. She found a way to leave the echo behind her and go straight for the sound itself.

In Geneva she had seen Mathias for a short time. He appeared to her somewhat numbed – stuffed with tranquillisers, she thought. He had said: 'I'll soon be out. I'll be like before Ioanna.' Mathias was always aware of his state and always in his reactions there was a dose of calm bitterness.

She drew one of the many curtains that her mind had and Mathias disappeared somewhere in a private sanatorium in Switzerland. There was still some time before she would welcome him and in the meantime her plans for her new house would be put into practice. She lifted the receiver and dialled a number. Triantafyllos answered, his voice neutral and colourless.

'Is it you?' Ioanna asked.

'Madam, have you returned?'

'Since you hear me.'

'I didn't know.'

'All right. It doesn't matter. I'll be waiting for you at eleven tonight.'

The next day the newspapers were full of reports about the

arrival of the new Governor. The Colonial Office had decided to have a military man rather than a career diplomat. He was short, stout, with harsh features and penetrating eyes. His whole career had been in the army. It was said he had the experience of guerilla war because the last phase in his long military career was the crushing of the guerilla movement in Malaysia. Recently the British had crushed, one after the other, the guerilla movements of Africa and Asia. But in the end they left these countries – colonies because their victories proved very temporary.

A brief biographical note accompanied the photograph of the new Governor, who held the rank of Marshal.

At around twelve the Governor rang the Archbishop. The other side remained silent for some time. Surprise sprinkled with suspicion.

'Good morning.'

'Archbishop, in spite of the fact that I belong to the military I loathe bloodshed. Reaction towards my profession? Perhaps yes, perhaps no. It may be part of my unseen self that shows itself every time I come face to face with the possibility of bloodshed. Of course, in the end, if need be, professional habit wins the upper hand and the visible part of myself occupies the centre of the stage.'

'Difficult is the way for man, Marshal. For some.'

The Archbishop needed time to assess the intentions of the new Governor.

'For this reason, Archbishop, I propose we meet, brushing aside etiquette. We talk, man to man. Enough blood has been shed on this island.'

The conversation was reported in the papers. The essence of the report was the same in all the papers. The salt they sprinkled it with was different.

The meeting had been fixed for the same night at the Archbishop's palace.

The comings and goings from the governor's house to the Archbishop's palace and vice versa went on for three days. Harding made his proposals in the simple and straight way of a soldier. The Turkish factor had not yet been fully taken into account but it was not absolutely neutralised and there was always the possibility of being exploited. The military wing of the Organisation had been trapped in the dream of absolute clear victory – a handful of fighters had bent a whole empire – and it didn't bother them at all the fact that as in nature so in geopolitics there is no room for a vacuum. Vacuum means interruption and the main characteristic in nature and geopolitics is continuity. One leaves the other comes. As for the Turkish factor they didn't even see it or they pretended they didn't see it. Street vendors and auxiliary policemen, what role could they play?

For the time being a vacuum ought to be created – its filling would be automatic. The meetings were vigilantly watched by the Press. Rumours of what took place flew and for this reason it was decided they should be continued for a few days away from the limelight, with no statements issued. The Anglican Archdeacon's house was chosen. It was somewhere outside the walls of old Nicosia.

A few years before Nicosia had started breaking the chains of the walls that held her tied for centuries at the same place, and the town crept south and north, towards the hills of Troodos and Pentadactylos. To the east and west was a plain scorched for centuries by the merciless Mediterranean sun.

They had almost reached a formula for an agreement; there was always one point to be clarified. The Marshal had to contact London, the telephone imposed unsurmountable obstacles. He interrupted the talks for a while and left in a military plane. When he returned he brought a new formula. 'The last one. I want a simple yes or no.'

'We've got to study it. Many things are at stake for us to say a simple yes or no. However I understand the impatience of Her Majesty's Government.' It was agreed they should meet in three days at the Archbishop's palace. The Colonial Secretary would be present – the government wanted to underline the importance of this meeting as much as possible.

Somewhere inside him the Archbishop felt that the traps had been avoided, one after the other. But he was not absolutely sure. A meeting with the military commander. He didn't like that Leader with a capital L with which the other signed the Organisation's proclamations, but for the time being he had no choice.

He had arrived late on Saturday afternoon at the Kykko monastery. He was alone with his driver. In another car and from a different route his two advisers arrived. He attended the evening Mass from the Archbishop's throne with a bent head. The psalms did not even touch him. His internal world widened so much it left no room for external irritations. His two advisers, wrapped in anonymity, hid among the congregation and from time to time their eyes fell on the Archbishop, who gave the impression that he was deep in prayer.

At around midnight the monastery was surrounded by partisans. The Leader wore his characteristic beret, his guerilla uniform and his military pistol. Accompanied by his bodyguard he crossed the cordon and entered the monastery. They talked with the Archbishop until four in the morning. The Organisation would not accept the agreement. The Archbishop saw that a door was being opened and that with clever manoeuvring the traps would be avoided, one by one. The leader was adamant. He felt that the necessary vacuum would not be created. After all, it was in favour of this change he wanted to fight. He wanted the expansion from the east – the miasma – to stop. And the agreement did not provide the essential guarantees – only some vague promises.

Thus the visit of the Colonial Secretary fell into a vacuum, and a new round of bloodshed would start again.

Ioanna rang Manos. Manos came. She gave him a cheque for twenty thousand dollars. 'For the Archbishop. I'd like to meet him.'

'I'll do what I can, Countess.'

The cheque was handed through the usual channel – Manos saw the Archbishop for a moment. He was sent to the archpriest who gave him a rough receipt and murmured something about the meeting, and that was all. Manos asked persistently for the meeting but was told neither yes nor no. It remained suspended. Ioanna remained suspended too. She felt a strange pleasure when addressed or referred to as the countess. Now she could stand beside Madam Oriol without blushing or remaining silent. The meeting had to take place. Ioanna saw it as a door which should open. She had no idea where this could lead but her instinct never cheated her.

'Mano, have we got any news from the palace?'

'Not yet, Countess. Efforts are being made all the time but the thing stops somewhere.'

However, she received a letter. The Archbishop praised her patriotism. He blessed her and expressed the wish she should carry on her work. Makarios signed it himself in red ink, but there was no word about the meeting.

Every day she studied the Archbishop's programme of activities and whenever he was to appear amid a congregation Ioanna made arrangements that she should be exactly behind him or almost next to him. Most of the journalists were his friends and the newspapers began to publish photographs of the Archbishop with the Countess among the crowd. On these occasions Ioanna was dressed in dark colours, brown or black. She put on her black glassess too. In one or two papers Manos saw that in the caption to the photograph there was: 'Behind the Archbishop is the Countess Oriol de Samargan known for her patriotic feelings.' This was some kind of solution, but the meeting was still necessary. Mano's insistence began to yield results. Her face became increasingly more familiar and, in a way, associated with the liberation struggle.

On a table in a corner of the sitting room she spread the architect's plans. The deadline they had given in the advertisements for the submission of tenders was approaching and the tenders had started coming in. 'Others will be coming,' Manos said. 'Not many. The giants need giants.' And Ioanna understood and felt deep in her that she had become a giant. The house was her own creation. Both as a conception and now as an execution.

Today five tenders arrived. 'We'll have some more in the

coming two days,' Manos said. They were the last before the deadline.

Next to the table with the architectural designs Manos had placed a smaller one and on it an album with cuttings from newspapers that referred to Ioanna. After looking at the architectural designs she liked to go through the album and linger for a fraction of a second on herself, behind her thick, dark glasses. However the meeting she had asked for with the Archbishop had not yet been fixed and she was irritated.

Today's newspapers published a photograph of the Colonial Secretary, Lennox Boyd. Just behind him stood Harding: he gave the impression that he had been unwillingly trapped in a vain attempt to climb a mountain, but had come to a stop a little below Boyd's shoulders. What struck Ioanna were the minister's eyes. His glance held an indefinable cynicism. Under the photograph was Harding's statement: 'Because of the inflexibility of the Greek-Cypriot side the talks led to a deadlock. The last chance was lost. I am obliged to suppress the rebellion using every means. I have given seven days' grace to all those who have turned their arms against Her Majesty's Government to lay them down. I promise an amnesty; what's going to follow afterwards I wouldn't like even to think of.'

The Cyprus radio broadcast the announcement every half hour. For three days it was the first and last thing on the bulletin. The seven days passed with the English soldiers in their camps and the Turkish auxiliary policemen in their areas. And on the seventh day, at around ten in the morning, when Ledra Street and Metaxas Square were busy, the Cyprus right wing showed a special appreciation for dictatorships and Her Majesty's Government showed the necessary understanding. A donkey was set free – by whom, nobody saw, nobody noticed – and walked along Ledras Street towards the square. Instead of a pack saddle it carried two boards: 'My Marshal, I surrender' in both Greek and English. The donkey crossed the square and disappeared in the direction of HajSavvas cafe.

Two military trucks loaded with English soldiers stopped at the edge of a certain area. The English had divided Nicosia and the other towns into areas. Everyone was known by a letter: 'The fucking B area today.'

'Yes serg.' Within minutes B area was surrounded.

'Give'em the bloody exercise.'

And at the edge of the road a Black Maria appeared and from inside came Turkish auxiliary policemen wearing helmets and holding clubs. And the soldiers stood in a semi-circle and the auxiliaries stood gathered together and they stopped the exit by wire fences.

A loudspeaker announced: 'All men above eleven should gather at the centre.' The voice did not sound like that of a Turkish auxiliary but amid the helmets and the clubs it was difficult to distinguish a Greek face. 'You've got ten minutes at your disposal.' And from the half-opened doors men and boys emerged, dressed casually, with an indefinable fear hanging like an invisible curtain, and with defiance in their eyes. They made them stand against the wall with their hands up. There was absolute silence and absolute stillness. The Turkish auxiliaries searched the houses for men above eleven years old.

They stood for hours in the blazing sun, their hands up, their bodies aching with pain. One of the men collapsed and the soldiers dragged him out of the line and threw a bucket of water over him. Around noon they let them go home.

'Until the next time,' the loudspeaker announced.

The deadline for the tenders came and in a special file a number of envelopes were piled. Manos did his job well – at least the formal part of it. There were times when Ioanna stood in front of the table and stared at the plans and at the envelopes. Some underground routes took her back to the small village in Paphos, with the house of the foreign woman occupying important space in her subconscious mind. She had rung Mathias and told him about the tenders. His voice had sounded calm, like an obedient animal.

'My love, the house belongs above all to you. Then to me. Therefore, go on. In no time we'll be together again. My kisses.'

Ioanna was too moved to express what she felt at that moment. 'Thank you,' she whispered. I'll be waiting for you.'

Manos suggested they didn't open the tenders before two or three days passed. 'There's a kind of formality in the delay,' he said.

'I don't understand that quite,' Ioanna said, 'but since you think so.'

Manos proposed that at the opening there should be the architects, the legal adviser and one or two friends present.

'What about a representative of the company?' he asked.

'They wouldn't be interested,' she answered somewhat indifferently. She wouldn't like to give Madam Oriol a chance to offend her with a polite refusal.

The tenders were opened one after the other and Manos felt some kind of awe at the figures he read, but they didn't touch Ioanna. After all it would be others who would decide who would win the tender.

Things became very bad in Cyprus once more. The two or three weeks the negotiations lasted created a fragile climate of calm, sprinkled with a dose of anxiety and uncertainty. The streets at night were once more filled with people, this accumulated immobility was searching for a way out – as long as this thin crust of ice lasted. And after the failure of the negotiations, the same atmosphere prevailed, the difference being that day after day the anxiety and uneasiness with which it was sprinkled increased. And suddenly the thin crust broke. In Famagusta, in Hermes Street, two yards from the centre of the town, they killed a nineteen-year-old English soldier, a national service man. It was March and the days were longer. The orange orchards were in bloom and when a westerly wind blew the town was flooded with an intoxicating scent. No one knew how the English soldier found himself cut off in Hermes Street. However his feet carried him towards Hermes Street and there the bullet found him and killed him. And the westerly wind blew pitilessly carrying with it the smells and the sea saltiness. And it brought the English soldiers into the streets of the town and brought out the

Turkish auxiliaries from the Famagusta Gate under the shadow of the Othello tower. And the air was filled with shots, and the auxiliaries hit out with their clubs and shop windows were broken and men ran as if hunted. And the westerly wind blew pitilessly carrying intoxicating smells, and a bullet found a nine-year-old boy on the threshold of his house. A stray bullet – as if it were a dog. A dead nineteen-year-old English soldier and a dead nine-year-old Cypriot boy.

An English journalist sent a report to his paper the next day: 'Morning found Famagusta licking its wounds.'

The Archbishop felt he had to make another effort. He decided once more to go to the United Nations through Athens. The day before he had been warned by the Kykko monastery abbot that the English were getting ready to arrest him. 'You must postpone your departure.'

'On the contrary. If what you know is correct then I must hasten it.'

The black Cadillac set for the airport at nine. Without escort. Only he and his chauffeur. The plane left at nine-thirty for Athens. He was holding his sceptre and wore his cassock and a simple priest's hat. On his chest was a huge cross. The black car left the last roundabout and started climbing for the airport. He turned his head back. At the foot of the hill Nicosia spread. Two or three wooden kiosks were scattered along the road. Every few metres there was a military postguard, and an English soldier with his finger on the trigger. On some huge eucalyptus trees there was the slogan: 'Eat, Drink and Dance'. People are always the same in peace and in war. Somewhere, hidden behind the eucalyptus trees there must be the inn. And somewhere a military postguard. A forgotten board: 'Europa Hotel.' They should have started building it in 1955 but since then there has been only the board. Will it ever be built? the Archbishop wandered.

The road ended in a fork, one branch led to the civil and the other to the military airport. A military Jeep blocked the road. The Archbishop's chauffeur reduced speed until the car stopped. An English officer jumped from the Jeep, approached the Archbishop's car, greeted him with a light nod and said: 'Follow me.' The Archbishop remembered the Kykko monastery abbot. The English officer drove towards the military airport. Behind him was the black cadillac. A military transport plane was at the edge of the runway with its engines running. The English officer jumped from the Jeep. He opened the rear door of the black cadillac and pointing to the transport plane, he said: 'For your protection.'

The tenders were all opened. And after a five minute discussion it was decided to give the assignment to HAPO Construction Contractors for the round figure of £100,000. Manos and the legal adviser would see to the details. Her personal servant opened the door and brought champagne and glasses. The telephone rang. Manos picked up the receiver. His look changed.

'The Archbishop has been arrested along with the Bishop of Kyrenia, Polykarpos from Kyrenia and Father Stavros of the Phaneromeni Church,' he informed the others.

They hastily drank the champagne and one after the other left. Ioanna stayed there staring sometimes at the plans and sometimes at the opened tenders.

18

Mathias Oriol left the Geneva clinic and, without informing anybody boarded a plane for Nicosia. When Ioanna's maid opened the door she remained speechless for some moments and then ran to tell her mistress.

The Countess came down the way she was, with uncombed hair, with no make up on her face. She found him in the sitting room standing at the window staring at Pentadactylos.

'Mathias!' She threw herself in his arms.

He held her in his arms, he kissed her but he appeared rather cold. Ioanna knew this state. Each time Mathias recovered he was withdrawn. This could last up to a month.

'Not even a telegram,' Ioanna said plaintively.

'You know how I loathe messages. And then it was something absolutely normal. I went in and came out. Here I am.'

'We could have organised your welcome. We could have informed some journalists.'

'What for?' he stroked her hand. 'And you know that my anonymity is part of the whole process of detoxification. It's the one aspect of it.'

'All right. Shall we have a drink?'

'Not me. Forgive me.' She rang the bell and the maid appeared.

'An orange juice for Mr Oriol. Do you mind Mathias if I have a drink?'

'Not at all.'

She poured a strong whisky in a glass and sipped a little.

She felt its burning travel down – a burning that lasted for some moments and after that she felt something like serenity spread inside her.

Ioanna lifted her glass. 'To your detoxification Mathias.'

'I've got the feeling that I'm coming from somewhere far, very far. It's so pleasant to find you again.'

She put her glass on the table, took the orange juice from his hand, threw her arms round him and dragged him to the bedroom. Mathias did not react at all. The perfect resignation, this thought passed like lightning through his brain.

Ioanna closed the door and locked it. Mathias stood in the middle of the room with the thick carpets, the heavy curtains, the dim light on the table. Ioanna began to undress him slowly, with a skill almost professional. She kissed him, stroked him, threw off her own clothes. There on the floor Ioanna made love to him.

'I feel a sweet tiredness,' said Mathias.

'Rest, you've come back home.' And they remained silent.

In a short while Mathias fell asleep and his chest went up and down rhythmically.

'The well known businessman Mathias Oriol has returned from his business trip to Europe,' Manos published in all the papers. Mathias read it. His business trip. His mind almost stopped. But who cares, he thought and bypassed it.

'We've got to visit Agonos,' said Mathias. He had rung the offices of the company in Nicosia and asked them to send a car with a chauffeur. 'I've not sent a message even to my parents.'

Ioanna did not answer. She led him to the table with the architectural designs. 'Agonos number two. It's our home.'

His glance lingered on the plans. Something began stirring inside him. 'I don't much understand plans but it seems to me beautiful.'

'You know Mathias I've got' – she hesitated – 'an aristocratic title. Countess de Samargan. If you want one too . . .'

'I'm a true American. Just Mathias Oriol.' The tone of his voice left no room for doubt. 'At the clinics I go in and out. Those who have titles leave them at the desk. From there on they acquire new ones.'

Ioanna felt annoyed but she thought that for the time being any discussion would be a wasted effort.

The maid came in and announced that a car was waiting outside.

'Okay,' said Mathias. 'In five minutes we'll be down.' He looked at Ioanna with an apologetic tone in his eyes.

'We have to, Ioanna.'

'I know,' she said, turning towards the door. Outside the car was waiting. The driver opened the door for them and they sat in the back. In a short while the car was crossing the centre of Nicosia.

'I see the traffic is still thick.'

'Every time there's no curfew it is on the roads with renewed strength.'

The car was now west of Nicosia. It climbed a hill, passed by the airport and continued towards the plain of Morphou.

'The Torture. Every kind of delicacies,' said the tavern sign. Ioanna noticed the 'torture'. And the irony hit her brain. For the owner or the customers? Memories danced in front of her. They had come here on a night after midnight. They were five girls with five men. The Boss did not object if sometimes they left at half past midnight if there was no work. The Torture tavern waited for them and they laid a table outside under the August stars. A fresh breeze started blowing from the direction of Troodos mountain, and they drank ice cold wine, and ate the delicacies until three in the morning. They got into their cars and drove back to Nicosia, and each girl went to her flat, with her boyfriend.

Now the car was accelerating through the plain cut on one side by the Pentadactylos range and on the other by Troodos. The road ran through a grove of cypress trees. Two big Greek villages followed the small Turkish ones. And after that Agonos, with its few houses scattered by the sea, a sea that had lost its bluish colour and had acquired a strange rosy colour because of the detritus from the mine. And then the workers' houses began, low-roofed, built of cement. It was a struggle to keep them cool in summer.

Mathias had a feeling that an iron line split the workers' houses. The atmosphere appeared charged. 'Something, I think, has changed,' he said to the driver.

'The Greeks are gathered in the south and east, sir. The Turks to the west. It's the situation, you see, sir.'

'And what about us, what do we have to do with the situation?'

The driver didn't know if he could include himself into the we. 'The company doesn't. Men do.'

'Has the company approved of the split?'

'It has accepted it, sir.'

In the distance, where the sea was blue again, the horizon and the bare landscape were suddenly interrupted by the Seagull. The poles, driven into the ground, were still there, three or four, and the multicoloured lights like beads of a rosary hung from the wire.

'The Seagull still exists,' Mathias said to Ioanna.

'For the time being,' the driver interrupted. 'With the curfews it will be difficult for it to survive.'

They entered the drive and the chauffeur parked the car outside the main entrance of Agonos. Mathias got out slowly. Ioanna hesitated for some seconds, something held her rooted at her seat until the chauffeur opened the door for her, and she too got out. Mathias climbed the steps and crossed the entrance. There stood his mother alone, with her lip trembling and in her eyes misting. She embraced him and held him tightly.

'I've returned mother.'

'You look wonderful Mathias.'

'As much as I can, mother.'

Madam Oriol gave her hand to Ioanna. Ioanna took it and for the first time she felt a kind of vague sympathy for her.

'What about father?' Mathias asked.

'His morning meetings,' Madam Oriol said. 'With the current situation these meetings have become daily. We'll have lunch together.'

At noon, the four of them sat in the big dining room. Madam Oriol wanted to give some kind of formality to this lunch – to celebrate the return of her son. Once Mathias had uttered the phrase 'the return of the prodigal son' and noticed how much his mother had been annoyed. It was as if the existence of the prodigal son laid responsibilities on others' shoulders and he wasn't sure if his mother, deep inside, didn't have some feelings of guilt. Father didn't seem to care, at least he didn't show it.

'Father, I can see you're fine,' said Mathias.

'I'd have felt better if we could work as well and as much as we wanted. There's a rise in the price of copper. We must produce more, but at the slightest excuse sometimes half the Greeks and sometimes half the Turks stay at home. The bloody bastards.'

'Now is not the time for all this, Oriol.' Madam Oriol said. 'Mathias has returned, this is what matters.'

'Forgive me my son. I'm carrying the company to the table. You must join it now once more.'

'It'll take some time, father.'

Madam Oriol ate slowly and without appetite. She kept her eyes on Mathias. The maid brought a bottle of champagne.

'Will you drink a glass, Mathias?' his father asked. And without waiting for an answer he filled all the glasses. He raised his own. 'To your return Mathias. Agonos is a big part of our life and vice-versa.'

Mathias was not sure if he should drink. He took a sip and felt the champagne penetrating inside him.

They passed the rest of the day going round the offices. Mathias talked to employees and then explained to Ioanna. It was the first time he had taken her to the mine and Ioanna had the feeling she had climbed a step higher on the platform, that now her financial activities went hand in hand with the title of Countess.

At around eight they returned to the mansion and Mathias and Ioanna went straight to his old room. Madam Oriol had proposed the guest room but Mathias said: 'We'll sleep in my room, mother. A return should be as far as possible a return.' His mother insisted no more.

Mathias ordered a whisky for Ioanna. 'What about you sir?'

'Nothing for the time being.'

The whisky with a jug of ice cubes was sent up and Ioanna sat in an armchair and sipped it slowly. Mathias stood motionless at the open window and stared towards the sea. In the distance, to the left, was the Seagull. When he closed the window and turned round he found Ioanna naked in her armchair.

They had been lying for some time in Mathias' bed. It hasn't been too bad, thought Mathias. The return doesn't present so many problems after all.

'I'm hungry,' said Ioanna. Mathias dialled an internal number and ordered food to be brought to their room. 'And a bottle of champagne.'

It was past midnight but Mathias was not in the mood for sleeping. It was his second night outside the clinic and his brain could not relax. Memories were caught in a dance in his brain – a dance without rhythm. One leapt up and before settling at some sublayer of his brain, a second one sprang up and then a third and one mingled with another and he found himself entirely sunk in this whirlpool of memories. He couldn't get hold of them, but they got hold of him, they didn't give him a breathing space. He rose and peered into the semi-darkness, he tried to lean them somewhere, it was impossible for him to calm down. Then the blank spot from where there sprang temporarily a neutral serenity suddenly became full of memories again. The dance continued with the same intensity with short brief interruptions. He stood up, exhausted. He dressed as noiselessly as he could, he found the half-filled glass of champagne and he drank it at a stretch. He opened the door and went out. Ioanna did not even stir. He followed the corridors as if he had been programmed and went out by the central gate.

He felt the sea-breeze caressing his face and the dance of memories was cut short. Without realizing it he found himself near the metallic giant that was used for transporting ore to the small bay. Some lights, scattered here and there, marked the outline of the steel structure. Down at the bay a cargo ship was anchored. Night and sea were one and the dim lights of the vessel were the only human presence. He remembered the clinic in Switzerland. When he opened the window of his room he was calmed by the serenity that rose from the lake waters. At night all merged into darkness and he felt a strange uneasiness. He found himself in a vacuum that frightened him. There were times that this fear grew terrible and the night nurse used to give him a double dose of tranquilliser.

There, at the entrance of the mine, was some movement. The miners had gone down the pits some time ago. He tore himself away from the gigantic conveyor and found himself among the two wings of the miners' settlement.

Somewhere three or four men lay in wait. Sleepless. In the darkness. Maybe they felt cold. They didn't dare light a fire. Every now and then a shadow tore itself from the rest and noiselessly went round their own wing. On one side were the Greeks, on the other the Turks. They mingled again at the shifts. Their faces wore cold masks. Down in the pit when they struggled face to face against the rock the sweat loosened the straps of their masks and the invisible hands that held them opened. Neither Turks nor Greeks. Simply men in trenches who fought for the glory of Agonos.

Kalo Chorio was one of the area villages. Relatively small, about four hundred people all together. Three hundred Greeks, one hundred Turks. Troodos cast its shadow on one side and on the other the sea winds drenched it with their saltiness. They withdrew into their low houses early in winter time, they lit their fires or went to bed early. For this reason their productivity was increased. But as the children grew they left the village. They did not want to be digested by Agonos.

'Has Demitris left?'

'He has.'

'And Sunai?'

'He went to Hora too.'

'All of them go to Hora. We'll be by ourselves in the end.'

The teacher, Tounjai, didn't know Turkish. He taught

Greek at the elementary school. He himself had attended a Greek elementary school – a slim boy with a dark complexion and curly hair. To listen to the Greek teacher talk about the Greek revolution and wander among the heroes of twenty-one. He leapt from picture to picture and was lost in the corridors of history, and he felt neither Turk nor Greek. Just a boy who liked wandering.

When, sometimes, he stopped at the tiny chocolate brown face of Tasia he had the impression that this wandering would end somewhere. They had gone to the orchard and hunted butterflies and they ran over the furrows and the wild aromatic plants smelled and the butterflies flew from flower to flower and sometimes they held each other's hand and sometimes they split and stepped onto the muddy furrows. And suddenly she stopped and lowered her pants to urinate and he saw the incision between her legs, and he lowered his short pants too and his 'toy' became a piece of wood and she was pulling at it and he was caressing her incision. But then people came between them. He remained Tounjai, and she was Tasia, and they buried themselves the one into the eyes of the other and they realized how strong and inviolate was the human wall. Once Tasia had dared to speak about it. But her father, six foot tall, who dug the earth with formidable power as if he were sipping from it strength, without even raising the tone of his voice, as neutral as the towered walls said: 'Our family doesn't stomach the circumcised ones.'

And Tasia did not ever speak again. They both stayed as they were: Tasia a pillar of her house, now that her parents were old, to stand sometimes upright in the middle of the room and disappear in muddy furrows and be pulling at a boy's 'toy'. And Tounjay to become a student at the teachers' college in Morphou. The language of instruction was English. The students were neither Greek nor Turks, and afterwards each one was appointed to a school, Greek or Turkish, according to the language he spoke. And Tounjai, who knew Greek better than Turkish, was appointed to a Greek school. And towards dusk he wandered amid the streets of the village and sometimes disappeared in the open or half-closed windows of Tasia's house. And she saw him, standing erect in the semi-dark room. And they were expecting something, darkness to dissolve away and the doors and windows to be wide open.

And the liberation struggle began. And the walls became even higher, their foundations filling with human bodies.

The Greek bullies stopped him one evening. 'Teacher, you've got to go. No room in our schools for Turks.'

'Where shall I go?'

'Wherever you want. Plenty of Turkish schools.'

'But I write and read Greek.'

'Your business, your headache.'

And on another evening he was stopped by two tough Turkish men.

'Teacher, you can't stay.'

'Why?'

'There's no why.'

Turks on one side and Greeks on the other. But Tounjai stayed. He didn't know any Turkish to teach in a Turkish elementary school. And one night a bullet hit him in the middle of his forehead. It was never known which organisation had killed him, the Greek EOKA or the Turkish TMT. And Tasia was left coming and going like a shadow. Sometimes she stood in the middle of the room absentminded. She had the vague impression that Tounjai would emerge from a street corner.

And the Greeks were separated from the Turks. And on both sides they were on guard. With shovels, axes, pieces of wood. Their arms must have been hidden somewhere. They joined forces again down in the depths of the earth, amid the sweat and the dust. Down there, it was neither Turk nor Greek.

Mathias stood, a shadow between the two wings of the settlement. Human presence lurked in the night and silence, a match was struck, a cigarette glowed. And pairs of human eyes peering into the darkness loaded with the stalemate of expectation. He tore himself away and returned to Agonos.

He went in as noiselessly as he had come out. The doorman never saw him. He ascended the stairs and slipped into his room. Ioanna was still asleep. He took off his clothes in the darkness and buried himself in bed, next to Ioanna. For some minutes he felt his brain being emptied. Champagne still circulated in his body. He felt it flowing along some forgotten paths and he fell asleep. It must have been nine or ten when he woke up, but he did not realize it for the heavy curtains were drawn, the bedroom lay lazily in darkness. The door opened and Ioanna entered as noiselessly as she could.

'Are you awake?' she asked.

'Almost,' he answered.

Ioanna went to the window. She drew the curtains and a strong light rushed into the room: 'Shall we go for coffee? I've already had my first one.'

'Let's go,' said Mathias and he got out of bed.

The messenger found him in the dining room drinking his coffee with Ioanna.

'Your father wants you,' he said. 'He's at his office.'

'Okay. I'm coming.' He ordered another coffee and lit his second cigarette. 'There must be small problems,' he told Ioanna. 'Of course, I'm not in a position. I'll see you in an hour.'

'All right, Mathias. I'm going for a stroll.'

Ioanna entered the yard entrance to the mine. She was shaken by the noise, changed her mind, and headed for the railway. Two or three ships were immobilised at anchor in the bay. It's a question of time when loading will start, she thought. She saw the houses of the settlement stretching lazily in the sun under the sleepless eye of the metal giant. She walked towards the bay. She sensed the presence of the sea near her. The way she saw it from a distance she remembered her village in Paphos. She started walking towards the bay.

Mathias entered his father's office. His private secretary, a middle-aged American woman, said: 'He's expecting you, Mr Oriol.'

'Thank you.' For a moment he was surprised at the

mechanical way he pronounced it. He opened the door and went in. His father was sitting at his desk with a huge map of Europe and America in the background. Tiny flags marked fields of activity.

'Have a seat Mathias,' his father said. 'Welcome back to Agonos.'

'Thank you father. It has been some time.' He sat in an armchair. He wanted to sink into it but he checked himself.

'Mathias, you've got to start being interested in the company again. I'm getting old and from time to time I want to relax a bit. To lie lazily in the sun. I want to go home more often. I don't want Cyprus to finish me off.'

Mathias said nothing.

'Prices are becoming stabilized. War is becoming a memory. It's a question of time when they'll start climbing down. Our flags,' he threw a glance at the map behind him, 'will start covering a smaller area. In Bolivia they are talking about nationalisation. For the time being we're avoiding this. But for how long? Ten, twenty, thirty years. We'll find something. We've always found something so far. But state intervention is not a substitute for good administration.'

Mathias remained silent. He was staring beyond his father at the map and flags.

'Are you not going to say anything?'

But Mathias remained silent. Then he said: 'Father, you know my problem. Is it my responsibility?'

His father lowered his eyes but said nothing.

'Yet, I can't leave you alone. Neither can I leave mother.' He paused: 'I'll be coming to work here three days a week.'

The old man's eyes were flooded with light.

'I'm starting tomorrow,' said Mathias and rose.

'We must lay our plans for withdrawing from Cyprus. The ore is being exhausted.'

'Okay. Father, from tomorrow.' He started towards the door.

'Mother will be very glad, Mathias. I already feel the joy.'

He went out, and walked towards the sea. Near the port he found Ioanna.

'When are we leaving Mathias?'

'You're going on your own, Ioanna. I've got to work for three days at Agonos. The rest I'll be with you. At Nicosia.'

Ioanna said nothing. She took his hand and they started walking towards Agonos. In reality this role of a part time wife did not make her feel strange. It was already familiar.

Early in the morning Mathias gave orders for a car to be ready to take Ioanna to Nicosia.

In two days I'm coming too.'

'Anything you wish Mathias.'

At her flat the staff had gone on leave. Every time she was away Manos had instructions to let the staff go on leave. She walked to the sitting room and drew the heavy curtains. The light coming down the slopes of Pentadactylos flooded the big room. On the desk were the house plans. Soon construction work would start. She poured a little whisky and sat down with a cigarette. Then the doorbell rang. A young man stood there.

'The Countess?' Without waiting for her answer he handed her a note, turned abruptly and disappeared, almost running. Ioanna closed the door and unfolded the note.

'Countess, somewhere, at a remote place, we need a house. It will be something like an interim station. The Leader.'

She lifted the receiver, dialled Manos' number and asked him to come over.

Manos, sitting opposite her, seemed lost in thought.

'Are you sure, you don't want a little whisky?'

'No, thank you.'

She thought he didn't show any surprise when she told him about the note. He suddenly stood up.

'I'll send a message to the staff. In one or two hours they'll be here. I need some time for the house.'

In the afternoon he came back. Ioanna was still asleep, he said not to wake her. He sat at the desk. In an envelope he had various photographs, he took out one after the other and looked at them. At about five Ioanna came down.

'I found something,' he said. 'If you like it we can reach an agreement. Tonight if you wish. Whatever, you decide.'

She looked at the photographs. A house right at the top of Troodos. To the right, something like fifty metres away, the village houses piled one on top of the other. The pine trees reached to the edge of the road.

'How much?' Ioanna asked.

'Five thousand,' said Manos.

'It's a deal. Fix it tonight.'

'We'll meet the agent at nine at the Palm Club. I hope we don't have a sudden curfew.'

At nine the same night Ioanna de Samargan acquired a house at Troodos and the organisation had its interim station.

At around midnight Manos took Ioanna home. She was half drunk. Manos used his own key to open the door. He gave her the key of the house they had just bought. 'I'll see that more keys are made. I'll send them, don't bother about it.'

Ioanna went inside.

'Goodnight Countess.'

'Goodnight Manos. Fix it the way you know.' She went to the telephone. She lifted the receiver and dialled Triantafyllos' number.

19

The halcyon days of January had passed. The winter sun that had been warming people for fifteen days hid behind black clouds. It became almost dark at four in the afternoon. And the wind whipped incessantly through Troodos' pine trees. The village streets became deserted from five in the afternoon. Men squeezed round fireplaces, they drank zivania, they chewed grilled sausages, they listened to the eight o'clock news and they went to bed.

The car proceeded slowly along the deserted village streets. Somewhere, high at the top, English soldiers sleeplessly guarded the installations. There was no sound in the woods. Outside the village the car lights were switched off, the car turned and proceeded along the country paths that led to the house that had been bought by Ioanna. The door opened from inside. The driver jumped out. The back door opened and the man who was sitting at the back jumped out too. A seventy-year-old man wrapped in an old overcoat got out with difficulty and stood on his feet.

'It's bloody cold.'

They went in. In the dim light they could just see the scanty furniture. Time had settled on it like dust. The guard led them to a small room at the back of the house. A forty watt lamp spread a dim light that was strengthened by the flames that leapt from an iron fireplace set in the middle of the room. Time here was also solidified dust.

'Sit down mister,' said the man who had just arrived. 'We'll spend some time here for the time being.' The Englishman drew a chair near the fireplace and sat. The door of the small room opened and the guard came in. He was carrying a big wooden tray with bread, olives, halloumi and plenty of hot tea.

'Didn't know when or if you were coming. The message just said, wait for them. I've been waiting for two days.'

'What you brought is quite okay,' said the other one. 'Here, mister, you look a little thoughtful to me. Food, manjaro. Our boys in the condemned cells must be thoughtful.'

The Englishman, with an effort, stood up and went to the table and filled a cup with tea and drank it. 'A little whisky, if only we had it . . .'

'Mister, we don't have English luxuries on the mountains. Only English machinery and English soldiers.'

After the first cup the Englishman felt better. He filled his cup once again and took a slice of bread, a little halloumi and two or three olives.

'The bloody olives affect my stomach.'

'Cyprus caviare. Caviare ala Chypre, understand?'

'No I don't understand.'

The Englishman was one of those who had settled in Cyprus. He had come as a soldier during the Second World War. He wandered amid the mountains and the valleys, he sat for hours on the banks of the salt lake, either at Larnaca or the Acrotiri outside Limassol. He studied the birds. That January, he remembered, flocks of black swans arrived in Cyprus. Sometimes he settled at the foot of Pentadactylos and lost himself amid the twittering of the birds and the wild vegetation. With the end of the war he found a job with the Colonial Office. He asked, and was sent to Cyprus. At sixty he was forced to retire. He went back to England but was not happy. He sold whatever he had and came back to Cyprus. He bought a clay-brick house in a village outside Nicosia, and an Austin Mini, and lived on his pension, and studied the birds and the insects. He took notes and photographs.

The fire was almost out.

'Time for sleep.'

He now noticed the two rough beds.

'Cover yourself, because in the morning they'll find you stiff. I'll be in trouble too.'

The guerilla took off his boots and buried himself as comfortably as he could under the bed covers.

'Come on, before the light goes out.'

He took off his shoes and lay on the bed. The other stretched his hand to a switch and turned off the light. The fire embers still glowed. In a short while both were sleeping. Someone would be sleepless in the big hall.

At around eight in the morning the guard came in with an armful of wood. New face. The guard had changed during the night. Without saying anything he opened the iron stove, threw in some pieces of wood and lit a fire.

The escort peered from under the covers: 'What time is it, friend?'

'Eight,' said the other.

'Here, mister, are you alive?' he shouted to the Englishman.

From under the bedcovers there came a growl. 'Bloody shit. What you mean alive?'

The guard went away. In a while he came in again carrying a tray with plenty of tea, three or four thick slices of village bread and a little halloumi.

The fire heated the room. The guerilla leapt up, kicking away the bed covers. He put on his boots. He stretched lazily and yawned. He said: 'We've got a big day in front of us.' He walked to the window. He opened it and the cold wind rushed in.

'You'll freeze us,' said the Englishman.

'Sorry mister. Morning exercise.' He inhaled the air deeply, he did some exercises and closed the window. The Englishman started getting up. He drank two cups of tea. He took a slice of bread and a little halloumi.

'Cyprus cheese?' said his guard. He also took a slice of bread and a piece of halloumi. He poured himself some tea.

When the Englishman had finished eating he stood up and walked about the room. 'When are we going?' The guerilla looked at him. 'I've got to see somebody who can give us an answer.'

'Answer to what?'

'Why I'm here. I feel choked in rooms.'

'With your fire? Your tea? Your bread and halloumi?'

'You don't understand. It's the bloody air. The bloody atmosphere.'

'The prison cells are two by three. Half of our room. No heater. No cheese.'

'What have I to do with these cells? Bloody bastards on both sides.'

'But we have. We never asked for it. Understand, mister?'

'I understand only birds and insects. And I hate rooms. And low skies. And fogs. When are we going?'

'Sometime.'

'It's always the same bloody answer.' They sit on the temporary beds. Sometimes they change places and sit on some crudely made chairs. They stand up and make one or two steps or they in turn stop for a while near the window. Their eyes are filled with the cold and the loneliness of the pine tree.

'If we only had something to read,' the Englishman said.

'Are we going to turn it into a school? At least you can see the forest.'

'Through glass!'

'A few miles from here it's Platres E, mister. The nightingales won't let you sleep at Platres. When they put you in a truck you see nothing. You only feel the shaking as it takes the bends. And your fear is shaking along with you.'

'An army is always an army,' said the Englishman.

'When they throw you off the truck you've got three minutes to look at pine trees. And then it's the cement and the iron gear. And the red faces. Glowing from whisky and passion. Have you ever seen torturers?'

'Bloody machines.'

'Calculating machines. When they get you out of the iron gear you have eyes for nothing. A sack of flesh and bones.'

'Idiots. The Victorian age in the heart of the twentieth century.'

Silence spread heavy like the frozen silence of the forest. Even the wind had died down. When darkness fell they brought an English soldier. He was hardly twenty years old. Someone was pushing him from behind.

'Plenty of company. The first round is on me.'

'Have a seat,' said the one who was pushing him. 'And shut up.' Turning to the first guerilla, he said: 'Friend, I've brought him. We had some difficulty but in the end we managed it. I'm having some rest. If you need anything just let me know.'

'Okay. Now we have two chickens.'

'One chicken,' said the old Englishman. 'I'm a broody-hen.'

'I'm bloody thirsty and hungry,' said the young Englishman.

'Yes, mister. My young one's in a hurry. In prison, you know, you're hungry outside hours. Shit!'

The English soldier threw himself on a chair. The guerilla fanned the sleepy fire, opened the door and peering outside he whistled a signal. The English soldier was holding his head in his hands and was trying to think of a way out. But his young brain stumbled somewhere, in some narrow streets of London, some dirty but warm pubs. He didn't understand those mountains and pine trees, or the roads of Limassol or Nicosia.

'It was bloody Ireland. Now it's bloody Cyprus.'

'Tea is here, a little bread and halloumi.'

'Camomile tea. Cyprus cheese and Cyprus bread. Here, mister, tea for you too?'

The other one looked at him. 'I've no choice.'

And the young Englishman started eating slowly, without appetite.

The door opened and the other guard threw them a sleeping bag. He looked at the young one. 'Sorry friend. This is all we have.'

The soldier got into the sleeping bag and settled on the bare ground as best as he could.

It was dark when they woke them up, it must have been around five in the morning but dawn hadn't broken yet.

Everything was still. The guerilla with the moustache told the two Englishmen to get ready, quick. He dressed himself in a hurry and went out.

'What's going on?' the English soldier asked. 'Are we going to pay for Harding's stupidities?'

'The bastards at the Colonial Office. They refuse to enter the twentieth century,' the old man answered.

'I don't understand.'

'They don't want you to, why should you? The less you understand the better you serve.'

'Not even a cup of tea.'

Two guerillas came into the room, the one they knew and another one. Their military coats were buttoned to the throat.

'We're moving. Going misters.' In the eyes of the two guerillas a wild determination had been immobilised. They took their pistols out of the back pockets of their trousers and ostentatiously put them in the inside pockets of their coats.

In case, the one said to the other.

'I want to be treated like a prisoner of war,' said the young soldier.

They did not look at him. The old man kept silent.

The partisans opened the door and signalled the two Englishmen to move out.

'Where?' the old man asked. His question remained suspended.

They opened a back door and went into the forest. The wind was cold, biting, penetrating. They walked in silence. They could just see the narrow path that crept like a snake in between the pine trees.

The dark face of the night became a little paler. At a certain point they were blindfolded. No matter how much the old man tried to protest, how it was possible to shut someone's eyes in the forest – eyeless in so much magic – he failed to move his guards.

'Top secret,' said the young one with a hint of sarcasm in his voice. They crashed into bushes. Sometimes a thorn hooked their bare flesh. When they took off the blindfolds they found themselves in a hideout, six by four. From somewhere light entered.

'Sorry friends. Here we stop.'

'I'm a prisoner of war.'

'What's he saying?' asked the second guerilla.

'War prisoner,' said the old man.

'Write a card to Harding. He does not understand prisoners of war. We are sometimes soldiers, sometimes guerillas, according to what suits him.'

'And what happens to us?' the old man asked.

'Send a card to Harding. He has the luxury of taking decisions. We simply react. Understand, mister?' His eyes were cold.

They sat down on blankets while the two guerillas went out. They heard whistling.

'The wireless of the forest,' said the old man.

'I don't understand.'

'So much the better.'

In the corner there was a radio. The old man switched it on. They heard: 'Two Englishmen, a civilian and a young sodier, have been kidnapped by the terrorists. It is assumed they will be used as a bargaining tool.' He switched off the radio.

'I'm a prisoner of war,' the young one said again.

'No prisoners of war in the heart of the mountains, my friends,' said one of the guerillas as he entered.

The old man had heard something about guerilla camps and hideouts in the cafes he went to for a coffee.

They remained silent. The guard had his eyes half-closed.

'You got a girl?' the English soldier said suddenly.

'We've got it only for pissing. What about you?'

'In Cyprus no. In England, yes.'

The old man pressed the radio button again. 'The Queen has rejected the appeal for mercy. The Minister of the Interior, in a message to the Governor, said: 'Her Majesty sees no reason why she should interfere with the course of justice.' The radio broadcast a Greek song. Then: 'The exetion has been fixed for the morning of the day after tomorrow.'

The old man remained silent.

The young man said: 'They're going to execute them in two day's time!'

'Girls plenty in England, eh?' said the guerilla.

'In England. What happens here?'

Heavy silence reigned. The second guard came in.

'Your turn.'

The other one examined his gun. He went out without saying a word.

'What about us?' said the old man.

'I'm waiting the way you do,' said the guerilla. 'From one point of view we're in the same position. Waiting.'

'What about beyond waiting?' said the old man. 'We shall receive, you will give.'

'We've been given these roles by others,' said the guard.

The radio interrupts its music: 'Auxiliary policemen are asked to present themselves at the local police stations. For three days all leave of absence is cancelled.'

The young Englishman tried to read the old man's eyes.

The radio had been silent for some time.

The three of them have their heads leaning on the walls of the hideout. Their glances travel in the limited space without crossing each other.

The prison Governor is accompanied by five officers – warders. They always see they are two paces behind, observation of hierarchy has something ritualistic in it. He goes into the cell. The young man sits at a corner – his glance flies beyond them. And the Governor reads in his language a piece of paper. The translator translates mechanically as the Governor reads. But the young man does not even rise, his eyes remain motionless.

The same thing will be repeated in the second cell.

The Leader issued the order. Execution will be simultaneous. An eye for an eye, a tooth for a tooth. Biblical phrases dress the order somehow – the same way as the dry, neutral tone of Whitehall.

*

The CHAPO (Charalambides and Polydefkis) House won the tenders for Agonos. Both of them had started from very low apprentices, assistants, masters, contractors. They swam in sweat in the heart of summer, they felt the edges of their fingers numb in winter, their buttocks received kicks, they washed plates with an apron round their waist, they swept yards under the hawkish eye of their mistresses, but they did not give in. They stole a sack of cement, a few bricks or tiles for some extra pieces of work they did and they put aside whatever they earned to buy a small piece of machinery, a concrete mixer or something similar. With the 1953 earthquakes they found themselves contractors at a Paphos village. The first profits made them completely independent from their masters. And they lay the basis for the construction house of CHAPO. Gradually they added to CHAPO, land-developers written in Greek letters – so that they wouldn't provoke the anti-British feelings of the public.

Their headquarters were found on the first floor of a small block of flats. They had made a huge desk in the shape of a Greek Π. They both sat at the head of the desk, and the clients sat on the two sides and in the middle there was room for the messenger to come and go, bringing coffees, teas or orange-juice.

Agonos No. 2 on a small hill at the eastern side of Nicosia, slowly began to rise. As Ioanna was looking at it from the foot of the hill one day, an idea went astray from somewhere and crossed the corridors of her brain. Agonos could become the monument of the struggle. But she didn't dare think of it again.

20

Manos wore a short-sleeved shirt, thin trousers and sandals. He had a camera on his shoulder. He had climbed to the top of the small hill where Ioanna's house was being built. He felt it was his duty to follow the building step by step.

He must have taken ninety or a hundred photographs of the site. He had already filled two albums, but had not yet shown them to the Countess. He kept them for a surprise present.

He looked down below. The market was busy. Curfews have recently become rarer, he thinks. The English react in a rather numbed way. And our side are very careful in their attacks. Very selective.

The workers have already made progress. The contract provides for completion by May 1959.

He took the path that would bring him down to the market. In a short while he was lost among the crowd. He passed by the American consulate. Consulates were part of his life, rather his work, for Manos belonged to the rare category where life and work are one and the same thing. The press officers in both the American and the Greek consulates were his friends. He visited them almost daily to have coffee with them, to smoke a cigar with the first one or a Greek cigarette with the second. Often they talked for some time, he told them what he knew and they told him what they regarded as their news.

Before 1955 he used to visit the Public Information Office.

He had become friendly with the man in charge, a short, stout Englishman of around fifty. Then, at the start of the struggle he cut down his visits until they stopped completely.

'Hullo, David.'

'Hullo, Manos.' Without asking he lifted an internal phone and said in Greek, with an American accent: 'Coffee, please.' He offered Manos a Cuban cigar. 'How is business, Manos?'

'You know, with the papers all the time you've got something to do. The Greek newspapers have become terribly sensitive concerning the Cyprus problem. You know this too. As for Agonos it's coming along fine. American-Cypriot project.'

'What do you think of the situation?'

'Something's being done under the surface.'

'No need to be a soothsayer. It's too obvious.

'The mobilisation of the Turkish factor and the adoption in practice of a division policy by MacMillan have trapped Makarios and the Greek government. I'm not quite sure to what extent. When negotiations with the English failed Lennox Boyd told Makarios: 'May God help your people'.

'And you think the moment has arrived you need God's help?'

'And his representatives on earth.'

'Where do you see us?'

'In politics just as in parapsychological phenomena there are things you can't see. The fact that you can't see them doesn't mean they don't exist. And here lies the fascination of the whole thing. They exist and yet you don't see them.'

'I had the impression that the legends of the time left you unmoved.'

'To the extent they're legends, yes. To the extent they hide reality, no. However, there's professional silence too.'

The woman brought the Greek coffee and Manos chewed on his cigar.

'I don't know. I just feel it. You know that at the end of the First World War Smuts, the South African leader, said that the old world had died without the new one having been born. Your people seem to believe the opposite. The new world has been born while the old one hasn't died yet.'

'Not even if you had been a Marxist.'

'Nature abhors vacuum. It's the same with politics. And the creation of a vacuum sometimes becomes a persistent objective so that a need to complete it is created.'

'And Makarios? What attitude will he adopt?'

'What he didn't do last year he'll be forced to do this year. Even gods obey necessity, and here it's not about gods but people. The Attorney General is going to Seychelles. Makarios is in touch with Barbara Castle. Where labouring is somewhat difficult the Labour Party plays some kind of a role.'

'And what about the Greek government?'

'Have they got any choice? They are part of the new world that was born so that the death of the old one is promoted. Averof and Karamanlis have secret talks with the Foreign and Colonial Offices. And the Turks too.'

'And here, what are the possible reactions?'

'AKEL is not in a position to react. And the fighters are split into small armed groups. And after all the place is strikingly ready for a compromise.'

'And the comromise?'

'I'm not in a position,' Manos said, 'to know how far we're ready to go. Scylla and Charybdis, don't forget, are Greek conceptions. How much room for manoeuvring do they leave? And in our time the ancient conceptions are presented iron-clad, trapped in the splitting of the individual, therefore more merciless.'

David showed him a short article in an extreme right wing newspaper. It was about the Faneromeni oath, the blue dream of the fighters. 'They have missed the train. It left them behind in 1950. It will be others who determine what happens. And these others are forced to act within certain invisible frames.'

'There will be no reaction?'

'There will be spasmodic and impotent reaction. The whole affair has been decided, my friend.'

'By whom?'

'By invisible brains. But they themselves are not gods. And the calculating machines are likely to make mistakes.'

Manos rose.

'Why are you in a hurry?'

'I'm not. I drank my coffee, I smoked my cigar. We've covered today's news. We even went a bit further, we entered tomorrow's area.'

'Manos, we must have lunch together one day. Next month I'm transferred to our Embassy in Ankara.'

'The process of upgrading has started. Whenever you feel, ring me.' Manos left.

Curfews had become rarer. The auxiliaries had been discreetly withdrawn from the streets. The soldiers were posted everywhere, are at the hospitals, the airport, the ports but especially in the streets and roads, both in the towns and in between them. Recently the English obliged all Cypriots over twelve to have an identity card.

John Moravia, nobody knew why they called him Moravia, most probably because his grandfather was of Italian origin, was a lawyer. Riding his bicycle he went every morning to the Courts Square in Limassol, where his office was. There he always found Antonis, his clerk, a short man who suffered from a chronic distortion of his spine that forced him to turn his entire body when he wanted to look in a certain direction. Only his face was untouched by the distortion. He lived for Moravia's office. His quick brain was divided into tiny compartments from which he drew the files of every case. He also lived for his wife and daughter. He knew nothing else except his office and his family. He had brought his wife from the distant village of Tylliria, settled her at his house and very rarely let her out of it. They had a daughter of seventeen who was already six feet tall.

'Good morning Mr Antonis.'

'Good morning Mr Moravia.'

'What have we got today?'

Antonis began to enumerate the cases. Then said: 'You

must not forget your article for the *Popular Platform.* It has, without fail, to go to the printing press today.'

Moravia noted down cases he had to look into. He saw he had nothing important for that day, closed the internal door, isolated himself completely and wrote the article. He called it 'Historical Compromise'. He wrote that the armed struggle, from now on, would lead to a nightmarish blind alley. No other way than compromise existed. There was also a disguised reference to Venizelos and Ataturk.

His article, on the front page of the *Popular Platform,* caused a sensation. At the Courts Square it was discussed in low tones. Someone cracked a joke: 'Moravia is heading for a ministry.'

Of the armed groups which operated at the foot of Madaris, three or four were known as uncompromising. They were under the direct command of Iranos who had graduated from the Officers' School. His first taste of battle had been the armed struggle against the English. He believed that in a Greco–Turkish war, the Greek army would be in Istanbul in twenty-four hours.

Iranos read the article carefully. He cut it out, put it in a black frame, wrote under it the word 'execution' and sent it to the leader. He was one of the few who had direct access to the leader. The answer was not crystal clear, but Iranos read between the lines. And he made up his mind. He put on a pair of glasses, stuck a blond beard on his chin, took a high school pupil who periodically apprenticed himself as a guerilla to one of the groups, and went to Limassol.

He stayed for two or three days at one of the organisation houses and instructed some to watch Moravia's movements. There was nothing in Moravia's habits that required watching. Every morning at seven-thirty he came from the northern area of Limassol, used side-streets to avoid the traffic, and arrived at his office at around a quarter to eight. In one of the side streets Iranos, with the apprentice guerilla, lay in ambush. Nearby a Matchless motorcycle was parked.

When Moravia appeared on his bicycle Iranos gave the pupil a light push. The boy took one or two steps forward, stood in the middle of the road and, when Moravia approached, he took out his pistol and fired at him from a distance of two yards.

The body sprang up, as a ball, hit a wall and fell to the pavement.

The Matchless was fired with Iranos in front and the pupil seated behind. Outside town they left the motorcycle at a safe house and took the bus for Madari. Before the roads were blocked they were already at Kalo Chorio. They left the bus and went on foot to the hideouts at Madaris.

The next day the headlines screamed: 'Well known lawyer shot dead in the street'.

They said he was extremely smart. He had hidden depths, like an iceberg. He had been under suspicion many times but the English authorities never managed to present convincing evidence and the courts always ordered his release. Last time they kept him in a special wing of the Central Prisons on the basis of an order which gave the governor the right to call for indefinite detention of any suspect. The suspect could be kept in prison until the Queen ordered his release.

Vrasidas – that was how he was known to the organisation – had the appearance of a student. He organised commando raids.

He slipped through the Nicosia streets with his companions with a nimbleness that surprised everybody, locals and foreigners. He studied the plan of a raid for two days. He isolated himself completely. He shut himself in one of the rooms he kept in Nicosia and towards the end of the second day he made up his mind.

When his guard – usually a pupil who sat at a desk studying his lessons, always with a pistol at hand in a drawer – saw him opening the door he understood that the conception of an idea was coming to an end. Shortly the birth would take place – and as with every birth, it would be accompanied by pain and blood.

This man, who could execute three men one after the other, without feeling anything; who could see companions killed next to him and justify it to himself as historical necessity, this man did not know how to behave in front of a girl. Instead of feeling sexual paroxysm in his legs he felt the opposite. But during the nights when he was alone under the blankets, he was continually aroused. Lefki, he had created her in his imagination, was a girl with thick black hair and thrusting breasts. He had seen her on two or three occasions from a distance.

Now, in prison, they kept him in relative isolation. They let him out twice a day, two hours each time. He went to the lavatory, he had a shower, he was shaved at the prison's barber shop, and there, he learned that the barber, one who was serving a long imprisonment, had been recruited as a member by the organisation. In the afternoon he walked round the yard under the austere eye of the warder. His only contact with the other detainees was a shaking of the head, a smile, a raising of the hand, a glance full of meaning.

The barber slipped him a note one day. Vrasidas understood that it was a special message from high up in the organisation. When they led him back to his cell he waited for some time until he was sure that the warder was occupied with something else. He took the paper out quickly. 'Agreements – compromise is imminent. Compromise equals betrayal? Will the priest cheat us? The uncompromising.'

He understood that the message came from Iranos, but the real sender was the leader. Now he was almost sure that the majority of the fighters in towns would follow the priest. The people too. With the fighters in the mountains things were different. He knew that the uncompromising would be in a relative majority.

His mind was hooked on the word compromise. And suddenly he saw it with another word – survival. It meant, he thought, government. And government does not exist without ministers. The priest would be alone at the top. He wouldn't accept the leader next to him, and the leader wouldn't like to stand at his side. Iranos would follow the leader.

He knew his obstinacy well and his political shortsightedness. But there was the other one, Karaiskos. He had known him since school. He never kept much company with him, he read poetry, he studied music and loved the theatre. He was one of the first to join the organisation and had reached one of the highest posts. He inspired the confidence of both the priest and the leader.

When he had to select his deputy the leader preferred Iranos and Vrasidas felt wounded. He was sure that, for Karaiskos, this meant nothing. His brain, under the impact of the word compromise, started working unusually fast. He knew that the English would not set him free until the last possible moment. Yet, the game would start from now. He began walking up and down in his cell, like a caged tiger. He had the nimbleness of a wild cat but he lacked the power of a tiger. He couldn't afford to stay in prison any longer. He felt Karaiskos becoming a deep wound inside him. From some half-talk of comrades he knew that Karaiskos met Lefki from time to time. They read poetry together. They never talked about the struggle. A bitter smile cracked his lips: Both Lefki and a ministerial seat.

He walked up and down again. Then he stopped. He made up his mind. He cut a piece of toilet paper and on it he wrote: 'A blanket and a pair of pincers. At eight.' The lavatories were numbered from five to fifteen. Next morning he gave it to the barber. In the afternoon the barber stood at the door of his shop and stared at the yard. Vrasidas was on his afternoon exercise. The guard's instruction was that Vrasidas should never stop. He must be on the move all the time. The barber looked him straight in the eyes. Vrasidas understood. The blanket and the pincers were at eight.

At around five he told the warder that he felt ill and asked to be taken back to his cell. He had his own way of causing fever. He swallowed a piece of soap. His fever lasted for about six hours. He sweated from top to bottom.

The warder put his hand on Vrasidas' forehead: 'You're burning,' he said.

In a short while he suffered an attack of diarrhoea. And

the warder escorted him every half hour to the lavatory. He brought him a jug of water and gave him some pills.

To begin with the warder escorted him to the lavatory, but around ten a cold northern wind started blowing, and the warder escorted him only to the gate of the lavatory block, leaving Vrasidas to cross the short distance by himself. Then he led him back to the cell. Vrasidas knew the habits of the warders quite well. At around eleven they drank hot tea in a cosy corner. The last time he opened the door of the block Vrasidas noticed how anxious the warder was to return to his tea. This time he spent ten minutes inside the block. He returned and saw the warder slumped in a chair. He closed and opened the door of the block to give the impression that he had returned, stayed motionless for one or two minutes and, when he saw there were no reactions from the warder, he returned to the lavatory. He waited for five minutes, then he climbed through the small window, holding the blanket and the pair of pincers. The barber had cut the blanket in eight thick strips, joined together. Like a wild cat he climbed up the rough external wall and reached the base of the barbed wire. Every time the moving searchlight neared him, he leaned his body against the wall and let it pass over him without touching him. With the pincers he worked fast, and piece after piece the barbed wire was cut, leaving an opening which became bigger with every click of the pincers.

With the blanket-rope he found himself at the foot of the external wall. The warder would be dozing until one, so he still had at his disposal sixty whole minutes. Walking against the wall he reached the last corner. As soon as the searchlight beam passed he crawled fifty yards to the nearest tree. From there he vanished into the night.

They started looking for him, but it was already too late. In his hurry he had gone into the side streets of Strovolos and a lorry driver gave him a lift. For the time being he didn't care where he was heading he only wanted to be away from Nicosia. The lorry driver made one or two attempts to start a conversation but he was stopped by the other's silence.

Now, amid the hills at the foot of Troodos, Varsidas felt

sure that he had made it. Nicosia was already half an hour or an hour behind him. At a bend he told the lorry driver: 'Here.'

The lorry stopped at the side of the road and Vrasidas jumped out with a nimbleness that surprised the driver. Then he set the engine in motion. Vrasidas waved him goodbye and followed the path that led down to the valley. It must have been eight or nine. He wanted to listen to the morning news bulletin. He smiled. The cat with the power of the tiger. He remembered the Esso advertisements. A huge tiger with its front feet raised: 'Put a tiger in your car'. He had put a tiger in his body.

He had to walk for about an hour, and it was past eleven when he reached the camp. Vrasidas met Karaiskos sitting at the entrance of a cave.

Karaiskos jumped up and shook his head. 'I heard it on the news. I didn't have an idea where they would take you.'

'They didn't take me. I've come by myself,' Vrasidas said. 'I didn't have time to inform anyone. I'm hungry.'

Karaiskos went into the cave and brought olives, a piece of halloumi and bread. For ten minutes Vrasidas ate without talking. From time to time Karaiskos cast a furtive glance at him. Over his face there hung what a teacher of his had once described as 'a veil of thoughtful silence'.

'I've got Rufus inside,' Karaiskos said suddenly. 'The organisation doctor talks about nervous breakdown. Someone else from the town talked vaguely about schizophrenia. He laughs and talks continuously. Seven days ago his complete isolation was ordered. His state has become worse. They are afraid lest we sustain some losses as a result.'

Vrasidas wondered at Karaiskos' desire to talk. Silence fell again, solid, like a partition.

'The day before yesterday his transportation here was ordered. In complete isolation. He and I. I give him tranquillisers every three hours. As soon as he tries to get up I give him a tranquilliser of ten milligrams.'

Rufus was a big lad with blue eyes and black hair. This unusual feature attracted many. He laughed with such openness that he disarmed everybody. His father was a retired policeman. Rufus was his only child and his sole support. He had married at a rather mature age, and had some difficulty in producing an heir. He took his wife from one doctor to another, and after both had suffered, she bodily, he psychologically, they had their only son. Constas made plans for his son's studies. He would use his retirement lump sum and he and his wife would try to make ends meet with his small pension and with what he earned giving driving lessons. All day long he waited for a customer at Courts Square in an old black Ford. He kept a big notebook where he entered his pupils' names with their addresses. Somehow Constas made a living. He put his pension aside for his son's return after his studies. But when the boy disappeared from the sixth form of high school, Constas felt his life become empty. The message that Rufus had joined the armed groups of the organisation did not change the situation. For five years he sat in his black Ford and waited, he knew no other way to fill his emptiness.

As the English tightened the ring round the guerillas' camps they always discovered something, sometimes accidentally and sometimes as a result of treason. And Rufus' fate was sealed. They could neither keep him nor set him free. And the responsibility fell on Karaiskos. At the camp a grave would be dug and in the archives he would be classified as 'missing'. In the meantime he would be kept under complete sedation and isolation, for recently he developed a tendency to go out and start shouting. A lot of disconnected utterances.

'He must be executed,' said Karaiskos.

'And the grave?' Vrasidas asked.

'Behind that bush,' Karaiskos made a gesture. 'I should have done it.' He stood up without saying a word and led Rufus outside the hideout. 'You can help me to bury him.'

Rufus' eyes blinked in the sudden light. But beyond his mechanical reaction the sedation circulated in his veins and arteries. His mechanical laughter had been frozen into an imperceptibly bitter smile. Behind the bush two shots were heard.

Vrasidas walked towards the bush. He saw Rufus lying on

his back. Karaiskos had thrown his pistol away and was standing as if petrified. Vrasidas dragged the corpse to the grave. He took up the shovel and silently started filling the grave with soil. Suddenly, he raised the shovel and hit Karaiskos on the head with all his force. He fixed his glasses, cast a last glance at the two bodies and began to walk away.

The organisation found them two days later. They put the second body in the grave and filled it. The mystery of the two dead men nagged at them but separation of the fighters into uncompromising and those ready to yield left no room for thorough investigation. Thus Karaiskos was put down as a suicide. A report was sent to the leader. There was something in it he didn't like, but for the time being he preferred to bury it in his archive, a black box which he always carried with him. When they announced Karaiskos' suicide to his father, the latter took off his priest's hat and after a few minutes of terrifying silence he wiped the sweat that was formed in thick drops on his forehead.

'The Karaiskos do not commit suicide. They fall fighting or are executed.' He walked towards the church. Months afterwards when whispers started, Vrasidas was riding high. How could he be reached by whispers?

The English began a game that would secure them what they wanted. They had managed to split a lot of geographical unities – it wouldn't be difficult to split Cyprus too. There was a lot of travel to the Seychelles; the possibility of partition started taking concrete shape with the MacMillan Plan, and the Archbishop was set free to go to Athens to be in the centre of fermentations and pressures. And the English Labour Party, through Barbara Castle, underlined the necessity of compromise.

Foot, the last English Governor, was now able to ride his horse and wander in the fields of Strovolos behind the governor's house in safety. The guerilla groups began to disband. They gathered their arms and came down to the towns, and each one headed for his own house.

For the time being there was no room for celebrations.

The leader, wearing a thick pullover and his characteristic beret, left in a Greek military plane for Greece. Constas, in the car he used for driving lessons, drove round the streets of Nicosia whenever he heard guerillas were coming to the town. Every time he saw a group of guerillas arriving, and stopping for a little while in a side street, and then scattering but without Rufus, he remained rooted in his old Ford while the sweat formed thick drops on his forehead.

The English soldiers discreetly withdrew to their two bases in Dhekelia and Acrotiri. A smaller base existed at Nicosia's military airport and it was from this one, every morning that the group of soldiers who manned the Governor's House garrison set out.

Priest Antonis, father Karaiskos, saw the guerilla groups come down, pass by the small church and then be swallowed in the centre of Nicosia, and his heart was wrung. In his waistcoat pocket, which he wore under his cassock, he kept the short letter the leader had addressed to him: 'Your son fell carrying out his duty'. Some rumours had reached him that his son was found hit with a shovel next to the shot Rufus, but they never told him the place. Somewhere near Troodos, between Macheras and Madari.

He opened the door of the small church and went in. He threw the stole over his cassock, he placed one or two tiny pieces of coal in his incensory and lit them. He threw in a little incense, lit two or three candles, and in the semi-darkness, started singing a commemoration mass for his son. He acted both as a priest and a chorus.

And the guerilla groups passed outside the church. Without any pre-arrangement all of them headed for the centre, crossed Metaxas Square and then scattered in the side streets. And people lingered on the pavements, to see them come.

Manos visited the central offices of the Contractor. The house must be finished as soon as possible.

'Some overtime will be needed. Will you undertake the extra cost?'

'Any idea how much?'

'I don't know. After carrying out the work we'll know. On the other hand your architect will be in a position to issue certificates. What we need is that you undertake the obligation.' He pushed over a printed piece of paper. Manos signed on behalf of Ioanna.

When he returned to his office he got her on the phone. 'The house will be ready by March. This is the time when the Archbishop will be returning.'

'Perhaps you should organise an opening ceremony.'

In the morning the tension began to mount. It stopped and continued and then it began slowly to rise, a few centimetres, a few metres, until it became a vertical pillar. And the people gathered along the streets, from the airport to the Archbishop's palace. From time to time guerilla shock groups paraded in the streets – some were wearing their black berets at a tilt, others at the backs of their heads.

Some voices had been heard about perjury but now amid all this freed emotion, in this subconscious deliverance from fear, there was no room for objections, and the voices did not go beyond the whisper stage.

And then they saw him, erect in his car. Pale. Fragile, leaning on his pastoral crosier.

From the balcony of his new palace he spoke to the crowds. 'Brothers, we have won.'

The last English Governor stood at his side. His face was a mask of serenity.

'Brothers we have won.' He started and finished the speech in this way. When they retired to the big hall for a coffee and a cigarette the Archbishop turned to Foot: 'Those who were inside the rails are candidates for Ministers and those outside candidates for Members of Parliament.'

The crowd began to disperse. They carried with them the echo of 'we have won' and felt a kind of satisfaction, the foundations of which were eroded subconsciously by mistrust.

The house was ready. Ioanna gave instructions to a young electrician who connected everything to a time switch and thus, every evening at eight, all the lights were switched on and the house, on top of the small hill, with Pentadactylos as a backdrop, lost its material existence in its own light and underlined the end of the curfews.

Manos had talked to some people in the Archbishop's circle about an official opening ceremony but the reaction was discouraging.

'It's better if we avoid it, Countess.'

'They don't regard us worthy enough, you mean?' she said, bitterly.

'It's not a question of regarding us as worthy or not,' said Manos.

'If the General was here,' she shouted.

'The General has other problems now. He has saved Cyprus and now he's going for Greece. With the proclamation of the Cyprus Republic something could be done.'

'Fifteen or sixteen months, it's a bit too long,' observed the Countess.

Every two or three days a photograph of the new house appeared in the papers.

'The Oriol-de-Samargans move to their new house.' This with very few variations appeared under the photographs.

Manos employed new people to complete the staff.

'Whenever you decide we are ready to move there,' he said one day. The staff entered the mansion and cleaned, polished, and moved the furniture around. They left an hour before the lights came on. The switching on of the lights was like an impersonal ritual.

And on an evening in the middle of March, a little before eight, Ioanna, Mathias, Manos, some close friends of theirs and the staff gathered at the entrance of the house. Ioanna looked at Mathias. 'Our house,' she said.

'Very beautiful,' he answered.

Manos brought two bottles of champagne, one for Ioanna and one for Mathias. Both of them proceeded right and left of the central entrance and broke the bottles of champagne on the wall. They were launching the house into time – this was what Mathias told her when he proposed it. And she liked it. At the same moment the time switch functioned and the building was turned into something weightless and illuminated and they all went in and drank champagne and ate to satiation point until the early hours.